SPICED

PIPPA GRANT WRITING AS

JAMIE FARRELL

Cover Illustration by Julie Bonart of Qamber Designs
Cover layout & typography by Qamber Designs
Editing by Jessica Snyder

DEAR READER

When I started Blissed *(Misfit Brides Book #1), I had a clear vision for three stories: Natalie's, Lindsey's, and Kimmie's. Then Pepper walked onto the page, and I knew I had a fourth heroine on my hands. (Having so many requests for her story certainly didn't hurt! Thank you!) Dahlia and Merry came along as well, demanding stories of their own, and suddenly what started as a series of three books continued on past my wildest expectations.*

This book has a lot of characters in it, because I can't tell Pepper's story without revisiting all of Bliss's past heroes and heroines, and I can't tell a story about a woman with ten sisters and two brothers without acknowledging the role growing up in a huge family played in her life. Therefore, I've put a handy little cheat sheet on the next pages to identify Pepper's family and all the past heroes and heroines of the Misfit Brides. Although "little" might be an understatement.

This book is my love letter to those of you who have fallen in love with the Misfit Brides. If you're new to the series, I hope the char-

acter list will help you catch up. If you've been eagerly anticipating Pepper's story, I hope you'll have fun with all of our old friends too.

Thank you so much for reading. It's a pleasure and an honor to have space on your bookshelf.

Jamie

THE BLUE FAMILY TREE

Herb and Violet, aka Mom & Dad

Basil (the priest)

Rosemary (the oldest daughter, married, with four girls)

Ginger (next oldest, married, with three girls)

Tarra (engaged when you turn the page)

Saffron (former band member for Billy Brenton, married, with a baby)

Pepper (our intrepid heroine)

Cori (the first of Pepper's younger sisters)

CJ (hero of *Blissed*, married to Nat, children are—well, you'll just have to keep reading)

Margie (the scientist)

Poppy (the first twin)

Rika (the second twin, though she still disputes birth order)

Sage (the veterinarian)

Cinna (the baby, bartender at Suckers)

(Gran is Violet's mom.)

Past Misfit Brides Heroes and Heroines

---

*T*ony Cross had smiled through dog drool, a flat tire, and accidentally discovering Bliss's elderly nudist colony tonight, all for the sake of drumming up business. But he wasn't sure he could smile through this last stop of the night.

"Stripper's here!" a girly voice shrieked.

He'd known this day would come—he *did* live in the bridal capital of the Midwest—but until tonight, he'd managed to avoid the bachelorette parties. Not that he objected to bachelorette parties. He simply objected to a bachelorette party at *this* house.

The brown oak door on the turn-of-the-century two-story foursquare next door to his own house swung open. Two redheads, a brunette, and that floppy black species-confused dog grinned at him from inside the screen door. All of them but the dog were in pajamas, party tiaras, and boas in all colors of the rainbow. And all of them— even the pint-sized dog—were eyeballing his package.

And by *package*, he didn't mean the four pizzas rapidly cooling in the winter night.

At least it wasn't *her*. "Pizza delivery."

"Oh, he's going to role-play! I wonder how many of those are sausage." The leader of the pack—a petite green-eyed redhead in blue leggings and with Captain America's logo on her T-shirt—flashed him a come-hither grin that did nothing for the blood flow south of the border.

Not that he'd expected it to. Blood hadn't flowed there in...he didn't want to talk about it.

"One supreme, two pepperoni, and one vegetarian," he said. "As ordered."

She popped the latch on the screen door and snagged his pizza insulator box while the brunette grabbed the mutant dog. "Come on in, *pizza man.*"

"Just need a signature and that box, ladies." He hit them with the famous Cross smile.

Big mistake.

The first redhead crooked a finger at him. "The box for your shirt." It was rapidly getting passed deeper into the room. He'd lost three other insulators this week, and he couldn't afford to be any shorter with Super Bowl Sunday coming up.

Three more women lingered in the back of the room. A brunette with glasses lifted his insulator. "Weird box for props, but I like the theme."

"Check out the way his jeans fit. Those aren't going to be easy to rip off. Think they have snaps on the side?"

"Just need a signature from Ginger Johnson," he repeated to the redhead in charge.

Yes, he'd just said *Ginger Johnson,* and every one of the ladies within hearing distance was snickering now.

He would've snickered too, but he wanted to get out of here before *she* realized who was on her front porch.

"Take it off, pizza man!" A birdlike woman in polyester pink pants up to her saggy parts and a sparkly tiara atop her tight white curls pushed into the doorway and shoved the door wider. She jiggled her bosom, shimmied over to him, and twirled her pink feather boa like a lasso. "Where's my purse? I got me some twenties, but only if you let me see that six-pack."

"Just delivering pizza, ma'am." He gave a subtle sniff. Margaritas? How many had Betty White's cousin here had tonight? "If one of you can sign this—"

Her talons reached out, and there went his receipt clipboard. "Ma'am—" he started, cutting himself off when she shoved it under her shirt.

"You want it? Come get it, big boy. Wouldn't mind if you wanted to give me a peek at your sausage, if you know what I mean."

"You *guys*. Seriously. I didn't need a stripper." A brunette in a veil decorated with miniature penises approached, towering over Granny. "Although, he *is* pretty cute."

Cute enough to be mistaken for a thirty-five-year-old stripper. Life goal achieved.

Not. "Ginger Johnson?" he asked.

"She's in the bathroom," a redhead in unicorn pajamas called from the couch, where she was holding up her phone.

Videotaping him.

What was it they said? No publicity was bad publicity?

He should've moved closer to Chicago. Or downstate. Or to Minnesota. "Ma'am, I'm going to need that receipt signed."

The old lady angled away, moving her lower jaw in a weird way that made her teeth clack.

"If she'd listened to us, she would've been Ginger Blue-Johnson," piped up an unfortunately familiar redhead in coffee-themed pajamas. Cinna Blue and her perpetually mischievous smile would've been his type if she looked any older than seventeen. And if she wasn't Pepper Blue's sister.

"Ginger won't mind if you get started," one of the older women said.

"Yeah, she hates strippers. I guess I would too if I'd had to watch Mom get a lap dance at my bachelorette party, but—wait. Ginger hired you?"

"Whoa, hey, he really *did* bring pizza," another voice called from deep inside.

3

Seven sets of eyeballs latched onto him.

Ten years ago, this would've been a wet dream come true. All these women in pajamas wanting him to take his clothes off. Minus Granny, of course.

Ten years ago, though, his equipment still worked.

But that was before Tabitha. And not even the twin redheads were inspiring any movement in his happy parts tonight.

"What in the world?" One more brunette stalked into the room.

His jaw clenched, his pulse rattled, and—oh, *hell*.

No.

Not a flipping *chance*.

Pepper Blue herself, the neighbor of his nightmares, the woman who owned a dog that thought it was a rabbit, who never had a hair out of place, and who was practically second-in-command in the bridal world of Bliss these days, was *not* causing a stirring in his, ahem, *stir stick*.

She was in a green feather boa, thick chestnut ponytail, and fitted red plaid pajamas as she stepped down the stairs. She planted her hands on her curvy hips and turned a schoolmarm frown on the other women.

The pajamas.

It had to be the pajamas.

"Who ordered a stripper?" she demanded.

"Ginger," the old lady said.

"Ginger ordered *pizza*," Tony said.

She blinked at him then, really looking for the first time since she'd taken charge of the room.

"Are you a stripper?" the apparent bride asked.

"Not since college."

"I bet you still got it, sonny." A hand smacked his ass, and Granny winked a wrinkly wink at him. "C'mon in. Show us some sugar."

"Gran, hands off the pizza man." Pepper wove through the other women, frowned at her grandmother, and held out a hand. "What's up your shirt?"

Granny flashed a grin that made her eyes look twenty years younger and added another pound of wrinkles to her cheeks. "You wanna see?"

"No one wants to see your tassels, Gran," said the bespeckled redhead in black and white pajamas with Einstein heads printed all over them.

"Spoilsport," the redheaded unicorn twin muttered.

"Hand it over, Gran." Pepper snapped her fingers. Her lush lips were set in a line, her bare feet planted wide, toes painted a delicate pink.

But over it all, she had brilliant green eyes that betrayed more than a hint of amusement. "You're keeping Tony from his job."

"I'd give him a hundred to drop his pants and let us see the goods."

"Sexual harassment can get you five to ten in the slammer. Think of all the great-grandchildren you'll miss. And who'll lead the conga line at weddings? Plus, I hear if you die in there, all you get is a state-issue coffin."

Granny finally quit moving her jaw, and her teeth—*dentures*—clacked together. "Hush your tongue."

"And Poppy got it all on tape. She's still mad about that fake snake you gave her for her birthday when she was thirteen."

"Yep. Holding on to this for blackmail," the unicorn-pajama-ed redhead confirmed.

They were all nuts, and something about seeing Pepper smiling and natural and relaxed was doing more bad things to his lower hemisphere. He eased back on the porch. "Just drop it by tomorrow," he said to Pepper.

Not because this wasn't entertaining.

But because he could no longer deny what that stirring in his pants was. *That* hadn't happened in so long, he'd thought he was permanently broken. And he didn't know how he felt about it happening *now*. For *her*. Nor did he want *this* audience if he went full mast.

Or if he didn't.

"Gran..." That warning note in her strict librarian tone sent a whole flood of interest pooling in his groin so fast an unexpected pain shot through his testicles. His pulse fired up to heart-attack levels, and his heart jackhammered against a boulder growing in his throat.

"Tomorrow's fine," he said gruffly. He lifted a hand, a wave good-bye, a brush-off, and retreated as fast as he could.

He'd lived in darkness for more than a year now.

And despite the *everything's fine here* smile he gave to the world, he wasn't ready to come out.

PEPPER BLUE WAS WAGING a mental war with herself over pizza.

She'd never been a pizza-for-breakfast kind of woman, and starting the day with that many carbs—not to mention the grease—would wreak havoc on her glucose levels, which could wreak havoc on her hormonal levels, and then her stress levels would explode, and *poof!*

All her hopes and dreams would drown in a circle of crusty, cheesy dream killers.

But that pizza was calling to her.

It sat on her black granite countertops in her renovated kitchen, the lid propped open against Gran's old mushroom canisters, four perfect pieces with congealed cheese mocking her.

You know you want me, the pizza said. *You neeeeeeed me.*

You're nothing more than an ugly test, she silently fired back. *Don't doubt Super Pepper's willpower. But soon...soon you will be mine.*

Can I have some? Sadie silently begged at her feet.

"Neither one of us should," she said to her sweet terrier mix. It was the double bacon. She could resist a supreme pizza. She could resist a Hawaiian pizza. But this was a supreme pizza, minus the pepperoni, with double bacon on a wood-fired crust. She hadn't had pizza in

6

months, and this pizza smelled like what she imagined the palace of heaven must smell like.

"It smells like dog barf in here," Margie announced behind her.

She straightened and flipped the pizza lid shut. Probably needed to throw it away. It *had* sat on the counter all night.

Right next to the red pizza carrier her sisters had stolen from Tony last night.

Her nose wrinkled at the thought of her obnoxious neighbor. "Are you sure *you* don't smell like dog barf?" she said. "Have you showered today?"

"I'm well acquainted with my own body odor, and that smell is not me." Margie leaned over and sniffed in Pepper's direction. Her red hair shifted in the messy knot atop her head, and the Einstein on her shirt was crooked. "Not you either. Why are you up and showered this early?"

"I need to run into the boutique." She waved at the pizza carrier and clipboard. "And return that. Anyone else up yet?"

"Negative."

Pepper met Margie's gaze, and a slow smile crept over her lips. "None of them?"

"If you're planning a whipped-cream attack, I feel obligated to remind you that this is your house, and you've just indicated a need to leave the premises while our sisters are still here."

"Whipped-cream attacks are for amateurs."

When Margie responded with a rare smile of her own, Pepper dove for her lower cabinet and went to work grabbing supplies. "Not a word," she whispered.

"About what? Gran did it."

Ah, Gran. She was a handful. Barely been five feet tall, not even a hundred pounds—and at least three of those pounds were wrinkles. Those white curls on her head weren't her most stubborn feature either. She'd raised six girls and had twenty-nine granddaughters. The woman lived for the privileges that came with age—speaking her mind, bossing around her progeny, and seeing just how much she could get away with.

One day, god willing, Pepper would be just like her.

Though she'd probably refrain from hitting on Tony Cross. Not that she could entirely blame Gran—Tony *was* ruggedly handsome with his dark brown lady-killers, thick dark curls peeking out from under his red hat, and a perpetual five-o'clock shadow two hours past its prime.

But his cat liked to terrorize poor Sadie, he had a revolving string of women coming to his house, and he'd turned her down flat when she invited him to join the Bridal Retailers Association.

Arrogant Grumplestiltskin. He wouldn't be her neighbor long if he didn't try to fit in here in Bliss.

She and Margie snuck their supplies into the living room, where half their sisters were sleeping.

"That's just mean," Margie murmured while Pepper shoved a can of Spam into Ginger's overnight bag. Of the thirteen Blue siblings, Ginger was the one most vocal about her hatred of the canned meat that had been a staple in Mom's kitchen when they were growing up.

"She hogged Saffron's baby at the bridal shower," Pepper whispered back.

"Ah. So now you're even."

"Exactly."

Margie lifted a blow-up goat from a gift bag near the door. "Shall I dispose of this?"

"*No!*" Pepper forced her expression back to neutral. If Margie—or anyone—suspected she wanted the goat for herself, she'd have some explaining to do. And she was *not* ready for explanations. "Ah, I mean, tuck it in with Rosemary. I want to see her freak out at the idea of another girl."

"You do realize this goat doesn't have magical fertility powers."

"Hush. Rosemary believes in it."

"I honestly struggle with the concept that I'm actually related to you people."

Poppy stirred in her sleeping bag, and Pepper and Margie both froze until her breathing evened out.

They hadn't had a sisters slumber party since Saffron got married two years ago. Before Pepper had moved here and bought into Bliss Bridal, before her brother married Nat, her co-owner at the boutique in downtown Bliss, before she'd realized her PCOS was rapidly aging her out of being able to have children while all her ex-boyfriends were getting married and starting families of their own.

She'd never regretted moving to Bliss—she loved the people, the boutique, her house, even if she would've preferred a better next-door neighbor. She loved the nonstop weddings, the annual Knot Festival in the summer and Snow Bride Festival in the winter, the goofball Battle of the Boyfriends every February.

She even loved the bridezillas.

But lately, she'd been riding so many hormones and, for the first time in her life, the terror that came with a legitimate fear of failing the biggest project of her life, that she hadn't felt like herself.

Seeing Gran and her sisters helped.

So much.

Last night had felt so normal. Laughing. Teasing. Dancing.

And when she was finally ready to tell them about her IVF proce-dures, when this last attempt proved to be the successful one, they'd support her. Babies were sacred in this family. Sperm might not have been, but babies were.

She wouldn't have the husband. But she'd have her family. She'd be a mom.

Almost everything she ever wanted.

Almost.

TONY WAS NODDING his head to some classic Metallica and portioning off pizza dough on a stainless steel table mid-morning Sunday when someone knocked on the back door. He wiped his hands on a towel

9

and headed through Pepperoni Tony's state-of-the-art kitchen to answer it.

And immediately wished he hadn't.

He leaned into the doorway and smiled at his unexpected visitor. He was reasonably sure she liked him even less than he liked her, but hell if he'd let her see she bothered him. "Pepper, you're looking lovely this morning."

Lovely with her thick chestnut hair, proper businesswoman coat, and nothing but *I don't want to be here* written in her bright green eyes. She swept a quick glance down his body, and—

Nothing. No twinges, no twitches, no pole movement at all.

"Nice apron." She lifted his red insulated bag. "Your clipboard and the receipt are inside. My apologies for my sisters. And my grandmother. It was the tequila. Honestly, you're lucky she wasn't naked."

"Never been one to object to bachelorette parties with naked pillow fights."

"So sorry. We saved that for after you left."

Despite her dry delivery, he tried to picture her and her sisters shrieking naked and flinging pillows at each other while goose feathers floated through the room. Testing...testing... Nope. Still nothing in his happy places.

Hallelujah. And possibly he needed to have his prostate checked.

"Let me know next time there's a repeat performance." He winked. "Pizza's on me."

There went the smirky eyeball. She glanced past him, her neck craning a smidge, and her nostrils wobbled. "Right."

"Did you just sniff my kitchen?"

Her eyes widened. *Caught.* "No."

"You did."

"I—it smells very nice." She closed her eyes, and this time, she inhaled deeply, chest rising, chin tilting, and a soft smile teasing her lips. "Like pizza crust."

This was where he needed to have a snappy comeback. *If you like that, wait till you get a sniff of my sauce.* Or *Didn't take you for the cheesy kind, but I got something gouda for you.*

But he couldn't form the words.

Because all of his blood had suddenly surged south, and for the first time in months, his equipment was fully up and running, springing to life like a caffeinated squirrel coming out of hibernation and sprinting off for the first romp of the year.

Fuck, that hurt. Hurt so damn good.

On the one hand, maybe he didn't need his prostate checked after all. On the other...*Pepper Blue?* His junk needed to get it together.

He snatched his insulator before she noticed the party growing in his pants. "Yep. Better get back to it. Thanks. Tell your grandma I'm looking forward to next time."

The last thing he saw before he swung the door shut was bewilderment knotting one of her brows. He dropped his head to the cold, hard door and sucked in a breath.

And another.

And another.

He hit his head against the door a few more times for good measure too.

Pepper Blue was an uptight bridal-town princess-in-training who liked to attack his cat with a squirt gun. She was smart, savvy, and sophisticated. The kind of woman a guy married, not the kind of woman a guy took home to test out his first boner in over a year.

Figured.

It just figured.

11

---

2

*P*epper's sisters had been cleaning the last of the bachelorette party mess when she'd left for the boutique, and she'd thought they'd all be gone before lunchtime. With the exception of Cinna, the baby of the family, none of them lived in Bliss. The older sisters had their families—and in Tarra's case, a fiancé—and the younger sisters had exciting social lives. They'd all needed to get home after the bachelorette party fun.

So when Pepper returned mid-afternoon, she was surprised to find Margie and Sage waiting for her in her living room.

And they weren't alone.

"Good, you're here. Sit." Gran was in a baby-blue pair of polyester pants and a Bro Code boy band T-shirt under a neon green cardigan today. She was playing with the fringe on Pepper's green chenille throw, but it wasn't her fingers that had most of Pepper's attention.

No, that went to the fluffy white miniature poodle licking herself on the ivory rug over the wide-plank hardwood floors.

"Where's Sadie?" she asked. Her dog was sweet as honey and she loved humans, but she didn't do well with other canines. Mostly because she thought she was a rabbit.

"Hiding," Margie said. "George thought she was a chew toy. We put Gran's suitcases up in the spare bedroom."

Gran wasn't as quick as she'd been last night, but she still scooted herself off the plush couch with the pluck of a fifty-year-old. "Young lady, I'm here to break your losing streak. I'm not leaving until you're married or I die trying to get you to the altar."

Pepper's lips parted, but no sound came out.

"She's been kicked out of another senior living facility," Sage said. The second-youngest of the family, she was a veterinarian and typically spent her time on the floor with the dogs. That she was giving George a wide berth, sitting in the easy chair across the room with her legs tucked under her, didn't bode well. "Which she couldn't tell us *last night* because she *didn't want to ruin the mood.*"

"No one else volunteered to watch her?" Pepper said to her sisters.

Gran harrumphed out a snort that would've made even Basil proud. "I'm experienced, not senile and in need of a keeper. And you, young lady, need my know-how."

Given her penchant for goosing young men, Pepper couldn't entirely agree on her not needing a keeper. "I couldn't possibly ask you to put your life on hold for me."

"Ginger tried that once. Didn't work for her either. And look where she is now."

Ginger, third oldest and the one most likely to play martyr at family functions, was married to a high school math teacher and had three daughters rapidly approaching their teenage years. "Are you talking about the part where she has a family of her own, or the part where she hides Oreos in Raisin Bran boxes and goes to 'book club' once a week to escape said family?"

Gran wagged a gnarled finger topped with fluorescent blue nail polish. "It's a sign a woman's doing a good job if she has to hide her cookies and run off once or twice a week."

"You could use the assistance with your love life," Margie said. "We considered having the twins take her, but..."

"But all three of them would end up hitched to strangers in Vegas," Pepper finished.

"Such sass from a girl who's managed to train fifteen boyfriends to be good husbands but couldn't keep one for herself. Where's your tuna? George is hungry."

"Tuna?"

"He's recently decided he's a cat. Also, we're going to need your computer. I got you registered on that timber thing, but it says you need a smartphone for the best experience."

"*Tinder?* You registered me for *Tinder?*"

"Yep. Got you a profile on MisterGoodEnough.com too. But don't you worry, honey. I won't make you do this alone. I'm gonna be right with you, double-dating the whole way."

"We stayed to try to stop her when we realized what she was doing," Sage said. "And don't worry about those emails from CyLord the Borg God. We canceled that date."

Pepper squeezed her eyes shut. Dating was absolutely out of the question right now. Probably for the next nine months. At least. "Gran, this is really sweet of you, but—"

"Ah, ah. Don't go thanking me yet. Don't want to jinx my magic. Now, there's a nice man named Walter who wants us to go on a date with him and his grandson tomorrow. Clear your calendar, honey. We're fixin' your love problems and getting you hitched. Shouldn't take more than a year or two."

A year or two?

More like nine days. Nine days until she'd have her positive pregnancy test.

And then Gran would want to stay for an entirely different reason.

"You're not on one of those baloney no-carb diets, are you? I need to make some biscuits for dinner, and you need your energy if we're going to snare you a man. First mission is to get you a date to Tarra's wedding."

"I don't—"

"I think you should ask the pizza man," Sage said. "Did you see the look on his face when you walked in last night? It was like he was seeing the sun for the first time."

"He squinted in pain?" Margie said.

"No, dummy, he was worshipping her with his eyes."

"And he has a nice ass," Gran said.

He did have a nice ass, but Margie was right. Tony Cross was *not* boyfriend material, and he didn't want to be.

Moreover, *she* didn't want him to be. What kind of guy slammed the door in a woman's face? She'd *complimented* his kitchen. And she hadn't had to stop by his pizza place. She could've just left his crap on his doorstep. She'd been doing the nice thing.

The jerk. "You want a pizza-delivery guy to be my baby daddy?" she said to Gran.

Tony was more than the delivery guy, but Gran didn't have to know that.

Also, Pepper's baby daddy, god willing, was a thirty-year-old doctor with no family history of cancer, diabetes, or heart disease, who had made a donation to a sperm bank so that single women like Pepper could be mothers.

And as soon as she found out that this last attempt at IVF had been successful, she'd tell her family. Until then, she didn't need their worries or judgment.

Or their help with her love life, which was officially on hold indefinitely.

"Shoot, we'll take the pizza-delivery guy. You've had *fifteen* ex-boyfriends marry the next woman they met after you. At this point, you can't be too picky," Gran said.

Sage nodded. "You take care of yourself so well, what difference does it make what job your soul mate has?"

"Soul mates are a concept fabricated by Hallmark and perpetuated by pop culture," Margie said.

"One day, Ms. Know-it-all, you're going to land smack dab on the lily pad of love," Gran told her. "Until then, you can keep your negative nelly thoughts out of Pepper's life. She needs some help here."

"Gran, you're welcome to stay, but I don't need help with my love life."

"You kinda do," Sage said. "Dating is the only thing you're *not* good at. And nobody knows you better than we do. We just want to help. We never get to help you with anything."

"On that, I can agree," Margie said. "Feeling useless to aid a dear sister is demoralizing."

"You're demoralized because I don't need your help?" Pepper didn't buy it for a second. Margie was super smart, working at some sciency business so complicated, no one understood what she did. She didn't need to help *Pepper* to know she was making contributions to the world.

"Growing up being told all about how you changed your own diapers at six months old and were training the goats before you could even talk? Yes. Also demoralizing."

"You don't actually believe that."

"While I acknowledge the story was a myth cultivated by our eldest sisters to encourage feelings of inadequacy and squash any thoughts of superiority in the younger half of the family, feelings are not always swayed by logic. Alas."

"At least let us find you a guy who won't leave with one of the cousins," Sage said.

An unexpected sting burrowed into her eyeballs. Not at the reminder of what her date had done at the last family wedding—or her next date at the subsequent wedding of her former date and her cousin —but because her family loved her.

They wanted to see her happy.

And when her test turned up positive next week, who better to share impending motherhood with than her grandmother? And her sisters?

She swiped at her eyes and surreptitiously sniffled. "Who needs a man when I have you?"

"Nice try, missy," Gran said. "We're finding you a man."

"I still think we should start with the pizza guy," Sage said. "She saw him today, I know she did, and she's not telling what happened."

Margie shook her head. "She'll do far better if her prospective mate is of a similar socioeconomic background, but given that Pepper never fails at anything, if she finds him sexually attractive and intellectually stimulating despite his career choice, she could potentially make it work and be his sugar mama."

"So this week's for reviewing dating profiles," Pepper said, because arguing was useless. She could play along. Play along and stall until she had that positive pregnancy test.

Gran and Sage shared a look.

"You betcha," Gran finally said. "Time for research. Go grab that computer doohickey, and let's get to work."

This was a good thing, Pepper told herself as she headed up to her bedroom to rescue Sadie. Gran might've been headstrong and inappropriate at times, but she was fun. And she loved her family, and she'd be thrilled to be getting another great-grandchild.

Having Gran move in wasn't exactly in the plans, but this latest houseguest would be a great distraction from dwelling on the state of her uterus for the next nine days.

TRAFFIC WAS slow at Pepperoni Tony's Monday at lunchtime, and Tony was beginning to worry.

His first shop over in Willow Glen had taken off immediately when he opened it five years ago. His pizza was damn good. It sold itself. Here in Bliss, his was the first brick-oven pizzeria in town. His customers all told him they'd be back, his Yelp ratings were fantastic, the atmosphere oozed warm Italian family, but he was barely breaking even.

Possibly because most of his customers were out-of-towners.

Brides and grooms and their families shopping for wedding supplies. Guests in for destination weddings. The occasional weirdos who swung through town just to take pictures of the massive wedding cake monument at one end of the main drag, which locals called *The Aisle* instead of Main Street because it fit the theme.

But out-of-towners didn't make for good repeat visitors.

Today, he was balancing double duty as busboy and extra server in the dining room. Red-and-green stained-glass lampshades hung over every booth. Family photos and customer artwork covered the wood-paneled walls, though there wasn't yet as much artwork as he would've liked. Red-checkered curtains hung on every window. Butcher paper served as tablecloths, encouraging kids and adults alike to color while they waited. The kitchen was behind an exposed brick wall that added as much flavor to the décor as Tony's secret spice blend did to the pizza sauce.

On his fourth trip out to deliver a pizza, he spotted a familiar face waiting for a waitress at one of the back booths.

A familiar *local* face.

"Lindsey." He put on his best *everything's great* smile, because she'd not only been one of his most loyal customers back in Willow Glen, she'd also gotten him out of giving Tabitha a single red cent in the divorce. Which meant she also knew every gruesome detail of his divorce, which still left his teeth on edge.

He nodded to her and the dark-haired couple in the red vinyl booth across from her. "How's the pizza?"

"As if you have to ask." She smiled back, one hand resting on her pregnant belly, and his gut bottomed out. It had been over a year since she worked his case, but she'd sent him a note a few months back that this building was coming on the market if he was still interested in expanding outside Willow Glen—translation, getting the hell out of Willow Glen—and he'd been able to purchase it quickly and quietly. The lady had a do-gooder streak in her. "But I do have a complaint about the menu. I didn't see any avocado."

"Pizza's fancy, salad isn't."

"I meant on the pizza."

"She's disgusting," the guy across from her piped up, prompting

18

his companion to shush him. He grinned at her.

"Like a chicken bacon ranch with avocado?" Hell if Tony would turn down an opportunity to make a local customer happy. Especially *this* one. Not only was she a popular native daughter, she was married to an international country rock sensation. One word from him could have this place flooded.

Lindsey shook her head. "Like pepperoni and pineapple and avocado."

"Okay, yes, she's disgusting," the dark-haired woman conceded.

"Tony, have you met Max and Merry? Max is moving into the building next door, so you'll be neighbors."

"The garage?" he asked.

Max nudged Merry's shoulder. "Merry's garage. I'm the hired help. Fixing up old cars."

"You are so much more than the hired help." Merry fluttered a hand against his bicep, her sappy smile making Tony's gut roil a little more.

This was the downside to life in Bliss. Not that he was opposed to love—he just wished his heart could hibernate like his dick had most of the last year. "You do oil changes?" Tony asked.

"For pizza? Hell yeah."

For pizza and for putting the word out among more locals. "Great." He looked back at Lindsey. "Let me know when you're coming back. I'll get an avocado just for you."

She gave him a quick once-over with her light brown eyes, as though she were looking for evidence of how he was holding up and how business was doing. "Have you joined the Bridal Retailers Association yet? They have a preferred list of local restaurants that goes out in bridal welcome packets."

And there went Pepper Blue invading his thoughts. "Been a little busy."

She didn't call him on the lie, but her face relaxed into blank-lawyer mode even though he knew she'd been out of the lawyer business for almost as long as he'd been divorced. As if she knew he'd been asked and had turned it down. Which she probably did, given the size of this town and the people she was related to.

"You should get on that," she said lightly.

"Good chance right now." Max pointed to something behind Tony. "Pepper's the one you need to talk to."

"Is that her grandmother?" Merry whispered.

Lindsey looked too. "Yes, that's Goosing Granny."

"What's the guy got on his hands?"

Tony blew out a slow breath and turned to look. Yep, there was Pepper, sitting at the table right beneath the picture of him as a four-year-old, on a leash, dressed as She-Ra while his sisters walked him. He hadn't noticed her, but then, he hadn't been looking. Her dark hair was swept back in a fancy ponytail, emeralds dangling from her earlobes, a brightly patterned green scarf draped over a fitted black shirt. Her outrageous grandmother, in a sweatshirt proclaiming her the world's best bungee jumper, bounced and clapped beside her—though her white curls, he noticed, didn't budge.

Across the table were two men—one hunched, gray, and balding, his lips curling in, his belt buckled about nipple level, chin at his chest as it moved slowly up and down, the occasional snore emanating from him.

The other was young, with a thick head of straight jet-black hair combed back, in a plaid shirt and a blue tie, a T-Rex puppet on his left hand and a stegosaurus puppet on his right. "What kind of pizza do you think we should have, Mr. Pointy Teeth?" he said in a falsetto voice.

"Anything raw and meaty, Steggy, my boy," he answered himself in a deep growl.

"You should eat your vegetables, Mr. Pointy Teeth," the stegosaurus said.

"I'm a carnivore, and I'd rather eat this lovely humanoid," Mr. Pointy Teeth said. He chomped toward Pepper, who blinked an imperious irritation that she'd aimed at him a time or two. "I can chomp five hundred pounds in a single bite. That means I could eat two of her."

"Isn't he fun?" Granny Grabby-hands said. "Noah will *love* this. You have to introduce Drew to CJ and Nat."

"He thinks I weigh two hundred fifty pounds," she said, and if Mr. Pointy Teeth and the oblivious dummy he was attached to didn't recognize that *I will eviscerate you first with my eyeballs, then with my tongue, and I'll finish you up with a knife in your thigh* tone, then he guessed Steggy was the smartest of the bunch.

"Did her grandmother really move in with her just to find her a date to her sister's wedding?" Merry whispered.

"That's what I hear," Lindsey replied just as softly.

"Someone should save her from this. Max—go save her."

There was a part of Tony—no small part—amused at the idea of Pepper taking Dino Man to a wedding.

There was another part of him—a stupider part—suggesting she needed a save. And that if he saved her, she'd owe him one. And that he could do this without his lower extremities getting involved. And that he'd break Max's friggin' neck before he'd let *him* be the one to rescue Pepper Blue.

His feet were moving before his brain could engage. He swung a chair from the next table around, straddled it, and propped an arm behind her chair. "Hey, gorgeous."

She swung around to face him, and her eyes widened. They were brighter than the sparkles in her ears, multifaceted with flecks the color of spring amidst the deep green, despite the *what the hell are you doing?* flashing through them. She blinked once, her lush ruby lips parted, and in an instant, the *what the hell* turned to *I might not like you, but* thank you.

"Hey, yourself." She tucked an errant, minuscule wisp of hair behind her ear. After the briefest hesitation, she reached her neck out, leaned into him, and brushed a kiss against his cheek.

His lungs hung suspended in his chest, unable to pull in air despite the hammering of his heart. His skin was tight, his stomach a tumbling vat of lava, and a tremor started in his knees and worked its way up his thighs, which felt as though he'd just squatted the entire building a thousand times.

"Thank you," she whispered before she pulled back, but her hand rested on his, and now his arm was on fire. *Good* fire. The kind of fire that funneled to his stomach and beelined to his groin. That wasn't a measly, bendable tent rod poking his zipper. That was a whole freaking flagpole.

Dammit.

Out of the corner of his eye, he saw her grandmother's jaw drop, and her top denture fell out.

"Steggy," Tony said without taking his eyes off Pepper, "you wanna grab that? Mr. Pointy Teeth's arms aren't long enough."

A moment of silence pulled his attention across the table. Up close, he realized her date was skinny, with a long face, plaid shirt, and wimpy irritation curling his lip. "Who are you?"

Tony reached across the table and shook Mr. Pointy Teeth's tiny hand. "Tony. Nice to meet you, Mr. Pointy Teeth."

Pepper snort-whimpered.

Granny Grabby-hands recovered her denture and worked it back and forth over her gums. She wagged a gnarled finger at Pepper. "He refused to strip for us!"

The old dude snuffled loudly and jerked his head up. "Chicken strips? I thought we were having pizza."

"Excuse me, but the ladies and my grandfather and I are here on a private date," Drew said. His dinosaur puppets were chomping on the edge of the table. That'd be an interesting insurance claim. *Damage occurred as a result of being gnawed on by dinosaurs with cloth teeth.*

"You told me you weren't dating the pizza man," Granny said.

"We wanted to keep it quiet for a while," Tony said.

"While it's new," Pepper agreed. "Because of...you know."

Oh, shit. What was *you know*? And did it matter? This was a onetime deal.

"*You haven't told him?*" Granny shrieked.

"Geez, Gran, I haven't asked him to marry me yet, either. I usually save all that for at least the third date."

And there went Tony's flagpole. More like a tadpole now.

"You propose on the third date?" Mr. Pointy Teeth's puppet master said. And the tool sounded *interested*.

"Not anymore," Pepper quipped.

"On that note," Tony said, "I need to get back to work." He pushed back from the table, executed a perfect chair spin to put it back at the table behind them, and touched Pepper between her shoulder blades. The contact sent a ripple of heat up his fingers to his forearm. "Later, beautiful."

"Can't wait, schmoopsy-kins." She flashed a smile, her focus directly on his nose.

He saluted the puppets. "Mr. Pointy Teeth, Steggy, nice to meet you. Gran, hope to see you again soon."

The words tasted like granite dust, but his smile felt real enough.

Joking around with a woman and her grandma, interrupting an awkward date—this was the most normal he'd been in almost two years. Since before his mom got sick, before Tabitha and—just before.

One of his waitresses was with Lindsey and Max and Merry, but Lindsey was giving him a funny look.

The kind that prompted a bone-deep, whole-body shiver. He pushed it off and cocked a finger at her. "Avocadoes?"

"Grocery store's right down the street."

Satisfied customers all around.

Life was good.

———

PEPPER USHERED Gran into the back of Bliss Bridal Boutique mid-afternoon Monday, still answering increasingly more difficult questions about Tony.

Tony. Tony with the crinkly-eyed pirate smile, the hilariously quick wit, and the remarkably simple solution to her dating problem.

If only he wasn't *Tony*.

Gran stopped in the doorway to the small office across from the kitchenette in the back of the boutique. "What's his last name?"

Crap. What *was* his last name? How did she not know her neighbor's last name? "For a woman who wants more great-grandchildren, you're being remarkably picky."

"You can learn a lot about a person from his last name."

"Whose last name?" Natalie, Pepper's sister-in-law and business partner at the boutique, waddled from the desk to the filing cabinet that was almost as tall as she was, dressed in a chic purple maternity dress that made her look like a fashionable grape.

"Pepper's boyfriend," Gran said. "He's a pizza-delivery guy."

Nat gave Pepper a half-squint before widening her stance and squatting to open the bottom drawer. "You have a boyfriend."

"It's...new."

"It's good to cast a wide net to catch the best fish, but you should've told me," Gran chided. "Poor Drew."

"*Poor Drew* wouldn't have noticed if your hair had been on fire."

"Who's Drew?" Nat asked. "I'm confused."

Gran plopped into the office chair and gave it a spin. "He was *supposed* to be Pepper's date at lunch today. He's a doctor."

"Of paleontology," Pepper clarified. "Gran set me up with Ross from *Friends*. With puppets."

Nat snerked. She shifted her weight and went one drawer up. "Dinosaur puppets? Does he do birthday parties? Noah would love that."

"See?" Gran stuck her tongue out at Pepper. "Some people can appreciate the unique."

"Does Mom know you got your tongue pierced?"

"YOLO, sweetheart," Gran said. "Tell me more about this pizza man."

She would've loved to, but *his cat is a demon and he slammed his door in my face yesterday and I have no idea why he'd pretend to like me today* wasn't the best start if she wanted Gran to quit setting her up on dates.

Having a fake boyfriend? Brilliant.

Tony as said fake boyfriend?

Insanity. And that was putting it nicely.

She turned to her sister-in-law. "Nat, you need some help?"

She was digging through the drawers, contorting her pregnant body and grunting. "Can you carry this thing for me for a few days?" the petite brunette joked with a point at her bulging stomach.

Pepper's own womb ached. *Soon.* Soon, that would be her too. Then no more dates, no more contemplating fake boyfriends, no more panic over getting too old to have kids.

And no more eating salad when she was dragged to a pizza joint for lunch.

"Not a chance," she told Nat. "I know his father too well."

"Apparently so do I." Nat flashed a cheeky grin. "Kinda how we got into this mess."

"Lalala, not listening..." Working with her sister-in-law was a special kind of gift. More family. More fun.

Usually.

Nat's pregnancy had been a convenient excuse for Pepper's own hormonal mood swings the last few months. *Too much time around pregnant women makes me crazy*, she'd told Cinna after they'd had a verbal bitch-slap session a month or so ago. *It's like when women's cycles sync. I'm having sympathetic pregnancy hormones.*

Or you're just mean, Cinna had said. They'd made up a few hours later, Cinna had had her own monthly hormonal outburst four days after that, and life went on.

Nat straightened and blew out a breath that pushed her short, dark hair out of her eyes. "Heard you moved in with Pepper and Cinna," she said to Gran. Nat was a Blue by marriage, but she had an evil streak of her own. "Sounds like you're having fun."

"I'm trying to, but someone's a real stick in the mud. She won't let me paint my room fuchsia."

"I don't want the fumes damaging any of your preciously limited supply of brain cells," Pepper said.

Nat's cheeky grin got bigger. "Good luck if you're trying to teach her to lighten up and have fun," she said to Gran.

Pepper sighed. She could lighten up. She could have fun. She'd simply been preoccupied with personal issues she wasn't ready to share yet.

Also, she'd worked her ass off the last fifteen years to get here—successful business owner, upstanding member of a prosperous community, with the house and the dog and soon the family. "You know you're only my favorite sister-in-law by default."

"And I always will be." Nat gave her a shoulder hug that was heavy on the belly and light on the squeeze.

"Need a nursemaid?" Pepper said. "Gran's quite spry for her age. Loves to give advice. Has an adorable dog that'll bite your ankles if you do something so heinous as feeding it dog food instead of canned tuna. And she makes the best cornmeal mush I've ever tasted."

"That's disgusting."

"It was good enough for George Washington, it's good enough for my family," Gran declared. "And I make the best raisin pies this side of the Mississippi."

Nat shuddered. "I can't believe I'm about to say this, but I'd rather have Cinna."

"That can be arranged too," Pepper offered.

"Stop it. You're raising my blood pressure. Tell me more about this pizza man. You went to Pepperoni Tony's, right? Oh, wait—is this the delivery stripper?"

"He was never a stripper, and his name is Tony." As in *Pepperoni Tony's*, which Gran apparently hadn't picked up on yet.

Nat, however, probably had. "Your sisters liked him, I heard."

"So did I," Gran said.

"That's just because he gave you a lap dance." See? Pepper could be funny.

Nat wheezed out a bark of laughter. "Stop, you're going to make my water break."

"You have clients this afternoon?" While Pepper managed the showroom downstairs with bridal and bridesmaid gowns, Nat had her own space upstairs where she designed custom gowns and oversaw the alterations room. Brides were willing to pay a pretty penny for original gowns from Bliss, and the boutique was thriving.

"Alterations," Nat said. "The bride is this sweet seventy-year-old lady. Her daughters and future daughters-in-law are her bridesmaids. She has two with her today—the others didn't need as much work."

"Family fun."

"If you love tension and drama and one bridesmaid calling the bride names when she thinks no one is listening." Nat swiped the back of her hand over her forehead and sucked in an audible breath as though she were trying to squeeze air into a balloon while someone was sitting on it. "Have you seen a bag of fabric pencils down here? Noah used to color with them when I wasn't looking."

"The pencils in the bottom of the filing cabinet? I took those upstairs last week."

"Dammit. Now I have to waddle back upstairs." She propped her hands on her lower back and steered her belly toward the door.

"Text me next time. If you need something down here, one of us will run it up."

After Nat left, Pepper physically unplugged the internet from her work computer and showed Gran how to play solitaire before ducking out to check on the customers and bridal consultants on the floor.

She loved the boutique and had from the first moment she'd seen it almost two years ago. Rows and rows of dresses, satin and lace, bustles and tiaras and veils. Large dressing rooms surrounding a viewing area with a floor-to-ceiling mirror and ivory Victorian couches for the bridal parties. The lingering scent of wedding cake added an ambiance the other boutiques in Bliss couldn't replicate, thanks to the bakery next door.

The bridal consultants were well-trained, and many had been with the boutique since before Pepper had become Nat's partner, back when Nat was a single mom struggling to fit in on The Aisle. So much history here, so much warmth, so much excitement from brides embarking on their next stage of life. Not just in the boutique, but in the entire town.

Pepper popped back into the office to check on Gran as an ominous *thump* sounded upstairs.

She took the stairs two at a time and burst into the brightly lit, multi-mirrored alterations room to a sight that she honestly wished was more unusual.

"Ladies!" she yelled over the pandemonium. Nat held her belly, eyes bulging as though she were trying to suck in enough air to continue giving the two bridesmaids a talking-to. Usually, she would've had a mouthful of pins and still have been able to talk down any emotional or irrational members of the bridal party, but today, her gaze swiveled to Pepper with an undeniable *help* written in her expression. The two on-staff seamstresses were nowhere in sight.

"Let's all take a deep breath and—" Pepper started.

A pincushion bopped her in the cheek.

"She is too a gold digger!"

"If you don't stop saying that about my mother, I'll—"

"Oh, shove it. I didn't say they don't deserve each other."

"Stop! You're about to be sisters."

"I will *never* call that judgmental sack of crap my—"

Pepper stuck her fingers in her mouth and gave a shrill whistle. The three women paused, one with a handful of ripped peach satin, another with a fabric pencil clenched in her fist, the bride with eyes brimming.

"Save the drama for the wedding, ladies. Our job is to make you look good, not give you a practice run for the reception. And we'll be happy to add any damages to your bill."

The younger bridesmaid—a brunette in a floor-length peach satin dress gaping about her chest who was probably in her mid-thirties, if not older—pointed the fabric pencil at the bride. "She's marrying my father for his money, but she's not going to get a single penny of it."

Pepper stepped between the two of them and plucked the fabric pencil away. "Far better money than love. At least you won't picture them having sex."

The bride's daughter squeaked.

"Oh, *gross*," the apparent future stepdaughter whispered.

"That is none of your business," the bride, a pleasantly plump lady with forehead wrinkles beneath stylish short hair, informed Pepper primly.

Maybe not, but they'd stopped terrorizing the alterations room before they got to the scissors or the mirrors. "Put that fabric back where you found it, please. And you—if you're in a dress, you need to stay on your block. Nat, where do you want them?"

She turned to her partner, looking for further guidance.

All the blood had left Nat's face. Her lips were parted, hands clenching her belly, eyes pinched in pain.

"Pepper?" she whispered. She glanced down at the floor. "My water just broke."

$\mathcal{T}$ony should've known this was coming, but the commanding knock at his front door shortly after nine still took him by surprise. Lucky, his gray tabby rescue cat, streaked through the kitchen to hide behind the grumbling fridge. Probably needed to replace that soon.

The fridge. Not the cat.

He lowered the heat on his sautéing veggies, tossed the cast-iron skillet with his steak into the oven, and headed to the door. The worn wooden floors creaked, much like his bones after a long day on his feet. He'd been spending so many hours at Pepperoni Tony's, he hadn't worked out in two weeks. Hadn't eaten much more than pizza in four days, and last night, he'd almost shredded mozzarella into the cat's food bowl and topped his slice with kibble.

Hence the real dinner tonight followed by an early-ish bedtime.

Not on the menu? Sharing it with the woman standing on his porch, arms crossed, toe tapping, lips set in a grim line.

So much for that gratitude she'd shown him earlier.

"Pepper, such a pleasant surprise."

She wasn't in a coat, so either she wasn't staying long, or she was assuming he'd invite her inside.

"We need to make a deal." Not a question. Not *would you like to make a deal?* Nope, Pepper Blue simply decided something needed to be done, and that was that.

It set his teeth on edge. "I believe the words you're looking for are *thank you.*"

Her shark smile shouldn't have stirred his dormant parts, but there it went, sitting up with interest. *Dammit.*

"I believe the words *you're* looking for are *Why, yes, Pepper, I'd like to stay in business in Bliss for years, so I'd be happy to talk to you about a deal.*"

"Business is fine, thank you."

"Then maybe the words you're looking for are *I'm so sorry I've been pulling your ponytails instead of just telling you I like you, Pepper.*"

"Amusing, but wrong."

"Suit yourself. By the way, Billy Brenton was in town today. Lindsey specifically asked him *not* to go to lunch with her. She's waiting to see how you fit in with the locals before she lets him put his stamp of approval on your pizza."

She turned to go, and despite his ego's objection, he called to her. "Wait."

That expectant, *go on, tell me you'll give me what I want* look was annoying as hell.

But even without dangling the Billy Brenton stamp of approval over his head, he knew she was right. He needed to get in better with the locals if Pepperoni Tony's had any chance at all of surviving here.

And the only thing he knew for damn sure was that he didn't want to go back to Willow Glen. Especially as a failure.

He'd failed enough already.

He kicked the door open wider. "You had dinner?"

She didn't smirk—exactly—but she didn't smile either. "I have, thank you."

"Since you'll probably send your grandmother over next if I don't let you in, I guess you can watch me eat."

She stepped inside his house and glanced around the living room. No doubt judging his bachelor pad, complete with sectional sofa pointed at the big-screen TV, Cubs posters on the walls, old magazines on his listing coffee table, and scattered cat toys on the floor.

"Gran's busy," she said. "There was a catfight in the alterations room at the boutique this afternoon, and Nat's water broke right in the middle of it, so Gran's at the hospital, waiting."

Obviously her game was to confuse him until he agreed to something horrible. "Her…?"

"Water broke. Right there in the middle of the alterations room. One minute, the alterations room is in chaos because the grown daughter and future stepdaughter of the bride are at each other's throats, and the next, Nat's standing in a puddle of amniotic fluid."

Retreat. Run. Truck. Drive. Forever scrub the image of any woman's water breaking from his brain.

He hadn't needed the unwelcome memories of what had happened to *him* in a labor and delivery room. Felt like yesterday, even though he knew the kid had turned a year old in December.

Without waiting, she followed the smell of food to his kitchen and settled herself at the small wooden island that served as both kitchen table and spare counter space. He went back to his vegetables, ignoring the searing ache in his chest.

"Your deal's about a woman in labor?" he asked.

"My last fifteen boyfriends have married the next woman they dated after me. Gran's scheduling me for double dates from now until my sister Tarra's wedding in two weeks because she's convinced she can break my streak. Unless you agree to continue this ridiculous charade you started at lunch today. Which I'm very grateful for, by the way, even if it was the most insane idea I've heard in months."

She made his divorce sound normal and totally cured that dancing in his pants with just a few little words. "You sweet-talker you. How's a guy supposed to turn that down?"

"Have no fear. I probably won't even need you the full two weeks.

And since it's fake, there's little danger you'll actually marry the next woman you meet. Although, given the rate you go through women, you're sure to find one sooner or later."

"Better and better with every word." Why had he let this woman in his house again? And why had she been watching his house closely enough to see how many women he had coming and going since he moved in?

"In return, I'll spread word among Bliss's movers and shakers that you're a decent guy with a good product and that Pepperoni Tony's is worthy of being added to our preferred restaurant list."

He pulled the steak out of the oven, speared it with a fork, and slapped it on one of his mom's old Polish pottery plates. "And?"

"And what?"

"And what else? You're asking me to give up dating"—*ha*, dating, he had the world fooled, didn't he?—"and go to a wedding and probably kiss you in front of your family, and all you're going to do is say a few nice things about me."

"I could say not-nice things about you and get you blacklisted."

"But you wouldn't do that, because you're secretly a cream puff in a shark suit."

"Don't try me, pizza man."

"You want to, don't you?" He set his plate on the island, loaded down with steak and bread knots and sautéed beans and julienned carrots, and leaned his elbows on either side of it to put his face closer to hers. "You want to kiss me."

If she did, that desire was buried under about forty-eight layers of *you wish*, *gag me*, and *no*. "That line might work on your usual type, but I have absolutely no interest in engaging in *any* physical activity with you beyond the necessities to convince my grandmother to stay the hell out of my dating life for the next two weeks."

He was going to have to kiss her, if for no other reason than to annoy her.

Hoped he remembered *how*.

PIPPA GRANT WRITING AS & JAMIE FARRELL

"And, unfortunately," she continued, "Gran's sharp. We're probably going to have to feign deeper intimacy."

That party in his pants went into full rave mode while a string of his favorite foul words echoed through his head. The last year, he'd taken out friends' sisters, his sisters' friends, random chicks he'd picked up at the bar. Blondes, brunettes, redheads. Short, tall, curvy, slender. Waitresses and teachers. Scientists and business owners.

Better off single anyway, the men in his family had said. *Who wants one woman their whole life? Not a Cross man, that's for damn sure.*

A different woman every night was what his brothers expected, even if it made his sisters roll their eyes. But not a single woman he'd taken out had done for him what this obnoxious woman was doing right now.

He sliced too hard into his steak.

"I can handle my grandmother if lunch today was a onetime deal," Pepper said. "Whether we do this or not is your call. You have way more to lose. But since you started it..."

Maybe he was looking at this wrong. Maybe he should be *glad* his equipment was coming out of hiding for Pepper. Wasn't any chance he'd get attached. He could kiss her. Might even sleep with her. Take some pressure off.

All the physical perks, none of the heartache.

He dropped his knife, and it clattered to the plate. "We should practice."

Now that eyeball she was inspecting him with wasn't quite so cocky. "Being nice to each other?"

"I've met your sisters. I highly doubt they expect us to be nice to each other."

She laughed, a buzz went through his veins, and his groin throbbed so hard he might've flipped something vital inside out.

"An unfortunately fair point," she conceded. "We should get a contract drawn up."

Screw that. He stalked around the island. She *was* pretty, when she wasn't harping at his cat or looking down her nose at him. He could do worse.

"Chicken?" he asked.

"Revolted," she replied cheerfully.

He didn't believe her. And now he wanted to taste her. For the first time since he'd discovered just how much Tabitha didn't love him, a woman was honestly intriguing to him.

He wasn't stupid—commitment and good taste in women didn't run in his family, at least not on the male side—but a kiss wasn't a promise of love and forever. She didn't want either of those from him.

She wanted an excuse.

He hooked his hand behind her neck, watching those green eyes search his, wondering what she was thinking, what secrets she was keeping, and which one of them would regret this in the morning.

She didn't stop him.

No, she tilted her face up and closed her eyes. "If we must, I suppose we must."

He brushed his lips across hers, a feather-soft touch of his sandpaper to her velvet. The air moved against his skin when her lips parted in a sharp inhale. Her hands settled at his waist, hesitant fingers barely touching his shirt. He cupped her smooth, hot neck, all that thick, silky hair teasing the back of his hand.

She was warm and pliant, which he hadn't expected at all. Gentle kisses to the corner of his mouth. A brush of her breasts against his chest.

A groan rumbled in his throat, and he claimed her mouth like a savage beast.

He'd missed kissing. Touching. Mating.

Instinct demanded that he claim her. Mark her. Push her against the nearest wall and own her.

Brand her with his kiss. Ignite her skin with his touch. Pleasure her until she was ruined for anyone else. So she'd never kiss another man. Never love another man. Never fucking *look* at another man.

Never betray him.

Never leave him alone.

Never break him.

She gripped him tighter and whimpered into his kiss, a mewling *more* sound that sent savage fire through his veins, but which also sent reality crashing into his chest.

Not real, he reminded himself.

A distant memory of a laugh trickled through his head. Not his own laugh. Tabitha's laugh.

He broke the kiss with a muffled curse.

Pepper's eyes were black as night, her lips swollen, her chest rapidly rising and falling. "Okay then," she said. "Glad we got that out of the way."

His skin itched. His hair itched. His *heart* itched.

He couldn't do this.

Not if he wanted to stay whole.

She stuck her hand out, and on instinct, he took it.

"Pleasure doing business with you," she said. "I'll call you tomorrow to discuss the details."

He blinked, and she was gone.

Funny.

Same thing had apparently just happened to his sanity.

PEPPER WAS ON HER TIPTOES, reaching for her hidden bag of chocolate chips and trying to forget Tony and his kiss and the suddenly over-complicated task of pretending she liked him.

That they were dating.

Intimate.

This was *not* what she needed to be doing right now. She needed to be taking it easy. Not stressing. Not adding crazy hormones to the mix.

But she hadn't been kissed in months, and she probably wouldn't be kissed again for years, and if she had to give up kissing, that was quite the kiss to go out on.

Probably good that it came from Tony. If it had come from a man she could've actually liked, she might've been in danger of wanting more.

How many times in the last fifteen years had she gotten so wrapped up in a kiss, so wrapped up in a man, only to discover he hadn't felt the same? In her early twenties, she'd dated older men. Responsible men with solid jobs who owned their own houses and drove dependable cars, because those men would make good husbands and fathers, and there was nothing she'd wanted more than to have her own babies.

Not the way her parents had—crowded, rambunctious, and on a tight budget. Yes, there had been love. More than enough love and acceptance and encouragement. And she appreciated each of her siblings—even Cinna—more now than she ever had. But she still liked stability. Comfort. Excelling.

In her late twenties, she'd begun to date men closer to her own age. She'd been working at a big-box bridal store in St. Louis, and while she'd done well there, she'd known something was lacking in her own career.

Then, two years ago, she'd come to Bliss for Saffron's wedding and ended up falling in love with The Aisle. *This* was the professional home she'd been looking for. Her boyfriend—the one she'd been sure had been *the* one, and whom she *hadn't* taken to Saffron's wedding just in case—had asked casually a week later if she minded if he asked one of her friends out, and the sudden shock of having it happen *again* had been what she'd needed to make the leap.

She'd come to Bliss, asked around, discovered Nat's father was talking about selling Bliss Bridal, and she'd never looked back.

Except to occasionally wonder about where her love life would be if she'd put less emphasis on financial success and the image of the perfect life, and paid more attention to what her heart was telling her.

Tonight, her heart was telling her that had been one hell of a kiss.

And that was all she was willing to concede.

George launched into his yipping. Sadie was still hiding in Pepper's room upstairs, but she barked too.

Probably hiding under the bed, the sweet goober.

She dropped back onto her feet and pretended to be straightening the mushroom crocks beside the stove.

Both because she hated getting caught looking for her chocolate chip stash, and because she did *not* need the sugar or caffeine. By her calculations, the embryo should be implanting itself about now. Which meant it was even more important for her to chill out.

"Thought you were closing tonight," she said to the footsteps behind her.

"As if. I called in a replacement." Cinna dropped her neon-green shoulder bag on the counter and stuck her head in the fridge. "What are you doing here? Everyone's at the hospital. Nat's dilated to nine, and if she delivers in the next two hours, *you're* going to win the family pool. How often does that happen? *Oh.* You had a date with the pizza man."

"I didn't—"

"I can *smell* him on you. Sauce and mozzarella don't lie. But you might. Are you dating him? Or did you just tell Gran that so she'll quit setting you up with guys whose grandfathers she thinks are hot?"

"I don't need to invent a fake relationship to get out of going on double dates with Gran." She was such a liar.

Cinna studied her, then grinned. "Good. Then we can make your celebrity couple name official. *Pepperony*. So romantic. And fitting. Plus, it's like he named his pizza place after you, even though he gets double billing there. Neither of you will ever find a better match. Although, I guess if you found a guy named Steak..."

"Can a girl date a guy for a few weeks before getting a celebrity couple name?"

"Why? Are you thinking of dumping him already? It's the pizza-delivery guy thing, isn't it? If he were a billionaire cowboy, you'd be saddling up. Admit it."

Discussing this without twitching, flinching, or wanting to gag had to get easier.

Or possibly the gag thing meant the IVF had finally worked.

"You, of all people, know he's not just a delivery boy. Also, I should charge you more to live here," she told Cinna.

"You love me and you know it." Cinna popped the lid off the milk, gave it a sniff, and then chugged straight from the container.

Pepper made a strangled noise. "*What are you doing?*"

"Finishing the milk. By the way, Gran gave me grocery money. And she says we don't keep enough liquid nutrition in the house."

"You are *not* buying Gran tequila. Or gin. Not while I'm responsible for her."

Cinna took another swig, then slammed the empty jug on the counter and wiped her upper lip with the back of her sleeve. "She's hilarious when she's toasty."

"She's pushing ninety and dangerous enough as it is. *And* she grabbed my b-boyfriend's ass."

Dammit. She hadn't meant to say that. Cinna's instincts were razor sharp. She'd either call Pepper's bluff, or she'd tell the whole family.

"B-boyfriend?" Cinna said.

"Shut up. It's new." Definite twitching. "And I haven't used that word in relation to myself and someone new in a *long* time."

"Maybe Gran really is the antidote to your love life."

Not likely.

"Anyway, I don't care if you're real-dating him or fake-dating him. Remember Ginger's story? Gran moved in with her, so she asked Bruce to pretend to date her so Gran would back off. *Poof!* Six months later, they were married."

Pepper squeezed her eyes shut and counted to ten.

When she opened them, Cinna was still in her kitchen, and her words were still lingering.

"Come on. Let's go. Gran's been cruising the geriatric ward at the hospital, looking for single men with single grandsons, while we wait for the baby. She says you need a backup plan. Plus, I want to be there when CJ passes out."

And this was exactly why Pepper kept certain parts of her life private. She had ten sisters and two brothers, and though the human body was supposedly seventy percent water, every last Blue child was seventy percent mischief. God forbid an outsider joke about CJ passing out in the delivery room, but inside the family, it was fair game.

"Put me down for five on him staying upright with flying colors," she said. Because family bets were *so* much safer than discussions of her love life.

Cinna grabbed a pen from the magnetized holder on the fridge, then ripped a sheet off Pepper's grocery list paper. "Ten dollars, Pepper votes he'll pass out," she murmured.

"I said he *won't*. And five more says he cuts the cord."

"Hush. His ego's already too big for getting Nat pregnant in the first place. It's our duty to vote against him."

"I honestly don't know why he lets you work at his bar."

"It's my charm with the customers." Cinna grinned. She had the best of all the Blue genes—the red hair, the green eyes, the outgoing personality, and the stubbornness to get whatever it was she wanted. At twenty-five, she hadn't yet figured out exactly what it was that she wanted, but when she did, *look out, world*. "Come on. Get your coat. Even if he doesn't pass out, I can't wait to see his face when he has a girl."

George yipped at the back door again, so Pepper let him in. He promptly attacked Cinna's shoelaces. "Go on," Pepper said. "George needs as much attention as Gran, and I've seen as much of this birth process as I want to already."

"Fine. Stay here. But if Nat's within five minutes of midnight when she delivers, I'm giving Tarra the winnings. She's all in for a girl tomorrow."

George growled.

Huh. He was good for something after all.

"You cheat, and I'll have George pee on your sheets."

"That's so last week." Cinna grabbed a granola bar from the cupboard before spinning back toward the door with an impish grin. "Last chance. You coming?"

"Nope. I'm stopping by tomorrow when I don't have to fight all of you to hold the baby."

Cinna's lips parted. "Oh, that's low."

"Run along. Wouldn't want anyone to lie to you about when the baby's born."

"Hmm." She hefted her bag on her shoulder and gave Pepper one more once-over. "I'll give you this round. But if you're not at the hospital, you can't stop me from taking bets about you and the pizza man."

"Go for it."

Much to her surprise, Cinna let it drop.

When she was gone, Pepper eyeballed her chocolate chip cabinet again and then the fridge.

She still had leftover pizza. And much as she disliked the man who made it, the pizza itself still smelled delicious.

Probably because she hadn't had any in so long.

Not because the pizza was special.

Or the kiss.

Although, it wouldn't be *entirely* bad if he had to kiss her again. Let her ride that bike one last time.

"Seven more days," she whispered to herself.

Seven more days, and she'd have confirmation that she'd finally done this getting-pregnant thing right, and she wouldn't be dealing with a fake boyfriend any longer, and she could eat carbs again.

She hoped.

PEPPER KNOCKED SOFTLY and poked her head into Nat's maternity ward hospital room Tuesday morning. The mint green walls, wood-

41

paneled cabinets, and rocking chair gave the room a warm, cozy feeling despite the hospital bed and antiseptic scent.

Her womb gave a pang.

She'd be in here herself with her own baby in about nine months…wouldn't she?

"Can Auntie Pepper come in?" she whispered.

"No." Her brother CJ put no heat in the word. The big redheaded doofus grinned as he rocked a bundle of blankets that she suspected held her brand-new nephew.

She dangled a gift bag. "I brought presents."

"For me?" he deadpanned. "You shouldn't have."

"For the first Blue man born in thirty-two years. Nice job, princess."

"Auntie Pepper better quit calling me *princess* if she wants to hold you," he cooed to the baby.

"Could call you by your real name instead."

"And I can have hospital security see you out."

Nat laughed from the bed. Her short dark hair was smushed against the white pillows, but despite the bags beneath her eyes, she looked more at ease than she'd been in months. Pregnancy hadn't been kind to her petite figure. Already the puffiness in her cheeks was going down, and while she'd never had a pregnancy glow, happiness was radiating off her now.

"And flowers for mama," Pepper said, handing over the other half of the bundle of gifts in her hands.

"Oh, you shouldn't have."

"For what you've done for my family, we all owe you more than flowers. Taking care of this big doofus *and* giving us a nephew? You're a saint."

"Oh, stop." Nat pushed herself up and took the tulips with a smile. "How's business today? Any more bridezillas? Did you get my…er… mess cleaned up?"

"Maternity leave. No shop talk." Pepper took a squirt of hand sanitizer from a dispenser on the wall and angled over to peek at the baby. "Oh, he's beautiful, Nat. Has CJ let you name him yet?"

"Sitting right here," CJ said.

"Our negotiations are progressing," Nat said cheerfully. "Congrats to you too, by the way. I heard you won the family pool. The date part, at least."

"Miracles all around."

"I can't believe none of you bet on me having a boy though."

"With *eleven girls* in the family? Plus Basil? I'm surprised CJ's capable of making a boy."

Over CJ's feeble objections, she took the baby and studied his pinched eyes, the white speckles on his nose, and the lock of soft, dark hair peeking out from beneath the blue knit hat. His cheeks were plump and rosy, and his little lips were suckling as though he were already dreaming about milk.

She hadn't gotten to hold her sister Saffron's new baby at the wedding. Too many other sisters and aunts had vied for the honor all night, and at some point, it got easier not to fight.

"Hello, handsome," she whispered. Speaking any louder would've been impossible with the lump suddenly clogging her throat.

Maybe she could have a boy too. She and Nat worked side by side most days at the boutique, and their sons could play together too.

She blinked rapidly and swallowed hard. "Has Noah met him?"

When CJ married Nat a year ago, he'd gotten an instant family with both her and her son. Until the baby, Noah had been the only nephew in the family.

"Oh, yes," Nat said. "Grandpa brought him by an hour ago. He's in love. And he's already talking about making a dinosaur costume for the baby."

"With a dress?"

"No, he seems to be growing out of the dress phase." Nat swiped at her suddenly shiny eyes. "My baby's growing up."

"We can have more," CJ offered. "I like this one."

She tossed a pillow at him. "You weren't the one pregnant and in labor. You didn't push nine pounds of baby out—"

"But I give good foot and back rubs."

The baby yawned and wiggled. When he blinked big, brilliant blue, unfocused eyes up at Pepper, her heart melted into a pile of sappy goo, and she had to will back the sting in her eyes again.

She wouldn't have the man at her side to rub her back, but God willing, she'd still get a baby of her own.

4

*T*ony left the pizzeria in good hands just after lunch Tuesday and headed down The Aisle. He hadn't been here much since he moved to town—he'd come to Bliss because the market was ripe for its first brick-oven pizzeria, not because he loved the bridal crap—but he knew Lindsey and Pepper were both right about him getting involved here if he wanted to succeed.

He'd joined the Willow Glen Chamber of Commerce. And he was being stupid in shunning Bliss's equivalent. Good pizza wasn't always enough.

Which was how he found himself in a bright, cheery bakery just off The Aisle, trying to concentrate on the cupcake case and not the blonde proprietress's protruding belly.

Was *everyone* pregnant in this town?

"I didn't think you two liked each other." What was her name? Karen? Kami? *Kimmie*. Right. Kimmie. And there was an accusation lingering in her blue eyes. As if Tony had broken some unspoken rule of Bliss by coming in to buy Pepper a cupcake.

Probably had. "Misunderstanding."

"So your cat didn't attack her dog?"

He refused to let his shoulders tense. That hadn't been Lucky's fault. "She's a rescue. Had a hard life. Just needs a little love."

Kimmie blinked, touched her belly, and smiled softly at an athletic-looking guy working on a laptop in the corner. "Salted caramel fudge," she said. "And a sex on the peach cupcake for Gran."

There was a time when he was good with grandparents. Looked like he needed to find that part of his personality again. "Beach?"

"No, peach. It's on the secret menu."

Three minutes later, he was twenty bucks lighter and loaded down with four cupcakes and a chicken salad sandwich, and he still wasn't entirely sure how Kimmie had gone from flashing a sweet smile at him to upselling him so high. Probably needed to figure that out and put it into practice at Pepperoni Tony's.

He turned down the alley before he got to The Aisle proper, and made his way to the back of Bliss Bridal. Going in the front, with all those brides, wasn't his first choice, but he'd do it if no one answered in back.

Lucky for him, someone answered.

Unlucky for him, it was Granny Grabby-hands.

"Pizza delivery? Or are you really going to take your clothes off this time?" she asked.

"Cupcakes, and it's still not your lucky day."

"Hmph. You young people. So uptight. Do you have any grandfathers still alive? Are they single?"

"No grandfathers," he told her.

"Fathers? I'm pretty spry for my age."

"None available." But the thought of turning this woman loose to wreak havoc on his father was enough to make him smile for real.

Which was apparently the secret password for getting in out of the cold, because Gran opened the door wider and gestured him into a small kitchenette. She snagged the bakery bag from him and deposited it next to three other boxes that were suspiciously familiar.

As though he was about six hours too late with the cupcakes, because Pepper had gotten her own this morning.

46

Not that Gran minded. She dug into the new box and latched on to the peach cupcake. "Now, tell me all your secrets. Any criminal record?"

"Nope."

"Did you pass high school?"

"Yep."

"Are you really interested in Pepper, or do you just want her to do her magic so you can marry one of her sisters?"

Definitely the oddest question he'd ever been asked. And not one he was touching. "You ever have trouble telling them apart?"

"Never. Except maybe Pepper and Basil from time to time."

"Pepper and—*Father* Basil? From St. Valentine's?"

"Yep. Two peas in a pod, those two."

He didn't know much about the stiff priest up the road, but Pepper didn't strike him as *stiff*. Driven, maybe, but not stiff.

Especially not after that kiss last night. "It's because they're your favorites, isn't it?"

She punched him in the arm and laughed. "I like you. You're funny. How long do you intend to wait before sleeping with my granddaughter?"

There went that party in his pants again.

Not that it mattered. They'd both more or less agreed the only sex they'd be having would be as fake as their relationship.

Plus, nothing like underperforming a debut to ensure it wouldn't happen again. And send him back to limp-noodle land for another year. Which would undoubtedly happen. "That's one of those questions you're going to have to talk to her about."

"How many ex-wives do you have?"

His shoulders threatened to corner his ears again. One. And she was enough. "Six, if you count the five from my time in the cult. But don't worry—I left that life behind last year. Pretty sure only two of the wives are still looking for me."

"Aren't you a smart-ass." And by the sounds of it, she approved. "I can see why you and Pepper get along so well."

"And I can see why she loves you so much." Hell, he was starting to sound like his father, full of charm for the ladies. He stretched his fingers and made himself lean casually against the wall.

"Gran?" Pepper's voice wafted down the hall. "Dammit, I told her —oh. There you are." She stopped in the kitchenette, looked at Gran, then Tony, then back again.

"You have a visitor," Gran said cheerfully.

"So I see."

"He brought cupcakes."

"Very nice of him."

"Well?"

The two of them stared at each other while Tony watched the show. Gran was in a Maroon 5 sweatshirt and neon pink linen pants. Pepper was her polar opposite, so buttoned-up in her fashionable skirt and blouse that it was hard to see where the prim ended and the priss began.

Finally, Gran *hmph*ed. "If you're not going to kiss him hello, I will."

"I'm at work. And if I hear you've been touching Tony inappropriately, you'll be eating dinner through a straw for the next week."

He choked. "Did you just threaten to punch your grandmother?"

Pepper rolled her eyes, and *boing!* There went his joystick. Only she could make rolling her eyes look hot. "I threatened to hide her dentures."

"Ah. Much better," he forced out. This conversation should've been deflating his stiffy, but it wasn't. "She's being a perfect gentleman this morning," he assured Pepper. "No grabbing my nipples or anything."

Now she was visibly fighting a smile, and he was losing yet another round to his groin. Not just her eyes sparkled when she smiled. Her whole *body* vibrated with suppressed mischief.

"Glad to hear it," she said.

"Shoo," Gran said. "I need to keep interrogating him."

Pepper crossed her arms. "Gran—"

"So you'll be like this when you're ninety?" Tony interrupted. He winked at her. He might've been malfunctioning from the waist down this past year, but he'd kept his flirting skills sharp. "I could handle that."

"Could you handle taking her shopping for a new retirement home? I'm happy to pay for gas to Peoria and back."

"Need to get back to work," he said. "Just thought I'd drop off some cupcakes."

Surprise flashed over her features. Because *he* thought to bring her cupcakes? Or because it had been too long since anyone had? "Thank you."

"I'm off at eight tonight. Stop by my place. Dinner's on me."

Her expression went guardedly blank. "Sounds great."

"Are you going to kiss him?" Gran demanded.

"Would that make you happy?"

"Yes."

"Then no, I'm not."

Tony sucked on his cheeks. Pepper sounded like a prude, but there was enough pluck in her voice that he wondered if he'd been reading her wrong. "Not even one little smooch?" he said.

She flicked her hands at him. "Out with you, or I won't get my work finished today."

"I'm going, I'm going." But he paused on his way by to put a hand to her back and peck her on the cheek. Close to the corner of her mouth. Close enough to inspire memories of kissing her in his kitchen last night, which would probably make him indecent to be out in public, but her breath caught, and he knew she was remembering too.

At least there was something to like about his neighbor.

THE DRIVE from Bliss Bridal to Suckers was taking four hours too long.

Okay, they'd only been driving three minutes, and only had five more to go, but Gran was on Pepper's last nerve.

"I didn't think you were serious about the stripping pizza man." Gran was wrapped up in a winter coat so huge she practically disappeared in the passenger seat, which unfortunately wasn't stopping her from talking.

"If I'd told you I was serious about him, you would've demanded to know his sperm count," Pepper replied pointedly.

"It's an important thing to know about a man."

"You didn't know Grandpa's sperm count when you married him."

"You young people have it so easy."

She smiled. Gran had a point.

"*Your* grandkids will probably be able to figure out their mates based on the chips the government will put in their brains at birth," Gran continued.

If she had grandkids.

She had to have kids first. This time next week, she'd know for sure she was finally on her way.

"If you marry Tony, you could name all your children after pizza toppings."

"Mushroom? Olive? *Anchovy Blue-Cross?*"

"Ham," Gran offered. "Tomato. Mozzarella. And why shouldn't he take your name? You could be the Cross-Blues instead of an insurance company."

Pepper steered her car into the Suckers parking lot. Cinna was pulling a shift at CJ's bar tonight, so she was on Gran duty.

And not a minute too soon.

Except now that she'd dropped Gran off, she had three hours to kill before she could meet Tony to sync their stories. So she went home, changed into jeans and a sweater, and grabbed the leashes to take the dogs for a walk.

And then she indulged in a little online fantasy shopping.

Cribs. Strollers. Adorable little onesies. Booties. And she'd need a good camera too.

She'd had a weird sensation in the pit of her stomach most of the day that she'd been doing her best to ignore. It wasn't something she'd experienced her last two tries.

Which maybe meant this time *had* worked.

Not that she had any doubt.

Pepper Blue didn't fail at anything.

Her phone alarm pulled her out of her browsing spree. She shut down her tablet and hid it in the locked safe in her bedroom, where she'd stashed all of her fertility medications, test kits, and the medical and insurance bills she'd had delivered to Bliss Bridal's PO box. Cinna was a snoop, so she'd had to take extra precautions to keep her out.

She peeked out her bedroom window and spotted Tony's big black truck. Her pulse fluttered. Time to do this.

If she didn't, she reminded herself, Gran would probably come home with goodness only knew who from Suckers tonight. Better the stress she knew to the stress she didn't.

Since it was just next door, she made the dash over without putting on a coat. The night was frigid, and she had goose bumps even on her rear end by the time Tony opened the door. "Evening. You like weenie mac? Got a whole pot going. I'll share."

"Hot dogs and macaroni and cheese?"

"Yep. From the box. Best kind ever."

He was such a bachelor. "That's disgusting."

"Food of champions."

The scent of sautéed garlic and onions wafted out of the house, along with something else savory she couldn't identify, and she realized she'd seriously underestimated Tony's ability to blend in with her family. He could prank with the best of them.

"You can have the weenie mac. I'll take whatever that is I'm smelling."

"Sorry. The bacon-wrapped scallops are for my cat."

Her left eye twitched.

He grinned, and that fluttering that had been quivering in her belly all day fluttered harder. He pushed the door open wider. "Get in here before you turn into a Peppersicle."

Once again, she followed him into his kitchen. All the houses in this part of town had been built in the early nineteen hundreds, if not before, which was a large part of their charm. It compensated for the issues that came with older houses for sure.

She'd redone her own kitchen when she moved in, but Tony's kitchen hadn't been touched in at least fifty years. The cabinets were all worn wood, with a few missing knobs. The wallpaper was faded yellow-and-brown plaid, the countertops olive green, and the vinyl on the floor was peeling. The only thing new was the IKEA-style island where he'd kissed her last night.

Nonetheless, the kitchen smelled amazing. Her belly rumbled.

"Make yourself comfy. Wine?"

"No, thank you."

He pulled a glass from the counter beside the sink, filled it with water, and handed it to her before he went to a cutting board on the counter beside the stainless steel oven. His arms flexed as he chopped scallions. Steam rose from a stockpot on the stove, and a pile of scallops already wrapped in bacon sat on a plate beside it.

"Why are you doing this?" she abruptly asked.

"I like having dinner most nights."

"Why are you *cooking* for me?" she clarified, fully aware she sounded like an ungrateful jerk. She wasn't trying to be. But this felt entirely too intimate, and she had no room for intimacy right now.

"What a boyfriend's supposed to do, isn't it?"

"If this were real, yes. But it's not. No one's watching. So this really isn't necessary." Her stomach threatened to kick her, because *it* was a brazen hussy who'd trade food for just about anything, but she ignored it. "*Appreciated*, but not necessary."

"Afraid you might come to like me a little?"

"No." She sighed. And *this* was perhaps part of her dating problem. "That came out wrong. I don't *dislike* you. Most of the time."

In another time and place, he could've been adorably sexy with those dark pirate eyes and that wolfish smile aimed at her over his shoulder. "How very honest of you."

This was getting her nowhere. She wouldn't mind being friends with her neighbor—provided he kept his cat inside—but that kissing thing wasn't happening again, and he needed to know it.

"We should discuss a few ground rules," she said.

"Oh, good. I love rules."

Twitch, twitch, twitch. "First, no dates."

He dropped the knife and laughed. "No dates? How does *that* work?"

"I'm busy at the boutique. You're busy at Pepperoni Tony's. My family's seen you, so they know you exist. They'll be pressuring me to bring you to the wedding, I'll resist because it's what I do, and no one will question the validity of our relationship working until the wedding's over and I don't need you anymore."

He stared at her like she'd sprouted live chickens out the tips of her hair.

"Second," she continued, "no kissing or touching unless we happen to end up in the same public space and it would be expected."

"It amazes me that you're still single."

She dipped her fingers in her water glass and flicked them at him. "Third, no sex."

"Truly astonishing."

She sighed out a growl. He'd fit right in with her family.

He turned to the stove and lit a burner beneath a frying pan. "No dates, no kissing, no fornication. Got it."

Her rules, and yet, when he parroted them back to her, she felt... offended? Hurt?

What difference did it make that he didn't want to see her naked and roll around in the sheets? *She* didn't want it either.

Perhaps it would've been nice to have felt attractive though.

One last time before her life completely flipped upside down. For the best reason.

"Once the Blueper Bowl is over, I'll take care of the paperwork to get Pepperoni Tony's listed on the recommended restaurants list. And I'll tell a few people to drop by for lunch."

"Blueper Bowl?"

"Super Bowl, Blue family style. It's a train wreck. You're not invited."

"I do love a good train wreck. Is Gran coming? She's quite the lady."

"You realize the harder you fight these rules, the more likely it is you're going to meet the woman of your dreams after we have our breakup, don't you?"

His shoulders shook in a silent chuckle. "Not worried."

"You should be. My track record's impeccable."

"I've already met the woman of my dreams."

Her heart flung itself against her ribs. He was *using* her. And not just for her connections.

Fine. What did she care? "And she's resisting marrying you. Of course. Sure. Fine. We're using each other. This is perfect. I get everything I want, you get everything you want, and everyone's happy."

She gulped her water, her hand wobbling.

Even the sarcastic jerk with the evil cat next door could find love. So what was wrong with *her* that she couldn't? She had her contingency plans, and she *would* have a baby, but was it so wrong to have wanted someone to share it with?

She had a speck of dust in her eye. Or possibly a whole dust bunny based on the way the darn things stung.

Freaking hormones.

"Matter of fact, here she is," he said. "Pepper, meet Lucky. Formally."

A soft *meow* had her blinking at the floor.

That scrappy little fur ball with deceptively innocent golden eyes slunk into the kitchen from a flap in the back door, hugging the baseboard. Her gray-striped fur was clean, but she was missing half her tail and she had a limp.

"The demonic *cat* is the woman of your dreams?"

"She's quiet, she doesn't yell at me when I leave my clothes on the floor, and she doesn't hog the covers. Though space on the bed is another story. And she's not demonic. She's recovering from life on the streets."

"She tried to bite Sadie's ear off."

"What would you do if you saw a shaggy bunny twice your size bearing down on you?"

"Sadie wasn't *bearing down on her*, she was investigating an unexpected visitor in the yard."

"Perspective is everything. And if we're going to pull this off, you're going to have to learn to appreciate my cat."

"I can fake it. And you don't get to call Sadie a *doggit*."

Now his eyes were *twinkling*. He was a twinkly-eyed pirate wolf in a chef's apron. Metaphorically speaking, of course, since he was actually in a loose gray polo and butt-hugging jeans that she was also doing her best to ignore.

"Seems like the kind of endearment your family would like." He dumped the chopped vegetables on his cutting board into the first pan and tossed Lucky a leftover scallion. She batted it across the floor, went down on her front legs, rear end wiggling before she pounced on it. "Plus, what else do you call a dog that thinks it's a rabbit? A *punny?*"

She wished she didn't instantly get the puppy-bunny thing, but she *was* a Blue. Good jokes were revered above all else. Tonight, however, she appreciated finishing this conversation—and probably eating those scallops—more than she appreciated his zinger. "Regardless, it's illegal to marry a cat, so I hope you understand that you're putting yourself in real danger of meeting the *human* woman of your dreams."

She wasn't sure if that look was *don't be a dumbass* or *we're not discussing this*, but it was clear he put no stock in her secret superpower.

"I will *never* get married again," he said. "Period."

Again. Okay then. There was a story there, but she didn't need to hear it.

Probably.

He flipped a pair of tongs and put the first scallop in the pan. A sizzle and the aroma of *delicious* filled the air. "You ask me, you're getting the better end of the deal. I'm going to break your streak."

She didn't know why, but a shiver worked its way down her spine, and she blurted the first thing that came to mind. "I meant it when I said no sex."

"Won't hold it against you if you change your mind about that."

There was absolutely no way Tony Cross wanted to have sex with her. Still, an unexpected zing pulsed between her legs, and she squirmed.

If she *wasn't* pregnant—she blinked hard.

Nope. Not going there. She *would* be pregnant. She *was* pregnant. It was just too early for tests to confirm it.

"And we need to renegotiate this date deal," he continued.

Now he was just trying to irritate her. "Sure. You can come over and watch chick flicks with me and Gran one night this weekend."

"When you say *watch—*"

"No phone, no tablet, no books, no radio tuned into the game. No faking it."

His warm grin turned carnal. "Sweets, I don't fake *anything.*"

Hello, terribly, horribly tempting idea. Goodbye, better sense.

She should've called his bluff at the pizzeria yesterday.

"If I watch chick flicks, you'll go see my band play," he said.

"Your band."

"We rock a mean polka."

Dammit, now he was making her laugh. Also not part of the deal. "You're going to have to cook me dinner more than once if you want me to watch your polka cover band."

"Did I forget to mention dinner's going to cost you a kiss?"

Right. "You don't want to kiss me."

"Sure I do. Now. Later. All night. For breakfast. Mid-morning snack. After mid-morning snack."

"Mid-morning snack? Are we in preschool again?" She grabbed the water once more and gulped, because there were definitely hormones raging in her body now, and they had nothing to do with her fertility treatments.

"Why wouldn't I want to kiss you?"

"Because you don't like me."

"That's never stopped me before."

Oh, he was annoying.

Except…he wasn't. Because there was something in his brazen confidence that didn't quite feel real. As if he was *faking* it.

She folded her arms and stared at his back. "We're not having sex."

"Challenge accepted." He flipped the scallops, and the tantalizing scent of frying bacon tickled her nose. Lucky continued tossing and chasing the green onion bit about the room, adorably oblivious to the humans.

He *was*. He was either intentionally trying to irritate her, or he was making himself out to be far more of a playboy than he actually was. She didn't know *how* she knew.

Just that she did. "Who taught you how to cook?"

He slid another glance at her. "My mom."

His mom had passed away last spring, she'd discovered during her cyber-stalking. One of very few personal tidbits included in the article about the Bliss Pepperoni Tony's location opening. "You miss her?"

He grunted.

She might've grown up with mostly sisters, but she knew a *drop it* grunt when she heard it. "Sounded like you were close."

"You're right. We shouldn't have sex."

And he was a terrible subject-changer. But she quit pressing, because she'd found out what she needed to know.

He didn't want to trust her. He grabbed two plates painted with grape leaves. "Why do you want to get married?"

"I don't," she replied.

"You did."

"So? As my sister Margie would say, it's biology. And I've used my evolved brain to get over it."

He set a steaming plate of pasta, vegetables, and scallops on the island before her, then plunked a second plate down for himself and passed her silverware. The food smelled tantalizing and delicious, but when he sat across from her and fixed that too-observant look on her, she wanted to slink to the floor and bat around a scallion with the cat instead.

"If you were over it," he said while he twirled pasta around his fork, "you'd tell your grandmother dating is futile."

She speared a perfectly browned scallop and told herself the only reason she was still here was because she could eat his delicious scallops and bacon without touching the pasta. "She's diabolical. And she's old enough that she thinks she knows what's best for everyone, even if she can't be enough of an adult to keep herself from getting tossed out of retirement homes."

She bit into the scallop and nearly moaned in pleasure. Perfectly cooked, both scallop and bacon, with some of that divine cream sauce adding the perfect touch.

"Good?" he said with a self-satisfied smirk.

"Passable."

"Delicious."

"Most likely you're a one-dish wonder."

"I'm starting to see your issue with men. Aside from your taste."

What was wrong with her that tossing around insults with Tony was turning into the highlight of her day? "Present company included, of course."

She twirled the linguine onto her fork and sank into sheer bliss when the flavors met her tongue.

One bite. She could have one bite of pasta. And holy damn, the man could cook. "Is this all your mom's teaching?"

"All Mom." His eyes crinkled, but his smile held a hint of sadness.

She couldn't relate, and a selfish part of her didn't want to. She still had both parents and three of her grandparents. Gran had buried her one and only husband following a tragic accident when Pepper was four. Grief was something she'd only experienced in her repeated failed attempts to get pregnant this past year.

"You sure we can't have sex?" he said. "Because you look like my librarian fantasy come to life."

His words said *I'm a hornball*, but that *don't take me too seriously* light in his eyes said he knew how to deflect a woman's attention with a bad proposition.

She smiled sweetly. "How about you just fantasize about having sex with me, and we call it even?"

"Surefire way not to get dessert, Miss Blue. And if you like this…"

"Thanks for the offer, but I'm off cannoli."

"I really want to kiss that tart mouth again."

"If wishes were horses—"

"We'd all be eating steak," he finished.

They blinked at each other.

"You're a *Firefly* fan," he said.

She smiled back. "We had a marathon at the bachelorette party."

"So I shouldn't call you Saffron."

"First, I have a sister named Saffron. So definitely not. And second, I've already told you that I won't be your Mrs. Reynolds."

"Spices." He tipped his head back and laughed. "You're all named after spices. That's nuts."

"No, my aunt Petunia's kids are all named after nuts. Peanut does okay for herself, but Walnut… And don't ask about poor Pecan. It's so awkward when people mispronounce it. She's not a pee-can, you know."

"You are a funny, funny woman," he said softly.

"You're a pain in the ass. But you're hot and you can cook okay, so I'll pretend to keep you for a while."

He clinked his water glass to hers. "And we should have sex."

He was impossible.

But maybe not as impossible as she'd first thought.

———

"WHY CAN'T they all be skins?" Gran demanded. "I need to see Tony without his shirt on."

"Hush, or we're leaving." Pepper settled onto the bleachers of the community center between Gran and Kimmie Kincaid. She should've been at Bliss Bridal, or running down the solution to the ticket issue for Bliss's annual Battle of the Boyfriends this weekend, but Kimmie had popped in—waddled, really, poor thing—and mentioned a pickup basketball game featuring all the hottest men in Bliss, and Gran had insisted they come.

Since she would've gone by herself, Pepper hadn't had much choice but to come along.

And there was a part of her happy to see that Tony was making friends on his own. She hadn't called in any favors to get him invited here—apparently he'd taken Max a pizza at the garage next door, and that was that.

Friendship was so much easier for men.

"They can't all be skins," Kimmie said. "Poor Charlotte would bounce too much."

"They make sports bras in flesh colors." Gran lifted her shirt. "See?"

"Gran!"

Out on the basketball floor, Mikey Diamond did a double take, staring in horror at them, his bald head gleaming under the lights. Tony ducked in and stole the ball, dashing down the court, leg muscles stretching and flexing, his thick arm extending to toss in an easy layup. He pulled his shirt up to wipe his face as he jogged back to the other end of the court, showcasing hard abs and slick skin.

Pepper gulped.

Who knew making pizza all day could keep a man in such good shape?

"Eyes on the ball," Mikey's wife, Dahlia—another who had drunk the water in Bliss and was currently sporting a basketball-size bump of her own—called to him.

"His grandmother's cheating," Mikey called back.

"Such a dirty old man," Dahlia said with a smile. She was adorable, petite and dark-haired with glasses that made her seem far more innocent than she was. While Kimmie ran the best cupcake shop in Bliss, Dahlia owned and ran the ice-cream shop next door to Kimmie Cakes. The two of them had supplied dirty-themed ice cream and cupcakes for the bachelorette party, as they did for many bachelorette parties around Bliss. Dahlia nudged Gran. "Mikey likes you."

"We have a bond," Gran agreed.

"Goosing him at Saffron's wedding does *not* give you a bond," Pepper said.

Dahlia laughed and clapped her hands. "Oh, I wish I could've seen that."

"I can do it again," Gran offered.

"Do I need to warn Josh?" Kimmie whispered to Pepper.

"Probably."

"Oh! The babies are jumping. Want to feel?"

"Absolutely." She'd take any chance to nudge her own maternal hormones.

Kimmie took her hand and put it on the side of her belly. A bump slid across her palm, and once again an unexpected and unwelcome sheen coated her eyeballs. "Oh!"

"She's going to be a handful." Kimmie smiled. "I had a dream there were actually seven of them. I thought poor Josh was going to need a paper bag when I told him this morning. Probably I should've left off the part about three of them being frogs and the other four being cupcake flies that the frogs were trying to eat."

"You have the best dreams, Kimmie." Merry leaned into them. She was a relative newcomer to Bliss, with a life almost as interesting as Kimmie's dreams. "I never remember mine. Which is probably a good thing."

"You have more imagination in your pinky than I do in my entire subconscious," Kimmie replied. "I could never write books like you do."

Merry's whole face went red. She'd only recently publicly claimed being the bestselling author of Pepper's nieces' favorite series of books, and from what Pepper had heard, she was still getting used to the attention. "It's a good mobile career."

"But you're not leaving us," Kimmie said.

Merry flicked a glance at the court, where Max was on the skins team, and a familiar glow overtook the blush. "Not a chance."

"I haven't goosed him either," Gran announced. "But I got Tony when he came to strip for us."

"In your dreams, Gran," Tony called on his way past.

"Don't encourage her," Pepper called back.

He grinned at her briefly before focusing back on the game, and honeybees buzzed about her stomach.

It was a dang good thing she wasn't dating him for real, because the only thing she needed buzzing in her belly was a baby of her own.

"Speaking of Tony," Dahlia said, "spill."

"He lives next door. Moved to town a few months ago to expand his pizza empire, my sisters mistook him for a stripper at the bachelorette party, I went to apologize later, and it turns out that despite the two of us getting off on the wrong foot, he's irresistibly funny and needed some friends." There. That sounded convincing.

"With benefits," Gran added.

It was Pepper's turn for heated cheeks. "You know what goes good together?" she said, because *this* was what she was supposed to be doing in exchange for him playing her fake boyfriend. "Pizza, cake, and ice cream."

"Does he do dirty pizza flavors?" Kimmie asked.

"I'll put Mikey on it," Dahlia offered. "I don't know why he ever thought he was born to be a drummer. He was really born to be dirty and lead the sexual revolution."

"Do you know if you're having a boy or a girl?" Pepper asked.

"Nope, and God help us either way," she replied with a laugh. She suddenly bolted to her feet. "Yes! Go, Mikey!"

Mikey tossed the ball down the court to Josh, who flipped a backward layup into the basket.

"Beautiful shot, honey," Kimmie called.

He blew her a kiss.

Tony grabbed the ball and tossed it in to Charlotte. The two of them made their way across the court, talking softly, while Luke Hart, the last member of their team, dodged Mikey, Josh, and Max.

"Who's winning?" Pepper asked.

"You are," Dahlia said.

"Charlotte's team always wins," Kimmie offered.

"And she's pretty pissed at Max right now," Merry added.

"What? Why?"

"For not telling her my, er, secret."

Ah, that made sense. Charlotte ran the local bookstore. She and Pepper had invited Merry to a book club discussion of Amber Finch's Phoebe Moon novels before Christmas, not realizing, of course, that Merry had written them.

Life in Bliss was way more interesting than Pepper had thought it would be when she moved here.

"I love your secret," Kimmie announced.

"My baby's going to need a signed set," Dahlia added.

So would Pepper's. Five more days, and it would be official.

"Holy hotness, Batman!" Gran fanned herself. "I forgot my ones."

"Gran, they're playing basketball, *not stripping*," Pepper said.

Gran's eyes twinkled. "One team's halfway there, young lady. You know what would make this game even better?"

"If they were shirts and pants?"

"Dang right. Love me some jockey shorts at lunchtime."

That would put Tony on the pants-less team.

Pepper's thighs clenched. "You are a terrible influence on me."

"Only get one life. Gotta live it." Gran pulled her dentures out, popped two fingers in her mouth, and gave a whistle.

Tony glanced over at them. His lips parted at the sight of Gran, and he lifted his brows at Pepper. *Gotta love her, right?*

She couldn't help herself.

She nodded.

And then she laughed.

Having him as a fake boyfriend wasn't real, and he wouldn't have been her first choice, but it was definitely proving to be fun.

5

*O*ne of the biggest lesson's Tony's mom had imparted to him was to never show up empty-handed. So Thursday night, after getting a personal invitation to dinner from Gran, he knocked on Pepper's door with a plate of cannoli in hand.

Pepper threw the door open and dashed out onto the porch in jeans that hugged her long legs, a soft green sweater that brought out her eyes, and panic written in the tight lines around her eyes and mouth. The little white dog yipped behind the door.

"Gran's decided we're having two boys and two girls, all named after varieties of pizza cheeses, and that's only because I convinced her *Mozzarella* and *Provolone* were more classy than *Anchovy* and *Sausage*. If you fake puke right now, I'll have to take you home to play nursemaid all night. Man up, Tony. Start gagging."

How was a guy supposed to turn down an order like that? "That's the sexiest thing anyone's said to me all day."

"She brought a date for herself, and he smells like overcooked liver and onions." She was close enough for him to smell flowers and something sweet. Her fingers rested on his chest when she glanced over her shoulder. "Cinna's here. She'll keep him from getting frisky. But if this

is going to work, you need to toss your cookies *now*. Can't be me—
that'll keep us stuck here."

"If we go back to my place, are we playing hide the cannoli?"

"If you weren't doing me a huge favor, I'd have a few highly unflattering and rudely suggestive things to say to you right now."

He peeled the aluminum foil back from the plate. "What? My sisters and I used to play all the time. Whoever finds the most, eats the most. I should warn you, I usually win."

The door swung open, and Cinna poked her head out, dog in hand. "Hey, pizza man. You treating my sister right, or do I have to beat you with a slab of pepperoni? *Ha*! Pepper-ony. Get it?"

Pepper's eyes pinched. "I'm replacing her shampoo with honey tonight."

And now he was imagining her in his shower, honey drizzled over her body, his for the licking. Zero to full salute in oh-point-two seconds.

This woman was definitely good for him. At least, certain parts of him.

"Are you two coming in, or are you going to stand out here playing kissy-face all night?" Cinna asked.

"We weren't—" Pepper started, but Tony interrupted her by covering her mouth with his. He shoved the plate toward Cinna, mildly surprised when she took it, so he could wrap both arms around his pretend girlfriend and kiss her silly.

She'd left his house on professional terms the other night. A handshake and an insistence she could walk herself home, and a repeated reminder that she wasn't putting out for him. Yesterday, after the basketball game, she'd given him a quick peck on the cheek. He'd been hot and sweaty, and she'd been in a dressy pantsuit thing and needed to get back to work.

But they needed to sell this relationship to her family.

Yep, that was the only reason he was kissing her. Nothing at all to do with enjoying actually being turned on by a woman.

Her lips parted, and he angled his head to deepen the kiss. To taste the inside of her lip, feel the smooth surface of her teeth, let her tongue take the chill out of the winter night.

He'd never been so hard in his life.

Or so grateful to be sporting wood at all.

"Get a room," Cinna said.

Pepper pulled back. She swept a quick glance at him, and her cheeks went pink.

"Have to sell it, sweets," he murmured to her dangly emerald earring.

"Yeah."

That breathy quality in her voice made more blood surge south. He put a hand to her lower back and guided her before him into the house, subtly adjusting himself. As soon as he stepped across the threshold, the little poodle launched itself at him and made a go at his leg again.

"Just remember, I offered you an out," she whispered.

"And turn down an opportunity to hang out with three beautiful women? Never."

"Kiss-up."

"Happy to kiss you anytime you want me to."

She shivered beneath his fingers, then pulled out of his grasp. "Here, I'll take your coat. Gran and Eugene are in the kitchen. Hope you're up for Cards Against Humanity. And don't let Gran have any beer or tequila, no matter what she tells you, unless you want to see her in her birthday suit."

He swallowed a chuckle. When she turned away to hang his coat in the coat closet, he settled his hands on her shoulders and pressed his thumbs along her shoulder blades. "Relax. Just a night of fun."

She melted into his touch, and something more than his groin pulsed.

Might've been that dangerous organ in his chest.

"Thank you," she said quietly. Begrudgingly, almost.

And suddenly he wished he'd taken her suggestion to fake throwing up.

PEPPER'S KITCHEN was her favorite room, and she loved any excuse to be in it. Gone were the worn, fifties-style cabinets and eighties-style linoleum, replaced with custom maple cabinets and a dark cherry wood floor. She'd knocked out the wall between the kitchen and the small back office to expand the room into an eat-in kitchen, and she'd hung white lace curtains. Sadie had her own little dining area in the corner—with an added bowl for George now—and she'd splurged on an Amish oak table that reminded her of her parents' table back home, though she needed far fewer expansion leaves than they did.

Tonight, after the meal Tony had served her the other night, she was worried that her Crock-Pot balsamic chicken would taste like garbage in comparison. But there were compliments all around and burps from Eugene, whom Gran had apparently picked up at the grocery store pharmacy after he told her stories of his years in the Navy. Tony's cannoli—dirty man—went over even better, and by the time they settled around the kitchen table to deal out cards, she was honestly beginning to relax.

Eugene's hair was ashy and his brows were bushy enough that they probably needed to be checked for small field animals, but other than a few off-color stories from his time in the Navy, he seemed fairly tame for Gran's usual taste in men.

Gran had asked more requisite boyfriend-grilling questions—did Tony have any guns, were any of his bills overdue, and what size shoe did he wear?—but she hadn't mentioned marriage, children, or politics. Tony had handled every question with ease, and he hadn't once said anything she could even remotely construe as a sexual innuendo.

Except for maybe when he told Gran he polished his favorite baseball bat every day. That, she was fairly certain, was TMI. It had also put another tingle between her thighs.

Cinna added her own questions—Cubs or Cardinals, what was the secret ingredient in his pizza sauce, and was he *really* man enough to take on dating Pepper, knowing that every other man she'd ever dated had married someone else posthaste?—but otherwise, she behaved herself too.

It was oddly disconcerting.

George had retired to Gran's room for the night, so Sadie had come out to eat dinner and was now curled up at Pepper's feet. Tony's knee brushed her thigh when he scooted his chair closer. He'd said hello nicely to Pepper's pup, which had gone a long way toward making Pepper relax.

She couldn't fault him for being protective of his own cat when she was so protective of her dog. Especially after getting a look at Lucky in her natural environment. The cat *was* skittish, and apparently rightly so.

Now, the black Cards Against Humanity cards had been dealt, and everything around her suddenly felt homier than she could ever remember. Family, food, fun, and a snoring dog.

It *fit*.

Apprehension once more gripped her stomach.

Or maybe that was one more physical sensation that meant this last round of IVF had been successful?

"Is she old enough to play this?" Tony asked with a nod to Cinna.

"Afraid I'm going to kick your ass?" Cinna taunted back. "Don't worry about sheltering me. Gran taught me everything I needed to know about the birds and the bees before I was ten."

"Never too young," Gran said with a nod. "But everything she knows about cussing like a sailor came from her father's side of the family."

Eugene burped, and either dinner had improved the odd liver and onion smell, or she'd gotten used to it.

"You should get that checked out," Gran said to him. "Frequent flatulence can be a sign of underlying issues."

"Getting old is my underlying issue," Eugene said.

"Ain't getting any younger," Gran said. "Only a few years left for getting to know more great-grandchildren. I could set a world record, you know. You have any children, Tony?"

"Gran—" Pepper started.

"Legitimate or illegitimate?" he interrupted.

Pepper choked on air.

"Both," Gran said.

"None that I know of, but the aliens never told me what they planned to do with the sperm they stole from me back in 2010, so it could be in the hundreds."

The room fell silent, and even Sadie lifted her head to look at him. With his dry delivery, it was hard to tell if he was joking. But there was a little twitch in the corner of his mouth, a slight dimpling in his cheek that gave him away.

"He's a little odd, Pepper," Gran said.

"Someone has to take care of him." She ruffled his thick, dark hair, and instantly wished she hadn't. His dark eyes turned to her while her fingers lingered in his thick mane. *Hold on tight and I'll take you for a good time*, those eyes promised.

She dropped her hand. "Are we playing this game, or are we grilling the guests?"

Eugene burped again.

Tony slung a possessive arm about her shoulders. "Dunno about Eugene, but I'd rather not get cooked tonight."

He nuzzled her neck, which was definitely *not* necessary to sell their story. His breath ignited the nerve endings in her skin. She knew so little about him—just enough to pull off playing his new girlfriend. If this were real, he'd have about eighteen checks in the *cons* column. But he still managed to put butterflies in her belly and a solid bass beat in her chest purely by whispering a goofy joke in her ear.

She'd been calculating risks since her first foray into penny stocks as a nine-year-old. She knew better than to sink too many assets into ventures where she couldn't see a positive return on investment, and that knowledge had steered her through college, through her first job, and through buying into Bliss Bridal two years ago. Even this old house—which she'd fallen in love with at first sight—had been thoroughly inspected from its bones up before she bought it so she'd be prepared for renovation and upkeep costs.

Tony was the biggest risk she could take.

And she had too much else going on in life to indulge in crazy monkey sex with a pizza man.

But there was still a small part of her that wished she could be that girl who would.

"Seriously, get a room," Cinna picked up a black card and read it. "*Blank* is the quickest way to my *blank*."

Tony was the quickest way to *Pepper coming undone*.

Nope. None of her cards matched. She plucked *handcuffs* and *world domination* from her hand—this word-matching game was fun, and she knew Cinna tended to favor the *handcuffs* card. Fairly lame as far as this game went overall, but she was playing with her grandmother, an old man she barely knew, her baby sister, and her fake boyfriend.

She wasn't playing that *whips and chains* card for anything.

Or that horribly irreverent one about baby Jesus.

Tony studied her over his cards. His stubble was thicker tonight, his focus more intense, making him look like a wild pirate intent on pillaging a fair maiden. Impulsively, she pressed a kiss to his scratchy cheek.

He slammed his hand to the table.

But not before she saw his cards. *The old ball and chain, Chuck Norris, pussy willow, whacking off,* and *Cheetos shaped like my scrotum*.

Practically a grand slam of a hand for this game.

"Cheater," he murmured.

"You don't know Cinna well enough to win this round."

"Hush up and let the man play, and no cheating," Gran said. "You can learn a lot about a man by the cards he picks. Gotta make sure this one's good enough for you."

"I like your family," he said. "They make mine look normal."

"Was that a compliment?"

His grin sent her spiraling every time. "It's whatever you want it to be, sweets."

THREE HOURS LATER, Tony and Eugene had departed for the evening, and Pepper was waiting for Sadie to finish her business in the backyard so she could get to bed. Busy weekend coming up for Bliss.

Her cheeks were still burning from the card game. Gran, on the other hand, was already snoring upstairs.

"How much are you paying him?" Cinna asked.

Pepper spun away from the back door, hand to her chest. "My house is going to charity if I die, so quit trying to sneak up on me and give me a heart attack."

Cinna yanked out a chair and plopped onto it. Her red hair was tied up in a messy bun, and she'd changed into her coffee pajamas. "You forgave Tony for his cat attacking Sadie."

"Lucky's a rescue. Had a hard life. And it only happened once." She'd been worried about Gran. Not Cinna. This wasn't good. It either meant extortion was coming, or—huh.

Nope, she couldn't come up with anything other than extortion.

"You don't forgive men for anything," Cinna said.

"That's the most ridiculous thing I've ever heard."

"Yeah? Tell that to Brent."

"Brent?"

"Your high school boyfriend? The one you dumped because he told you he had ADD?"

Pepper opened the back door. Sadie did her bunny hop back inside with a happy doggy smile on her lips. She stopped just inside the kitchen and sat, tail wagging. *Bedtime, Mommy?* Heck yes, it was bedtime. She had a full shift at the boutique tomorrow, and she was volunteering with the Knot Festival committee to put on the Battle of the Boyfriends this weekend. She needed her sleep to keep healthy for the little one hopefully growing in her belly right now.

"Brent. Right. I dumped Brent because he was copying my homework. And you were two. How in the world would you even remember Brent?"

"Saffron told me. Also, didn't you dump Joey because he lied to you about his mother?"

Joey. More recent, and much more epic. "He told me his other girlfriend *was* his mother. And he married her two weeks after we broke up."

"Oh." Cinna wrinkled her nose. "No one would think less of you if you just joined a convent."

"As for Tony, I get it. He's just as protective of Lucky as I am of Sadie. Can't really fault a guy for loving his pet."

Ten sisters, ten distinct personalities, yet each of them had the same *I'm not sure I believe you* squint.

But more than any of the rest of her sisters, Cinna loved chaos. She loved a good story. And she loved being in the thick of pranks and knowing things no one else did. Probably because she'd spent her entire life being told she was too young for this, that, or the other thing.

"Mom's not having any luck finding a new retirement home for Gran," Pepper said. "I'm starting a group text message with the family to get volunteers for extra babysitters, and I'm dropping her with Basil tomorrow before I head into work."

"Just because she's old doesn't mean she needs babysitters."

"She needs babysitters because she's Gran. Left to her own devices, she'll invite all her friends over for Senior Citizens Stripping Class."

"Yeah, but it's not like she has access to YouTube to upload videos of it." Cinna sighed. "I want to be her one day."

Pepper smiled. "She's pretty special."

"Until she plays the *my vagina* card. Then I agree. She needs a babysitter. I thought Eugene was going to stroke out right there. Tony took it like a man though. You ever dated a divorced guy before?"

"Not to the best of my knowledge."

"Huh. Maybe he'll break your streak."

"I really don't care if he—" She stopped herself.

But Cinna was quick. "You don't care if he breaks your streak?"

Sadie went down on all fours and turned pitiful, *I'm tired* puppy dog eyes on Pepper. She sucked in a deep breath. "I don't care if he breaks my streak," she said slowly, "because dating with the sole purpose of finding a man to marry hasn't really worked out for me. So I'm trying something different this time."

"Just dating him for the sex, huh?"

"Yep. It's all about the sex."

"Try to keep it at his place. My virgin ears can only take so much." Cinna stood and stretched, then ambled toward the door. "Don't go crazy-Pepper on him, okay? I like him. Oh, also? I invited him to the Blueper Bowl Party. And he said yes. Night!"

She dashed for the stairs.

And left Pepper with that sinking feeling that her easy weekend had suddenly become infinitely more complicated.

She'd told Tony not to go.

Which almost definitely meant he'd show up.

THERE WASN'T much on TV, but Tony didn't care. He was content lying in his bed, flipping channels, his mind wandering back to the way Pepper tucked her hair behind her ear when she was nervous and how she always smelled like flowers and all the times she'd made him smile tonight.

And trying not to glance out his bedroom window toward her backyard.

Plus, if he moved, he'd risk disturbing Lucky. His little fur ball had curled up on his chest as soon as he propped himself on a mountain of pillows and snagged the remote for his big-screen TV hanging over his carved maple dresser. Her deep, incessant purr vibrated against his chest, and every time he stroked her silky fur, she kneaded her needle-point claws through his shirt to prick his skin.

She'd completely destroyed the roll of toilet paper in his bathroom today. The pen cup he kept on his desk had been upended, pens and pencils scattered all over the floor, and he'd dug six paperclips out of her water bowl.

Perfect, happy little kitty. She made his house a home.

Not quite the home he'd always wanted—the happy wife, noisy kids, two dogs terrorizing the cat and probably a hamster and a bird and maybe a pet snake too—but more of a home than he'd thought he'd have again after Tabitha happened.

His phone buzzed on the nightstand. Lucky lifted her head to give him a stern *you are not going into work tonight, mister,* glare.

"Just a text message," he told her. "They'd call if I had to go in."

She stretched out her claws and pushed the pads of her front feet into his pec, then settled her head back down with a kitty sigh. He dropped the remote and eased his phone off the nightstand to peer at the screen.

Did you tell Cinna you'd come to the Blueper Bowl Party Sunday night?

He almost laughed. For a woman with ten sisters, she was remarkably gullible. *Thank you for coming to my house tonight, Tony*, he typed back. *I'm so grateful to you for playing the part of the doting boyfriend even though it meant we all had to picture my grandmother doing the hibbity-jibbity with Eugene during that one horrible round.*

Her texting bubble popped up nearly as soon as he hit *send*.

Maybe he'd get lucky and she'd send him a boob shot.

His groin stirred.

You're a prince among men, Pepper replied. *Especially if you stay out of the Blueper Bowl party. This is legitimately for your own good.*

Screw texting. He hit her number, and she picked up before he heard the phone ring on his end. "It's four solid hours of family time. My parents will be there too, along with both my brothers and my three brothers-in-law and all eight of my nieces, plus the babies, and I halfway expect Sage to bring an animal, though I haven't heard what her latest pet is. Last time it was a turtle, which was a big improvement over the snake."

"I'm not worried. I'm bringing my family with me for backup."

She squeaked. No words, just a little squeak. Lucky lifted her head and sniffed at the phone, white whiskers quivering on either side of her nose.

Tony let himself chuckle. "You got played."

"I—*dammit*. She didn't invite you at all, did she? She's getting salt in her coffee tomorrow morning."

"You fix her coffee?"

"No, but I control the sugar bowl."

"That's why my sugar bowl is full of sprinkles. Nobody colors salt."

He could picture her tilting her head, debating with herself if he was serious. She burst out in laughter. He smiled and rubbed Lucky harder.

"They're green," he added. "My sisters won't touch it because they think I've let my sugar go moldy."

"If you show up at the Blueper Bowl, I might accidentally lose that paperwork to get Pepperoni Tony's on the recommended restaurant list. Don't think being invited to one basketball game means you're in."

She wasn't subtle, was she? Refreshing, if he were being honest. He'd never been able to read Tabitha's mind, and he'd thought he'd enjoyed the challenge, but now he didn't have the patience for bullshit. "Four biggest pizza holidays of the year—New Year's, Thanksgiving, Halloween, and the Super Bowl. I'll be working."

"Oh. Right."

"Happy to deliver something to my favorite customer though."

"Oh, stop."

"You're right. I like that chick over on Elm better. Gives better tips, if you know what I mean."

"Elm? Isn't that the street they call *Widow Row*? You know why those old ladies are tipping you, and don't try to deny it. But now I'm wondering if you were here tonight for me, or if you were here for Gran. Tony Cross, you like the cougars, don't you?"

Normalcy was highly underrated. This—outrageous conversations with a pretty girl who didn't want him after a fun non-date date—was damn near perfect. "I don't care how old they are, so long as they're tigers in bed."

She laughed again.

Home run.

"You busy tomorrow?" he heard himself ask.

And there was the awkward pause. The reminder that she was fun, but not real, and they'd already broken the no-date rule this week.

"I have to work," she said. "With Nat out on maternity leave, things are a little crazy at the boutique."

"Crazy busy, or crazy falling apart?" He'd seen both at Pepperoni Tony's. Some good, some bad, some his fault.

"Busy. Good. I like the crazy days. Reminds me of being home."

"Because having your grandmother and Cinna living with you isn't enough?"

"Compared to wondering if you'll find all your underwear flying on the flagpole when you get back in from feeding the goats in the morning, and not being sure who to go after for revenge, so you plot vengeance against twelve people instead, while proactively working to pin said revenge on one of those said twelve? Nope. Gran and Cinna by themselves are actually easy."

There was a smile in her voice, and his shoulders relaxed. Lucky purred harder on his chest. "Sounds like sheer insanity."

"You have siblings?"

"A few."

"They didn't prank each other all the time?"

"Never lived with all of them at the same time."

"You let that stop you?"

"I was a highly responsible child. Adulthood corrupted me. Speaking of, what are you wearing right now?"

"A red teddy and four-inch heels."

He bolted upright. Lucky leapt off him, leaving scratches down his chest, and scrambled under the bed. The lame come-on had rolled off his tongue with the practiced ease of a man who'd spent the better part of the last year convincing his family that his heart hadn't been shattered beyond repair, but he hadn't had as much recent experience with instant hard-ons. "Be right there."

"No, wait, I'm in a University of Missouri T-shirt and pajama pants with singing hamsters. Whoops. The teddy was last night."

"Slippers?"

"Toe socks with rainbow toes."

His chest ached, and not just where Lucky had scratched him. "Hair up or down?"

"In old granny curlers. I'm about to put a plastic bag on my head and apply a green face mask too."

The idea of watching Pepper go through a nightly routine—with or without the curlers—was so domestic, it should've choked him. Instead, he was getting harder with every word she uttered.

Nightly rituals were so intimate. Watching a woman, unguarded, in her own haven, with no more pretenses to keep up for the world at large, was more revealing than if she'd stripped naked.

I got so mad at my boss today, but I couldn't tell him without wanting to cry, Tabitha had confessed to Tony one night early in their marriage while he leaned in the doorway to the bathroom and watched her wash off her makeup.

I always wanted to be a teacher, but I'm not smart enough for college, another night. He'd offered to put her through school, to let her prove to herself that she *could* do it, but she'd declined.

Showing her insecurities. Her fears. Her lack of confidence. He'd tried to tell her she could do anything, but that he'd love her even if she never wanted to do more than work as a cashier at the dollar store in Willow Glen. She'd never believed him.

But she'd believed her *lover*.

"Not so eager to come over now, are you?" Pepper teased.

He swallowed hard. "Nope. I like my women dolled up and

stripped down. Speaking of, what are you doing after work tomorrow?"

"Prep for the Battle of the Boyfriends," she replied without hesitation.

At the mention of the insane annual band competition that Bliss had turned into a sappy love show, his boner deflated.

He'd sung his heart out for Tabitha and proposed to her at the Battle of the Boyfriends four years ago. Growing up in Willow Glen, he'd heard about the competition, but he'd never thought he'd enter himself.

Until he'd caught Tabitha sighing over a poster advertising it.

"You have fun with that. I'll drop some pizzas by on Sunday."

"You don't have to—"

"Need to be up early myself," he interrupted. "Thanks for a fun night. Tell Gran I'm looking forward to a rematch."

He hung up in a hurry, his chest an empty chasm of broken hopes and dreams.

She was fixing his manhood, but he was still too much in his own way for anyone to fix the rest of him.

6

*W*hen the lights dimmed in the Bliss Civic Center theater to start the show Saturday night, Pepper's volunteer duties for the Battle of the Boyfriends were more or less done. Tickets were collected, contestants were wrangled, judges were happy and in place, and best of all, Gran had been made an honorary judge and was seated safely in the spotlight between Will and Lindsey Truitt—last year's winner, an honor she still refused to talk about—and the Harts from the chocolate shop.

Pepper could've stayed to watch the show, but honestly, she wanted to go home, prop her feet up, and read a book. She lingered at the back entrance behind the audience to check her phone.

No messages from Tony.

Or anyone else, for that matter. She wasn't checking to see if *just* Tony wanted to text her. One of her siblings might've come to town early for the Blueper Bowl and forgotten she was busy tonight and needed to know how to get into her house.

Someone paused beside her with a heavy grunt.

"Checking on Tony?" Kimmie whispered. "Poor guy."

She slid a glance at her curly-haired friend. "Poor guy?"

Kimmie pointed down at the stage, where Max's sister-in-law,

Rachel, had just come out to kick off her duties as emcee for the evening. Max's brother, Dan, followed his wife, but no one would've mistaken him for having any real role tonight. Not when Rachel had the mic.

"He proposed to his girlfriend here a few years ago," Kimmie said. "I don't know much about their divorce, but it's never pretty, you know?"

Good thing it was dark, because Pepper was caught—again—with too little information about her fake boyfriend. She made a noncommittal noise.

"Right. Sorry. None of my business. I just—he was such a nice guy, and they came all the way over from Willow Glen to participate. I hate seeing bad things happen to nice guys. But, hey, he has you now."

Right.

He had her now.

"You've never dated a divorced guy, have you?" Kimmie's sweet face lit up with a smile. "He could break your streak."

"Are you and Josh coming to the Blueper Bowl party?" Pepper whispered.

Kimmie clapped a hand to her mouth. "Sorry. I forgot. Not talking about the streak. Yes! Yes, we're coming to the party. We stopped by Suckers the other night for coconut cream pie, and Cinna told us all about the tight end pool. And I really want to see the Blueper Bowl halftime show. Josh says it sounds like something from one of my dreams. We're both very interested. Hey, will Nat be there with the baby? I haven't had a chance to stop in and see her yet. Plus, I figured she's probably still recovering from all of your sisters coming to visit."

"You'll still have to fight the sisters tomorrow, but Saffron's coming with her baby too, so you might have a chance."

"I really just want to see Nat." Kimmie rubbed her belly. "It's a little scary, you know?"

"Gonna do great, sugar." Josh stopped behind his wife and kissed the back of her head. Inside, a screechy violin stirred to life. "And babies need their rest," he added quickly.

"Chicken," Pepper murmured.

He flashed his old playboy grin. "Damn right. Here. Help me get Kimmie to the car."

"I can walk myself," Kimmie objected.

"Not when your friends are trying to escape horrible music."

"Oh. Right." Kimmie flailed her arms wide. "Oh, Pepper, please help me too. I'm horrifically low on my coconut and cupcake consumption today. Woe is me."

"Have I mentioned lately how much I love you?" Josh said to her.

"I always love hearing it again."

Kimmie didn't stop at the love glow. She shimmered and glittered and outshone everything else in a three-state radius. Before Josh, she'd been mousy and beaten down by her overbearing mother. And much as Pepper was happy for her, hard as she tried to squash that green-eyed monster, her heart still ached in envy for what this unlikely couple had found.

She accompanied them out to Kimmie's car. She'd heard rumors Josh had traded his Porsche for a minivan, but she hadn't seen it yet herself. When she should've gone home and taken some doctor-prescribed rest, instead, she hit the grocery store.

She popped into her own house long enough to let the dogs out and love on Sadie, then she carried the grocery bag to the house next door.

There were still gaps in her story with Tony that she needed to know to accurately pull off this farce for the next five or six days, she told herself.

Not because she was using him to make herself feel less lonely while she waited for the pregnancy test at the doctor's office Monday morning.

Okay, maybe *some* to feel less lonely. And possibly because she didn't dislike him as much as she thought she did. Or maybe because she wanted to know if he was thinking about the Battle of the Boyfriends going on just a hop, skip, and a throw from his house tonight.

The front windows were dark, but his truck was in the driveway. His cat didn't announce her presence the way George announced everything from squirrels to snowflakes to the mailman. She swayed heels to toes after she knocked at the door. A hint of wood smoke on the crisp air made her wonder if he had a fireplace.

She didn't. It was the one thing her house was lacking.

That, and a huge master bathroom with a built-in whirlpool tub.

The door swung open. Tony was in sweats and a Pepperoni Tony's T-shirt. He hooked one hand around the edge of the door and swept a quick glance over her. "Is this a bribe or a threat to keep me from the Blueper Bowl?"

She sucked in a big cold breath of spontaneity. "It's a peace offering with a confession. There's virtually nothing I can't do. Except knit."

He lifted a brow.

And find a man willing to marry you, that obnoxious dark brow said.

His brow needed to shut up.

"Gran tried to teach me once," she said, "and I made this horrific uneven scarf of knots and frustrated tears."

"Your first problem might have been your teacher."

"She's a very talented woman. Your turn."

"My turn…?"

"Tell me something you're not good at."

"Because…?"

Because once again, she'd been caught having someone else tell her things she should've known about her fake boyfriend. She shifted her grocery sack to her other shoulder. "How much do you know about Bliss?"

"Crazy town. Lots of weddings. Should be a good pizza market."

"Small town. Lots of events. Good people with *excellent* memories about past competitors in all the goofball love contests."

His hand wobbled on the door, and it wasn't hard to visualize it shutting in her face. But when his shoulders sagged and his gaze dropped, she took the liberty of opening the screen door and letting herself in.

"You get married here too?" she asked quietly.

He shook his head. "Boat on Lake Michigan."

"I planned a wedding on a boat once," she said. "I was thirteen, and I had this *huge* crush on my sister Ginger's boyfriend's brother. He was on the swim team, so I asked him if he wanted to get married on a boat."

He shut the door. "Tell me he didn't marry his next girlfriend."

"I didn't *actually* date him," she said with an exaggerated sniff.

"How many weddings have you planned?"

"You first. Tell me a secret."

"I'm having fantasies about getting a Knitting Pepper action figure."

"A secret about *you*."

"That was about me."

She had a *lot* of work to do. She lifted the reusable cloth grocery bag. "I need your kitchen."

A spark of interest lit his dark eyes, and he hooked a finger into the bag. She pressed it shut before he could peek in.

"What's wrong with your kitchen?" he asked.

"I can't interrogate you properly there if you're here."

"You bake?"

"First place every year in my high school's bake-off."

His warm smile made his eyes crinkle in the corners, and her belly dipped. "And since high school?" he asked.

"Since high school, I've become a workaholic, forgot how to sleep in past seven in the morning, and can no longer stuff my face with mountains of cookies without feeling sluggish and needing to buy larger pants."

His smile turned wry. "Being a grown-up blows, doesn't it?"

"Depends on the day."

He trailed her into the kitchen and flipped the light switches for her. Clean countertops, empty sink and dish rack. The old refrigerator banged and chugged beside the radiator, which was incredibly poor planning on someone's part. She deposited her bag on the island and pointed him to a stool.

He leaned a hip against the island instead, just inside her personal space bubble, making her pulse do things her pulse wasn't supposed to do for men right now.

"Keeping me up past my bedtime, Miss Blue."

"Yes, yes, I'm a terribly bossy, inconsiderate person. You can take a nap tomorrow." She put a hand to his arm and pushed.

Bad move.

Because his bicep was hot, hard steel beneath her chilled fingers. Also, he didn't budge, and now she was in his personal space bubble. And she wanted to be closer. Closer to the heat radiating off his entire body. Closer to his delicious scent of earthy male and marinara sauce.

Closer to his wickedly talented mouth and his overgrown five o'clock shadow.

Her knees wobbled. She jerked back and dug into the bag.

"Do you ever take naps?" His words were a caress and an invitation. Goose bumps popped up along her arms.

"Naps are for the weak. Cookies, cake, or brownies?"

"What kind of cookies? And I didn't say the nap was for sleeping."

She plopped bags of flour, sugar, and chocolate chips onto the island. "Secret family recipe."

"Toll House, hm?"

"Mock my cookies and I'll go home, pizza man."

He stepped around her and reached into a cabinet. "Feeling feisty tonight?"

Was she?

Or was she feeling the weight of what that test would mean Monday morning? It would be positive. It had to be.

Who would she be if it wasn't? *What* would she be if it wasn't?

She'd done an impressive job of distracting herself this week, but tonight, it was proving harder.

She dropped a container of baking soda on the counter and turned to face him. "You own a successful business."

He didn't answer, simply eyed her as he set a blue flowered Pyrex nesting bowl behind her. If he was as much like she was as she was beginning to suspect, he definitely wouldn't call himself successful yet. Because Pepperoni Tony's might be a staple thirty minutes away in Willow Glen, but it hadn't yet taken off in Bliss.

"So you know the drive and determination it takes to be successful," she continued.

His nod came slowly.

"Do you ever turn it off? Because I don't. I can't. I don't know how. Failing—it sucks. We're supposed to learn from it. Not call it failure. But that's exactly what it is when fifteen men go on to marry the next woman they date after you. When you're thirty-five and alone and too *feisty*. Too high maintenance. Too stubborn. Too set in your ways. Too successful. Except you're just *you*, and you don't know why you can't find someone who'll take you just as *you*."

He was either going to run for the hills because she was crazy, or she could laugh and say *psych*.

Except that was her truth. She worked hard, she expected the best, and every time she'd gone through a breakup, at least one of her sisters had said some variation of the same thing.

Men are intimidated by you because you're just too awesome.

They didn't *get* it. They didn't get how failure affected her. How personal and terrifying all of her dating failures were. And she didn't know if Tony would get it or not, but he had guts, he had will, and he had his own relationship failure on a level her sisters had never known.

He leaned his elbows on the counter, his gaze on a point on the wall behind her. "My parents got divorced when I was six. Mom found out my father had another family on the side. Not even ten miles away. Both my older half-brothers are divorced. Sisters and half-sisters are decently happy, but they all bitch about their husbands. Tolerating shit is what Cross women do, and getting divorced is what Cross men do. Yay me. I lived up to family expectations."

A thick mess of something she didn't want to label *sympathy* welled up in her chest. He didn't have to tell her he'd wanted to succeed at his marriage. Because who didn't?

"No. I don't turn it off," he said finally. "Food's what I'm good at. I don't fail at food." He gestured to her. "Hence the reason you're here. So I don't fail."

She ignored the reminder of their deal. "I thought I failed right out of college. I have a math degree, and I had a job lined up with a huge consulting firm in St. Louis, but they went belly-up two weeks before I was supposed to start. I took a job with this bridal chain instead, busted my butt being indispensable in the corporate offices for six months, got promoted into a job in marketing, and I can't even do derivatives anymore."

The left side of his mouth hitched up. "I studied history."

"Slacker."

"Until I dropped out."

He eyed her, probably looking for a reaction.

She eyed him right back, because it wasn't a degree that defined a person. It was how hard they worked with what they had.

He nodded. "When I was about nine, I told my mom I was going to save my money to buy a car when I turned sixteen so I could deliver pizza. Told her I'd work really hard, and then when the right major pizza holiday came around, and I had a car full of pizzas, I was going to make a break for the Wisconsin border and eat every last one myself, and never come back."

Laughter rolled out of her. "You must've been adorable."

"My two older sisters used to dress me up like princesses and parade me around downtown on a leash. Life at my dad's place was worse. I just wanted to get away."

"And eat pizza."

"And eat pizza." His lips lifted in a smile. "And for the record, I've never turned down cookies either."

"Why history?"

"That involves an old family story with grandpa pants, four stuffed teddy bears, and a completely inaccurate recitation of Civil War history that I refuse to bore you with."

"That's enough. I'll fill in my own blanks from there."

He pulled out a drawer and handed over a stack of worn metal measuring cups. "You do that, and I'll have to find that scarf you knitted."

She laughed again. "Good luck with that."

"Never doubt the man with the pizza. It gets me everything from oil changes to invitations to basketball games to dirt on prospective employees."

She selected a measuring cup and measured out the right amount of flour. "These cookies are going to earn me all of those deep, dark secrets that you're still hiding that a fake girlfriend needs to know."

"Do your best, Miss Blue."

She nudged him with her shoulder. "I always do, Mr. Cross."

An honest smile lit his eyes. "Good."

For fifteen years, she'd been looking for a man who wasn't intimidated by her. Now, when she'd finally removed the need for a man from her life, life had handed her an obnoxious neighbor who just might fit the bill.

Life was evil like that.

PEPPER WAS RIGHT. She didn't fail.

The proof was in her magic cookies. If he wasn't careful, he really would spill all of his secrets. "Don't know," he said around a mouthful of his second bite of rich, caramel-chocolate goodness. "Missing something. Not enough vanilla. Why aren't you eating any?"

"I'm waiting to see if they kill you. Being in mourning over the death of a fake boyfriend will buy me way more time than you leaving Tarra's wedding with one of my cousins."

88

She swept crumbs off the edge of the island and turned to toss them into the sink. His kitchen smelled like chocolate and melted vanilla sugar, his cat was trying to squeeze into an empty butter box, and having a woman using his mom's old bowl and spoons gave his house a cozy feel that put him on edge.

She was allowed in the outer circle of his life, but she was flirting with those private caves he'd sealed off from the world. Knocking with her chilled hands, whispering a seductive *I'll be gentle if you open the door.*

But he wasn't letting his gullible heart out to fuck up again. "You want me to come to your sister's wedding?"

"No, no. Just a joke. We'll stick with the original plan."

Good. Much better. Neither of them wanted to do the awkward wedding-date thing. The awkward Cards Against Humanity with grandparents date, fine. But not the awkward wedding date.

She scrubbed at the cookie tray in the sink, and as he relaxed again, an ugly thought occurred to him. That maybe she wasn't joking. "One of your exes hooked up with one of your cousins at a wedding?"

"That would be a story, wouldn't it? By the way, if you get a delivery order for Suckers tomorrow, just ignore it. My family will launch the inquisition, and you don't have time for that."

Three cooling racks were stacked on his island with perfectly browned chocolate chip cookies, and that top tray was calling to him again. "I always pass inquisitions with flying colors."

"Had a lot of experience?"

"Not lately."

There were too many questions in the glance she tossed back at him. *How many of those women you've dated since your divorce were serious? Did you sleep with any of them? Introduce them to your family? Are you rusty? Does your equipment work?*

"Good cookies," he said.

"Of course they are."

There she went making him smile again. Even if he were in a place where he could consider honestly dating for anything other than show, to have a woman to talk about or bring along on the occasional family get-together, Pepper wasn't his type.

She was right. She was too successful. Too independent. He didn't have a single damn thing a woman like her needed, and he'd had enough heartache in his life from a woman who had needed so much more.

Not just Tabitha, either.

His mom had needed him. Needed him to be the man of the house, needed him to love her, needed him to take her to her treatments and doctor appointments, needed him to make those last final agonizing decisions for her.

Pepper wiped her hands on an old dishtowel printed with a faded rooster before leaning her elbows on the island. Her stretchy black cotton shirt dipped, and a hint of cleavage drained half his blood to his crotch.

"You've got chocolate—" She rubbed her thumb at the corner of her own mouth.

If she were really his girlfriend, she'd lick it off for him. Even as his fake girlfriend, he'd let her. They could keep this skin deep.

He rubbed the bristles on his chin. "There?"

"No, *there.*" She touched the side of her mouth again, and he went full salute.

"Here?" He scratched his cheek.

Her lips twitched up. *Fun.* This was fun. Hell, she'd been right. They were two hardcore business owners. They didn't do *fun.* She leaned farther across the counter, her shirt stretching tighter, his groin pulsing in sweet, welcome pain, those brilliant emerald eyes dipping to his mouth.

"You're a very bad man," she whispered.

"I'm a lonely, divorced workaholic with only a rescue cat for company," he whispered back.

She licked her thumb. His primal needs spiraled into a tight, focused arrow of hot, desperate desire. He didn't need cookies. He didn't need milk. He didn't need air.

He needed to kiss her.

She pressed her chilly thumb to the edge of his mouth. An hour of baking over a hot oven, and her fingers were still cold. He caught her wrist and turned his head, sucking her thumb into his mouth. Her breath audibly caught, and he sucked harder, swirling his tongue around her, tasting chocolate and Pepper.

"Very bad man," she whispered.

He released her wrist, but she didn't pull her thumb out. Her eyes were dark, her breasts rising and falling quickly, her long hair hanging out of her ponytail, dangling over her shoulder and brushing his arm. He sucked her thumb again.

Her eyes slid closed. He reached behind her and tugged at her hair tie, letting all that thick, silky hair cascade over his arms. Her thumb slid out of his mouth with a soft *pop*, and before his brain could talk him out of it, he pushed up to capture her lips with his.

Thick, lush Pepper lips. Warm, salty mouth. Slick, talented tongue.

She gripped the front of his T-shirt and pulled. A strong woman who knew what she wanted, and she wanted *him*.

His gut tightened. His heart was a hot mess. And he was about two seconds from completely losing it in his pants.

All because of a kiss.

His fingers ached to touch her skin. Learn her curves. Explore her hidden parts. Make her ache for him. Drive her mad with need for him.

Bury himself in her.

Lose himself in her.

Would she be hot? Wet? Tight? Quiet or loud? Could he make her scream his name?

Did he still know how?

Tinny music split the air. Pepper pulled out of the kiss with a gasp. "Gran."

He replied, he thought, with something coherent, but he wasn't in complete control of his mouth. Instinct demanded he grab her, shove

91

the cookies to the floor, and throw her on the island. Strip her. Pump into her. Claim her.

But she was dashing to her canvas bag near the doorway, hand brushing her mussed hair back, bending over and giving him the sweetest view of her heart-shaped ass.

He rubbed his throbbing erection through his sweatpants. So close. He'd been *so* close.

Still was. Another stroke or two, and he'd be finished.

He dropped back down on his stool, trying to even out his breathing while Pepper spoke into the phone. "Doesn't Basil have a key? I gave him a key—oh. I—yes. I'm just next door... No, no, it's no trouble."

She hung up a minute later and didn't meet his gaze when she looked at him.

Probably good, because he didn't like to be the one to flinch away either.

"Gran's locked out. I need to—thank you. For letting me hang out and make a mess of your kitchen. Hope you get lots of new business tomorrow. With the big game and all. I'll drop a few hints."

"Yeah. Thanks for coming."

Or not coming.

"I'll call you later this week. So we can get our stories straight. The breakup story, I mean. So they don't ask why you're not at the wedding, but don't take it out on Pepperoni Tony's." Her smile didn't reach her eyes when she gave a friendly finger wave from her side of the kitchen. "Thanks again."

He slid off his stool onto wobbly legs, too slow to stop her, not sure he knew what he'd say even if he'd succeeded.

But his dick knew what it wanted to say.

And for the first time in months, it was fully armed, ready, and not backing down.

Little victories.

So why didn't he feel like celebrating?

7

*S*unday night, three-quarters of Pepper's family gathered at CJ's bar to watch the game. He'd shut down Suckers to all but family and close friends tonight, since family and close friends put the bar almost at capacity.

This was one of her favorite spots in all of Bliss, and not just because the short-order cook made a mean Cobb salad. She'd celebrated buying into Bliss Bridal in the corner booth. She'd made friends with countless locals around the steel semicircle bar. And while she hadn't dated much since moving to Bliss, she'd had her share of tears-in-my-beer drinks with friends after discovering yet another ex-boyfriend was getting married, which she'd followed with two more tears-in-my-beer drinks after helping two of her exes' brides find their perfect wedding gowns at Bliss Bridal.

At this point in her life, her dating record was nearly a source of pride. Who else—besides Lindsey, of course, Bliss's resident matchmaker—could claim to have participated in the successful union of fifteen happy couples? And letting go of the traditional idea of the perfect happily-ever-after had freed her to set her own course for her future.

Tomorrow.

Tomorrow, she'd know.

Tonight, she'd soaked up love in the baby circle, getting baby hugs and snuggles and cuddles, and hopefully baby cooties. She'd rubbed Kimmie's belly, she'd rubbed Lindsey's belly, and she'd rubbed Dahlia's belly.

She'd done everything she could, and the next fourteen hours would be agony.

Too bad she couldn't use Tony as a distraction again tonight.

Too bad she'd turned chicken and fled last night. Once that test came back positive tomorrow, she wouldn't have a man's hands on her again for a very, very long time.

"I still don't get why Tony couldn't just hire extra drivers tonight." Rika slid onto the stool next to Pepper, her fruity drink half-gone. She was third youngest in the family—right behind Poppy, who had her by four minutes—but she was getting close to thirty herself. The whole family, growing up, getting older. "Aren't there Uber drivers around here?"

"In Bliss? No. And hiring extra drivers for one night of the year would be like me hiring extra bridal consultants for Knot Fest week. You buckle down and get it done."

"You're bringing him to Tarra's wedding, aren't you?"

"No, I'm bringing my other boyfriend."

"He needs to get his ass here so we can—*mmph*!"

A hand clamped over her mouth. Cori, next in birth order behind Pepper, flashed a smile while she muffled Rika. "Leave Pepper alone and let her enjoy having a boyfriend. *Eew*! Did you just lick my hand?"

"Yes, and you should wash more often. *Oh*! Look! That guy in blue touched that guy in red on the butt. I have that on my bingo card."

"Bingo!" Tarra called across the bar.

"Shut *up*," Cori called back. "Lucky pain in the ass," she muttered.

One of the babies let out a wail while the adults all laughed and groaned. Except Tarra's fiancé. He rolled his eyes.

Pepper's womb squeezed. The next family contest could be about *her* baby—gender, date, and how many hours she'd be in labor.

Gran squeezed up to the bar. "Your pizza man's late."

"He's delivering pizzas," Cori and Rika chorused with her.

"That's why I ordered up a dozen." Gran's wide grin was impossible not to smile back at, even as Pepper's shoulders headed up toward her earlobes.

She hadn't talked to him today. She assumed he knew better than to show up here—he'd been warned *and* threatened—but she'd been too chicken to call and confirm.

Because she'd been the one who fled like her pants were on fire last night. Who hadn't gone back when she could've.

"I made sure to tell them I only wanted the boss man to deliver to us," Gran said. "We need him for the—"

"*Touchdown!*" Cori yelled.

"That's a *first* down, not a touchdown, you dolt," CJ said from behind the bar, where Noah, his and Nat's six-year-old, was helping with the soda gun.

"They both have down in them," Cori retorted. "And you shouldn't call your son's aunt names in front of him. Babies deserve to grow up in non-hostile environments."

"What's a bolt?" Noah asked. His brown hair tumbled over his forehead, and his dark eyes were sparkling with curiosity. "Is that like a nut?"

"Exactly like a nut," CJ confirmed. He glanced at something behind Pepper, winced, and then swung Noah up into a football hold. The boy was slight—he had Nat's build, petite and small-boned—and CJ stood solid at six three, so he managed to pull off the awkward hold with ease. "Let's go score a touchdown in the ice-cream freezer in back. Don't tell Mom, okay?"

"Pizza's here!" Sage called from the door.

Pepper glanced in the mirror behind the bar, and she froze.

He hadn't listened. And now—

"Lock the door!" Gran crowed. "The stripper's here!"

Pepper glared at him. *I told you not to come.*

He answered with a stubborn, wolfish smile. *That was your first mistake.*

"Trouble in paradise?" Margie intoned beside her.

"Would you want your new boyfriend to meet the whole family *again*?"

"We're missing four siblings."

"Why am I explaining to a scientist that nine people still outnumber one by nearly a factor of ten?" She skittered off her stool and headed toward the door, but Gran was already ahead of her.

Her old bones could move quickly when she wanted them to. "Tony, my sweet boy. I brought Cards Against Humanity, but none of the other wusses here will play me."

"We respect you too much, Gran," Saffron's husband, Dylan, called from one of the booths.

"Oh, phooey. You're just not man enough to get beat by an old lady."

Tony put an arm around her, and Pepper's heart might've gone a little soft at the edges. "I don't understand why you're still single, Gran."

"It's by choice, young man. Don't go flirting with me. We need you to marry Pepper."

"We've only been dating a week."

"And you're not getting any younger," Gran declared.

"Hey, don't start the inquisition without me." CJ swung out of the kitchen, Noah-less. He leaned over the bar to poke Basil, who was watching with his normal affected boredom from the stool near the back wall, priest's collar stark white against his black clergy uniform. "You're up too, Your Holy Grouchiness. Come on. Time to quit being a father and step up and be a brother."

"I surrendered my brotherly duties to God twenty years ago, and I'm not taking them back now."

"Tony has pizzas to deliver," Pepper said to CJ. "We don't have time for an inquisition."

"Have you ever been caught in a compromising position with any farm animals?" Rika called.

"Rika—" Pepper started.

That smile growing on Tony's lips stopped her. It was the *I will win this game* smile. The *they don't scare me* smile. The *try your worst* smile.

"No, he hasn't," she finished. She reached his side and snagged his hand, but when she tugged him toward the door, he didn't move.

"Does a skunk count as a farm animal?" he asked.

"You've had sex with a *skunk*?" Gran said. Silence settled over the bar. Kimmie gaped. Her mother—here with Nat and Lindsey's father—seemed on the verge of a stroke. Even Mikey and Will—the Southerners in the group—seemed flummoxed. Sage—veterinarian of the group—stared on horrified, eyes wide.

"Sex?" Tony said. "No. I was behind it while my brother was trying to teach it to fetch. My nose was compromised for a week. And my clothes had to be burned."

Snorts and giggles went up around the room.

"I approve," CJ announced.

"Not so fast." Gran lifted a finger. "While I approve of his personality, I still don't know his sperm count."

"Why is it always the sperm count?" Margie said. "Why can't we ask about his IQ or his arrest record?"

"A man's not living right if he hasn't visited the slammer at least once. And gotten a prison bitch. And a tattoo. I got mine right—"

"Whoa, Gran—family-friendly establishment here," CJ interrupted.

"Gran, if Tony shows you his abs, will you let him get back to delivering pizzas?"

"Depends. Are they worth seeing?"

"I don't know."

More silence filled the bar. Pepper's cheeks went hot.

"You don't know?" Margie said in the silence.

"I don't know if Gran will think so," she amended quickly. "She has very eccentric taste, and she might be disappointed he doesn't have an extra nipple over his belly button."

She sent him a quick, silent, *you* don't *have an extra nipple over your belly button, do you?*, which he chose not to answer.

Instead, he linked his hand with hers and swung it.

"There's only one woman I strip for," he said. "Sorry, Gran."

"Then you owe me your sperm count. You get them tested. You told me so."

"Gran—" Pepper started.

"What if I come from a long line of thieves?" he said. "Or charlatans? Or internet spies?"

"You don't—" she started again. He hooked his hand behind her back and pulled her into him, pressed her head into his shoulder, muffling her, letting her whole body feel just how hard he was.

Hard chest under his red jacket. Hard abs. Hard—oh, *yes*.

That was what she'd left yesterday?

Priorities, she reminded herself. Being a mother would make the sacrifice worth it.

"Our genes can compensate for a lot," Gran said.

"What if he comes from a long line of *liars*?" Margie put in. "He *did* let Gran think he was a stripping pizza-delivery man."

"Is that one Nutmeg?" Tony said to Pepper.

Shrieks of laughter went through the bar.

"Hey, I know that joke," Nat called.

"Have you ever gone to a wedding with one woman and left with another?" Sage asked.

His whole body went stiff. Not *good* stiff, either, like that stiffness against her hip.

She shoved back. "And we're done," she announced.

"No," he said, quite distinctly, with more than a bit of annoyance twisting his features. "That's a jackass move."

"What about a Blueper Bowl party?" Saffron called. She was nursing her month-old baby girl at the musicians' table with Will and

Mikey and their pregnant wives, staring Tony down without blinking.

"Not at the Super Bowl, not at the Blueper Bowl," he growled. "I don't leave my date for other women. Period."

An approving murmur rolled through her family and friends, and a thrill at his words sent a hot longing zinging between her legs. She should've been indifferent—this wasn't real or permanent—or at least evolved enough not to get a thrill at feeling claimed, but protective caveman Tony was the sexiest thing she'd seen in months.

Hormones, she told herself. Early pregnancy hormones.

Which was exactly why he wouldn't be hers, and they wouldn't be rolling in the sheets. She gave one last sniff of his jacket—hot pizza and hotter Tony—and took another step back. "Thank you for delivering us pizza. Don't let us keep you from work."

"Not so fast, young lady," Gran said. "It's halftime."

"Dibs on the cucumber!" Cinna yelled.

"Tarra gets the cucumber," Sage yelled back. "She's pushing forty. She needs it most."

"What's with the cucumber?" Tony murmured.

"Just be glad it's not the goat," she replied. Dang goat. It was the only thing she *hadn't* tried. Not that she needed it or truly believed in it, but she would've taken it in a heartbeat. "And don't let them suck you into the middle of the group, or you'll never escape."

He flashed another of those warm, amused grins at her. "Who says I want to escape?"

"How could you *not* want to escape?"

He looked over her and swept a glance around the room. CJ had pulled out a box of vegetables, and the men—even the family friends— were picking from a box of animal-ear headbands. "Where are the elephant ears?" Mikey demanded. "I got the trunk—"

"Hush," Dahlia said with a laugh.

"Mighty good idea to keep quiet, Mikey," Will chimed in. "You show us that *trunk*, it'll give us proof otherwise."

Lindsey wrinkled her nose. "Now you hush."

"So this is normal family," Tony said quietly. "I like it."

That wasn't fair, making her heart meltier. Reminding her of how much she shouldn't take for granted.

"Give it another five minutes," she said.

"Get me the cheetah ears and a banana for these two," Gran called. She gripped Pepper's wrist with one frail hand and Tony's with the other. "Where's the karaoke machine and the camera? I want this one played at my funeral. Basil, don't you make me come flush you out of the bathroom. Pregnant ladies out front. Now, Mrs. Billy, don't you be shy. Singing ain't ever hurt anyone."

"Beg to differ, Gran," CJ called.

"She killed three cats with her voice alone last year," Mikey added.

Lindsey moved herself and her belly gracefully between the tables. "You're just jealous of my trophy."

"This is going on YouTube," Pepper warned Tony.

He glanced back at Will—Billy Brenton to his legions of country music fans—before shedding his Pepperoni Tony's hat and jacket. "I don't have a clue what's going on here, but I wouldn't want to look too cheesy," he said to Pepper's questioning glance.

His lips hitched up on one side, and a laugh bubbled out of her. "Or saucy?"

"You catch on quick, Miss Blue."

"Aw, now, aren't you two adorable?" Gran shoved the banana at Pepper and the cheetah ear headband at Tony. "Now line up. It's showtime."

They were jostled into line between the bar and the tables, facing a camera set on a tripod in the corner. The first chords of "Yellow Submarine" blared out of the speakers in the corners of the bar, eliciting a few groans that Gran shushed quickly.

"How—" Tony started.

"First rule of the family—you don't question the halftime show."

It had morphed over the years from the first family talent show—Saffron's fault, of course, for saying she could've done a better show than *NSYNC—and no one could agree on when the props had been added, but Tony was right.

The Blueper Bowl family lip-sync battle with weird headbands and random fruits and vegetables was Pepper's normal.

And she was dang lucky to have it.

———

PEPPER LEFT Suckers with butterflies in her stomach and a smile in her heart. She wouldn't interrupt Tarra's wedding week with the news that she was pregnant, but hanging with her family—and having Tony be such a good sport about the fake-boyfriend stuff—had been a great way to spend the night.

"He has a secret," Margie said beside her as they walked to Pepper's car.

"Everyone has secrets."

"Yes, but he has more than usual."

Pepper clicked her key fob to unlock her doors. Her taillights flashed in the dark. "How could you possibly know that?"

"Science."

"Science?"

"Science invented the internet, so yes. Science."

"Ah. You've discovered he's divorced."

Margie was four years younger than Pepper in birth order—CJ and Cori were between them—and she was the most analytical of her siblings. Everything was logical with Margie, but more, she had an old soul. She'd understood things about the world as a teenager that Pepper still struggled with in her mid-thirties. Were Tony a *real* boyfriend, she'd be worried about Margie's concerns.

"Yes, but I can't determine if his ex-wife is still alive. He might be a psychopath or a serial killer."

Then again, maybe the Blue genes were finally overriding Margie's analytical obsessions. "I'll make sure to swing by the police department tomorrow and ask for a background check."

They climbed into Pepper's car, and she cranked the engine. Now would be a good time to sow a few seeds of doubt so it wouldn't come out of left field on Friday when Pepper told the family she and Tony had broken up and he wouldn't be accompanying her to the rehearsal dinner or the wedding.

"Cinna knows something, but she's not telling," Margie said.

"Oh, please. One, she always wants everyone to think she knows something, and two, she's probably already taking bets on when we first slept together."

"Negative."

"What?"

"She's taking bets on whether Poppy will bring her boyfriend to the wedding, but she hasn't said a thing about you. Why do you think that might be?"

Irrational irritation knotted Pepper's shoulders. "Psychological warfare? She wants me to think she doesn't care?"

"Her past behavioral patterns would indicate it's because she's worried about you."

"She took bets on CJ and Nat, and he needed more worrying over than I ever will."

"He needed the goading. Also, she's matured in the last two years and may be more inclined to consider the repercussions of her actions."

"*Cinna?*"

"She might've mentioned a concern about you becoming an old maid and the toll your love life has taken on your mood lately."

An unexpected burn took up residence behind her nose. The mood swings were all hormonal, but the fact that Cinna had noticed and chalked it up to something being wrong rather than to Pepper being bitchy was touching. "How kind of her. But she doesn't need to worry. Obviously. I've found a successful businessman boyfriend who lives next door for easy booty calls. Life couldn't be better."

Margie snorted.

She was an exceptional snorter.

Pepper rubbed away the sting in her eyes and cranked the engine.

"He's my boyfriend, and he's a very nice man," she said, and she didn't have to reach hard for the overly defensive tone that would make Margie wonder if something was wrong.

"Because you like him, or because you don't want to know who Gran will deliver for you next?"

Both, along with her pregnancy test tomorrow.

"Because he's *different*." There. She was getting into this story now. "I've never dated a divorced guy who doesn't like to talk about himself before. Maybe this one will work."

"This guy doesn't sound like the marrying type. He wants to have a one-on-seven orgy with us."

"What? No, he doesn't."

"He asked again about pillow fights after the halftime show."

"He was *joking*."

"Seemed rather desperate to me. Like a man who needs to prove his virility by making crude jokes. Almost Mikey-ish."

"Oh, stop. Tony is *so* not Mikey-ish. And you know Mikey's getting some, in addition to being ridiculously happy with Dahlia, and he's *still* a dog."

"I applaud your attempts to break your streak, but this feels off. And you know how I feel about feelings."

Given half an opportunity, Margie would rationalize how *feelings* had led to global warming, every war in history, and—to quote her —*that awful cat website that started internet memes*. It wasn't a family gathering until someone spun Margie up over politics or human behavior. So if she was willing to embrace a gut feeling, Pepper had a bigger problem than Cinna failing to start a pool about her dating life.

"You think I should call it off with him."

"He's an unknown quantity with unknown motivations."

Her gut said he was everything he'd said he was last night—a lonely divorced man trying to fit into a new home. And her gut had been turned inside out by fertility treatments, IVF procedures, and the abundance of babies coming in Bliss these days.

"Be careful," Margie said. "Have fun if that's all you want, but don't... Just *don't*, okay?"

There were so many *don't*s, Pepper didn't even want to ask. They started with *don't get hurt* and ended with *don't do something you can't undo*.

Wise advice from the wisest of her siblings.

And after tomorrow, none of it would matter.

IT WAS NEARLY midnight before Tony collapsed face-first on his bed, still in his jeans and a marinara-smeared Pepperoni Tony's polo. Lucky leapt onto the bed on light feet and tiptoed across the quilt to sniff him, her whiskers tickling his face.

Good night for pizza sales. Good night for his business.

Good night for fifteen minutes of fun with Pepper's family.

The mere thought of her caused a stirring in his pants.

He was getting better. Back to normal. Healthy again.

Lucky pawed his cheek. He shoved to sitting and scrubbed his hands down his face. "Hungry?" he asked the cat.

She mewled and climbed into his lap, turning three times before leaning in to knead his thigh.

Not hungry, then. Just looking for affection.

He pulled his phone from his pocket and checked his email. His cheek twitched at a note from his sister—*You haven't RSVP'd to Bella's wedding yet, and you know she wants Uncle Tony there*—and none of the other emails held any interest, so he switched over to his text messages instead.

Nothing interesting there either.

Not like his favorite niece getting married too young to a guy Tony didn't know enough about. One more thing he'd sacrificed in the divorce—while he'd been playing the playboy over here in Bliss, he'd let too many people in his family drift away.

Or maybe he'd drifted away from them, and they were just trying to give him space.

But he wasn't going there tonight. Or ever, if he could help it. His thumbs hovered over the screen. Texting Pepper was veering into relationship territory, and they weren't in a relationship. Not really.

But she'd been a friend. A friend who let him kiss her. A friend who made the world seem brighter than it had been two weeks ago.

It was never wrong to text a friend.

She was probably sound asleep and wouldn't answer anyway.

Thanks for a fun halftime show, he texted, and he hit *send* before he could rethink it.

She was probably still irritated with him for ignoring her and delivering pizzas to Suckers tonight. He grinned to himself while he scratched Lucky behind her ears.

He'd forgotten how much he enjoyed playing the game. Pushing the limits. Testing.

His phone buzzed.

Thanks for stripping for Gran, she'd replied.

He barked out a laugh that sent Lucky skittering across the bed. She slowed on the far corner, hunched over and watching him, ready to pounce if he moved wrong. "Sorry, kitty," he murmured.

My pleasure, he typed back to Pepper. *What are you still doing up?*

The typing bubble appeared and disappeared about six times before an answer came. *Exciting day.*

Today had been an exciting day, or tomorrow would be an exciting day?

Her typing bubble lit up again. He stood and pulled his shirt off, watching the phone on his bed. His pants hit the floor next.

She was still typing.

Was she in bed? What did she wear to bed? Those flannel pajamas? Or did she strip out of them? Maybe she just wore the shirt.

With nothing beneath.

Nothing beneath.

Ah, there was that sweet feeling of his manhood growing to its full potential. He slid between his sheets and wrapped his hand around himself.

His phone dinged.

Thank you again for your help. You've been a really great friend. I'll make sure no one retaliates against Pepperoni Tony's when we break up.

He deflated in his own palm.

Right.

This was temporary. No more kissing her. No more hanging with her hilariously cool family. No more having excuses to talk to her.

Just as well.

She deserved a forever kind of guy, and he was done with forever.

Thanks. Sleep well, he sent.

You too. xo

He snorted. Kiss hug, huh?

In his dreams.

8

*P*epper didn't eat breakfast Monday morning. Her belly was already full of butterflies. She made herself maintain a dignified walk into her doctor's office, chatted pleasantly with the lab tech who drew her blood, and sat flipping through *Redbook* beside a potted plant in the muted waiting room. Any minute now, she'd be called back, and her doctor would tell her that this round of IVF had worked.

That she was going to be a mother.

The failed artificial insemination and her first two rounds of IVF were warm-ups. But this time, she'd done everything to the letter to combat the effects of her PCOS. She'd taken her pills at the exact same time every day. She'd maintained her blood sugar at normal levels without exception, even though it had meant passing up pizza and cookies and countless other treats. She'd taken her temperature six times a day and paid more attention to her natural rhythms than she would ever publicly discuss. She was the healthiest she'd ever been, and she'd spent enough hours with babies, between Saffron's new little girl and Nat and CJ's new little boy, that she was sure her maternal hormone level had never been higher.

Her first failures had been the emotional price to pay to make her appreciate today. The work she'd had to put in so that she could earn being a mother.

This test? Merely a formality.

She was sure she was pregnant.

She had to be.

After thirty minutes, the nurse called her back.

And thirty minutes after that, she left her doctor's office with a shattered heart and a gaping hole in her soul.

For everything else in her life that hard work could accomplish, it couldn't get her pregnant.

And according to her doctor, it probably never would.

SHE WOULDN'T CRY.

She was a hard-ass businesswoman. She had great friends. Great family. The sweetest dog in the entire universe.

A bright future.

Alone.

She sucked air through her nose while she sat in her car and quickly swiped mascara over her lashes. No eye contact with herself in the mirror—she couldn't bear the grief she might see, nor could she mask it if she acknowledged it. She had eight hours to get through at the boutique before she could go home and fake food poisoning and hide herself in her room all night.

Maybe the test was wrong.

Maybe her doctor had done it too early. Or they'd mislabeled the vial with her blood. Or—

Or she needed to accept that she was a thirty-five-year-old woman with polycystic ovary syndrome. No husband, only a fake boyfriend who wouldn't go with her to her sister's wedding this weekend and who didn't have the slightest clue she was trying to get pregnant.

Her options for motherhood were convincing a man to marry her so she could pursue adoption more easily, though she'd need to save a lot more money for it, or asking one of her sisters to carry a baby for her.

Her other option was to get out of this car, walk into Bliss Bridal, and make the most of the life she'd built for herself. Considering there were a dozen bridal consultants, five seamstresses, and two full-time support staff who depended on her for their jobs, she needed to get to work.

And then she needed to find a hobby. Be something more than a businesswoman, friend, sister, and aunt.

Find another way to leave her mark on the world.

She shoved her mascara back in her purse, applied a quick layer of lipstick, and forced herself out into the frigid morning. Her flats slapped the pavement on her way to the back door. The scent of cake wafted through the chilly air from the bakery next door and stuck in her nose, a little celebration in the midst of her desolation.

Pepper didn't *fail*. She learned, she adjusted, and she succeeded next time.

But for getting pregnant, there would be no *next time*.

Three of her girls were already prepping the shop for the day when she walked in. She called a greeting to them before settling herself in the office to look over yesterday's reports. Normally on a Monday, she'd peek at the distributor catalogs that had come in during the last week and flag the dresses she might want to stock for the next season, just to get her in the mood for selling dresses, but today, she was so over this whole idea of happily ever after.

She should've bought a tech start-up instead. Something far, far from people and weddings and babies.

Shortly after ten, someone knocked at the office door. Before she could double-check her makeup, voices swelled as the door swung open.

"Hey, how's it going?"

Pepper straightened, taking a blow straight to the heart at the sight of Nat weighed down with a purse, diaper bag, and baby carrier.

Guilt added the follow-up punch. Just because she couldn't have babies didn't mean she needed to be mad at women who could.

"Double digits, Nat." Pepper stood and gestured her to sit. "I really thought you could make it ten days before you showed up."

"TJ wanted to see where Mommy works."

"You realize Cinna will find his birth certificate sooner or later. You shouldn't have given her a key to your house."

"TJ *is* his name."

"You're a better liar than CJ, but I still don't believe you." She wouldn't cry. She wouldn't. "Hand over the baby and kick your feet up. Need anything to drink?"

Nat pulled a full water bottle from the green zoo animal diaper bag she'd brought in. "Someone won't let me leave home without water. And speaking of your relatives, the Blueper Bowl was fun last night. And Tony was a good sport. Lindsey told me he was a nice guy, but she didn't mention the smile and ass. You've threatened him with something worse than death if he dumps you and gets married right away, haven't you?"

As if that would make a difference. She bent over TJ's carrier and gently pried the soft yellow blankets back until she could see his little sleeping face. She barely resisted clenching a fist to her belly, and she had to swallow hard again at the burn in her throat and eyes. He was so sweet. So precious. So perfect.

A new generation to love and snuggle and carry on the Blue name.

"How's he sleeping?" she asked.

"Pretty much only in the car or when Aunt Lindsey or Uncle Will is holding him. Which, of course, is proof my family is just as awesome as yours." Nat tossed her jacket on the second chair. "Now, back to you. How did Tony really take the halftime show?"

She touched a finger to the baby's nose. Half of her wanted to offer to babysit every night, and the other half wanted to go throw up. "Can I pick him up? He's so cute. Look at those cheeks."

"You think Tony has cute cheeks?"

That was close enough to permission for Pepper, so she went to work unbuckling her new nephew and pulling him out of his seat. "The *baby* has cute cheeks. Quit changing the subject."

"We were definitely talking about Tony. So who's changing the subject?"

"You show up here with a baby and you think my latest boyfriend is going to be my top priority?"

"You haven't dated a new guy since before I got pregnant. So, yes."

Dating. *Crap*. She needed to let Tony off the hook. Go buy knitting needles and learn to be *that* aunt who made blankets for everyone else. Level with Gran, tell her dating was off the table right now. That she'd decided she didn't want a husband or family, and—*dammit*, her eyes stung. She buried her nose in the baby's blankets and inhaled his sweet baby-lotion scent while she tried to get herself back under control.

"You know he's divorced," Nat said softly.

She nodded. *Everyone* knew he was divorced, and apparently everyone thought that made him broken.

Nat, of all people, shouldn't judge.

"Want me to find out why? Lindsey's all *attorney-client privilege*, but I have my ways of finding out."

Tony's divorce was none of her business. "You don't trust me to talk to my own boyfriend?"

"I don't like not knowing about the men my friends and family are dating. And I don't know very much about Tony. I mean, I know the six feet, dark hair, always scruffy, fabulous ass part. I know he grew up in Willow Glen and Lindsey loves his pizza. But I don't know who he dated before or after his wife, why he got divorced, who his parents are, what his most embarrassing childhood moment is, and if that's actually his original pizza recipe."

"How many people's most embarrassing childhood moments do you know?"

"Here on The Aisle? Pretty much everyone under forty. You know Max Gregory, right?"

"Is there anyone who *doesn't*?" Max had been the primary topic of gossip since Merry arrived in town a few months ago. Between her secret life as an author, her father being a jewel thief, and Merry herself stealing Max's family's most prized jewel from their jewelry store shortly before Christmas, there practically wasn't anything else worthwhile to talk about in Bliss. "The entire *state* knows him by now. Probably the whole country."

"He serenaded Charlotte Russell with a really bad version of Bro Code's 'American Sweetheart' to ask her to homecoming our senior year. She thought that his singing was two ducks having sex outside her bedroom window, so she threw a bucket of water on him."

An unexpected laugh welled up inside her. "Does Merry know?"

"If she doesn't, she will soon. I hear Charlotte is trying to talk her into doing a signing at Once Upon a Page a few times a year, when she's not kicking Max's ass on the basketball court for keeping the secret."

"So what's your most embarrassing childhood memory?"

"You first."

"Not a chance."

Nat smiled. "That's what I thought. So, how many dates until you ask Tony to marry you?"

"I already asked. He said he's not buying the cow before he gets a sample, and I'm not putting out for a guy who calls me a cow."

"He called you a cow and you're still dating him? And wait—you *haven't* slept with him yet?"

Dang it. She'd screwed that up again. "Not all of us can have some emotionally wounded prince come riding into town to save our first-borns and their dinosaurs from evil fountains," she said pointedly. "And Tony has a unique sense of humor. It was funnier in person."

She hugged TJ closer. The little guy yawned and stretched, and a hollow pang cramped her empty womb.

"All of your Blue people think you're funnier in person," Nat said.

Pepper pressed a kiss to TJ's forehead. "Your mommy is making fun of me," she whispered.

"Only because I love you."

TJ scrunched up his face, blinked his dark blue eyes open, and let out a wail.

"I know, sweetheart. I don't like it when she laughs at Auntie Pepper either," Pepper cooed.

Nat sighed, but despite the crying baby, her lips were still curved up in a smile that forecasted trouble.

Pepper needed to buck up. Because life was going on with or without her.

TONY WAS elbow-deep in pizza dough, enjoying the hell out of getting his hands dirty. He did the paperwork because a businessman had to, but he lived for the cooking. With the mid-afternoon lull creeping in, he was catching up on getting tomorrow's dough ready and contemplating those cookies he'd stashed in his office after having two for breakfast.

"Looks a little dry," one of his crew said over the traditional Italian music coming through the speakers in the ceiling.

"Never doubt the master, kid."

"Yo, boss, got a lady looking for you," his cashier called from up front. "Something about that bridal fest crap."

Always something. "That bridal fest crap makes it possible for me to pay you," Tony called back. "Out in a minute."

He slapped his ten-pound ball of dough into a proofing bucket and stuck it in the walk-in fridge, then washed his hands before heading out front.

His cashier nodded to a slender woman in a black wool coat perusing the family photos—including a photo of him in a pink bunny costume—near the glass door.

"If she wasn't from The Aisle, man, I'd be all over that," his cashier murmured.

A brunette head twisted as though she'd heard the guy, but her wry brow-tilt changed to a quiet smile when her green gaze landed on Tony.

"Eyes on her face or you're fired," he murmured.

The kid ducked his head and grabbed a rag. "I'll get those tables wiped off, Mr. Cross, sir."

"Tormenting the hired help?" Pepper asked.

He looped an arm around her waist—he *was* her pretend boyfriend, after all—and smiled at her. There was something off about her. Her eyes weren't bright enough, her smile not quite authentic.

He could relate. Sleep had been elusive last night after her pointed reminder that this arrangement was temporary. "Always. What brings you in today? You had lunch yet?"

She pulled away and shifted her bulky brown purse to her other shoulder. "I'm here on business."

Despite her hip cock of unhappiness causing a flutter in his chest, a flare of awareness sparked below his belt. Her cheeks were tinged with pink as though she'd walked the eight blocks in the cold to get here. He couldn't see much of her figure beneath her coat, but the shape of her legs inspired thoughts that inspired more healthy, virile movement in his pants.

Looked like she might need to go in back and talk in private. Or... do other things. Like get naked.

"Business is overrated," he said with a wink.

She didn't smile back. Actually, her nose pulled a Rudolph, going shiny and red while she blinked quickly.

His instincts were screaming for him to hug her, and their ploy would've made a simple hug natural, but self-preservation demanded distance. He settled for cupping her elbow. "You okay?"

"Perfect." She treated him to a smile that was heavy on the unhappy. "Busy day."

He might not have been in the dating game for several years, but he knew the difference between a *busy day* woman and an *I'm displeased with you* woman. He slipped his arm around her waist and pointed to the grainy picture of two girls in terrycloth jumpers and

114

him doing a girly impression of her dog in front of an insurance office. "My sisters parading me around Willow Glen as the Easter Bunny."

A soft smile lifted the corners of her mouth. "You seem quite proud."

"Of course. I made that costume look damn good."

She rolled her eyes, but the smile growing on her lips made the tight band suffocating his heart loosen. "Modest much?"

"Just telling you what my mom said."

Her smile slipped, and she dug into her bag. "I really am here on business. Just need your signature on this to apply for the recommended dining list. I'll make sure it's approved."

He took the paperwork from her, an unease he didn't want to acknowledge clawing at his gut. "You sure you don't want something to eat? Pizza, breadsticks...you ever try gelato? Not as authentic here as you'll get in Italy, but I guarantee it'll make your taste buds sing."

"I'm good. Thank you." She hefted her bag on her shoulder once more. "And they need me back at the boutique." Her eyes flicked to the dining room behind him, where he was fully aware of his staff watching them. "Thank you for—for your help this last week, and for everything you did last night, but I need to suck it up and tell my grandmother the truth. I've taken enough of your time."

Panic slammed into his gut. "No."

She flashed him a pained smile. "You've been great. Above and beyond duty. Thank you, again, for your help."

"No, I mean *no*, you're not doing this." He barely refrained from stomping a boot. She *wasn't* doing this. He lowered his voice. "If you let me out of our arrangement, I have a few sisters of my own who will spend the next six weeks trying to set me up with potential dates for a family wedding."

There went another pained smile. "Doesn't seem like you'd have any issues finding a willing and able date on your own."

Dammit. A year of being a one-date wonder to give the appearance of a playboy enjoying single life, and now the only woman his body had reacted to since his divorce was shoving him off for that very reputation he'd worked so hard to cultivate.

"Four weeks," he pressed. "Those women—business—" *Hell*, he was screwing this all up. "Am I that much of a hardship? Four more weeks, a nicely staged breakup, and we'll both have more breathing room in the meantime."

She fingered the single emerald dangling from a short chain around her neck, lashes lowered so he couldn't read her.

"I'll quit with the asshole jokes, I promise." He wasn't desperate, he told himself. And this wasn't about *her*, exactly. The last week or so, she'd somehow become a friend. The fact that she was one of the few friends who didn't know why he was divorced, one of the few women —the only woman—who had inspired his equipment to work again was simply an added bonus.

And he had some oceanfront property here in Illinois to sell himself too.

"So you've been getting more out of this than I thought," she said.

"Just got the invitation reminder," he said gruffly. "I wasn't trying to use you. More than agreed upon."

"You're right. We both have secrets."

Ironic, coming from the woman claiming to be down because of a *busy day*. "Most people do."

She locked gazes with him, and her eyes didn't waver. She had high expectations. A demand that he be good enough for this task. But she also had something else—a belief that he could do it.

She wouldn't still be here if she didn't.

"All right," she finally said. "Four weeks."

Her right hand moved, but he was quicker, sliding in to let a kiss linger on her soft, cool cheek. "Thanks for dropping by, sweets," he murmured.

Her breath was uneven against his skin. "My pleasure."

It was a lie, but he'd bought himself some time, so he didn't care. He let her go. "Call me later," she said quickly before ducking out the door.

He turned around, and because the dining room was occupied by only a handful of customers, half his staff was unoccupied and staring at him.

His head server set her tray down on the counter and snagged a breadstick from a basket that hadn't found a home during the lunch hour. "Did you chase her away on purpose, or are you really that bad at picking women?"

"Why am I paying all of you to be here when there aren't more customers?"

"Because you're a softie."

Hell of it was, she was probably right. And when he got back to the pizza dough, his heart wasn't in it.

His heart was wondering what had gotten Pepper down today. As soon as he was done here today, he was sniffing out the truth.

9

*C*inna was working, and Gran had been invited to a seniors' Bunco party—"I'm gonna meet me a man without a grandson so you and me and him and Tony can go out on a proper date," she'd threatened, er, promised—so Pepper miraculously had the night to herself.

Well, her and the two dogs.

After a nice long walk with Sadie, and a follow-up walk with George, she plopped herself down on the couch with the bag of yarn and knitting needles she'd bought that afternoon, searched for a "how to knit" video on YouTube, and refused to consider the possibility of letting herself cry.

She'd followed all the doctor's orders for success. Diet, exercise, rest. She'd learned new stress management techniques to deal with the hectic pace at the boutique, and she was a damn successful breather now. She'd battled mood swings through months of hormone therapy. Don't get her started on the number of hours she'd spent with her legs in the stirrups or having her reproductive organs poked and prodded.

For her body to refuse to carry a baby?

Who the fuck did her body think it was?

Her fingers curled tight around the knitting needles in her left hand, and she yanked an unsuspecting skein of yarn from the plastic bag. Except the yarn got caught in the bag handle. The plastic crinkled and snapped with every tug, but it wouldn't give up the yarn from the handle. Sadie was already hiding upstairs, and even George beat a stealthy retreat out of the living room.

Pepper stabbed the knitting needles into the bag. She ripped the handle apart. The yarn sprang loose, and she threw it at the TV.

A sob the size of Texas rose up from the pit of her stomach, clawing its way up her ribs and jamming itself in her throat.

Why was her body broken?

Science could put a man on the moon, but she couldn't do the one thing women were biologically born to do.

If her body couldn't have babies, why couldn't she have lost the instinct to want them?

A knock startled her. The words *go away* formed on her tongue, but shame made her swallow them.

Her problems weren't anyone else's fault. Not Gran's, not Cinna's, not her family's. Not whoever was at the door, be it the UPS man, a neighbor, or an ax murderer. Though if it was an ax murderer, he'd picked the wrong house on the wrong night.

She blew a slow breath out through her mouth. Whoever it was would go away. And those knitting needles weren't going to unstab the plastic bag and other skeins of yarn by themselves. But her fingers wouldn't unclench to do the job.

The knock came again, this time accompanied by a dark shadow swaying toward the window.

Dammit.

They could see her sitting here. And they apparently *weren't* going away.

She marched across the living room to the small foyer and flung the door open. "What?"

Tony's eyes flared wide, and his mouth parted. He stood there sexy as sin with his dark jacket, jeans that hugged his muscular thighs, and tousled hair. Strong and virile and probably perfectly capable of fathering as many children as he could ever want.

If that damn sting in her eyes didn't learn who was boss real quick, she—

For once, she didn't know what she'd do. Not like she could threaten her own eyeballs.

He stepped into the house. "You okay?"

No, she wasn't okay. She might never be okay again. "Yeah, I—oh. This?" She wiggled her fingers toward her face, undoubtedly red-eyed and puffy-nosed. "I was reading."

And if he believed that, maybe he should've stuck to delivering pizza instead of opening his own chain.

"On purpose?" he said.

Her chin tilted up, and while she knew her bitch face was coming out, she couldn't stop it. "These are happy tears. Good book."

His lips twitched, and she couldn't decide if she wanted to hug him or kick him.

He took the question out of her hands when he came the rest of the way in, kicked the door shut behind him, and wrapped her in a tight hug. His body radiated heat, sucking her into his orbit as though he were a universe all his own and she were the central solar system. Scents of pizza and leather tickled her nose, and while that sob tried to suffocate her lungs again, a long-forgotten desire flared to life.

"Thanks." His breath tickled the roots of her hair. "I needed this."

Oh, she had too. More than she'd realized. More than she wanted to admit. Her sisters had hugged her this weekend. Gran had hugged her before disappearing into the seniors' center. A bride had hugged her at work today.

But no one had hugged her like *this*. Intentionally. Thoughtfully. Not out of habit, but because it was necessary.

She wiggled her arms beneath his open jacket to loop them around his back. Her cheek settled over his heart. The steady *thump, thump, thump* in his chest was a reliable, soothing rhythm battling the chaos raging in her own body.

Tears threatened again and her breath dragged unevenly, but she refused to let the grief win.

He smoothed a firm hand up and down her back. The tension she'd held behind her shoulder blades put up a fight, but it was no match for his steady care.

If she let herself relax, she'd cry. No, she'd sob. Wail. There would be no demure tears sliding gently down her cheeks. She would ugly-cry. With a blotchy face, snotty nose, and gaspy breaths.

She latched onto his words—*I needed this*—because it was all she had.

He needed her.

He wasn't related to her. He didn't work for her. He wasn't buying something from her. She'd flat-out told him she wouldn't have sex with him. Ran away, even, the last time he kissed her. But here he was, asking for a simple hug.

Did he need a hug? Or did he understand she couldn't ask for this for herself, and he wanted to offer her comfort and affection for no other reason than that he was a good man?

A tremble started in her core, and suddenly the hug wasn't enough. She needed a solid connection. Grounding. An anchor.

To escape from herself. From her brain.

She grabbed him around the neck and pushed her lips to his. His arms tightened around her middle, holding her in a granite vise while his mouth opened to her. His tongue stroked her lip. She whimpered into his kiss.

This. This kiss, this connection, this escape was everything she needed.

She raked her hands into his hair and sucked his lip into her mouth. He pushed her against the wall, a rough rumble in his chest vibrating through her clothes and sending sparks racing over her skin.

Her fingers twitched, her lips tingled, and an inferno roared to life deep in her belly.

She wanted to have sex with Tony.

Tonight. *Now*. Why couldn't she? There was absolutely nothing standing in their way.

Except, apparently, him.

He wrenched himself free. "Pepper—"

Her heart dipped to her belly. "I changed my mind." Before her brain could catch up, before he could argue, she yanked on his hair and attacked him with another kiss.

How long would it take to get him naked?

Her nipples tightened into needy points, and she felt an unmistakable swell of hard male interest growing against her belly.

George yipped, claws clicking against the wood floor. His furry body leapt on her leg. "Down," she ordered, her voice strong and clear, all hints of sobs and tears beaten back by pure carnal desire.

"You want me to go down on you?" Tony said.

Looking in his eyes was like falling into a chocolate river, warm and delicious but fluid and unpredictable.

"Yes," she breathed. Who *was* that woman? She was sexy and breathless and panting. Would he pick up on how long it had been? Or did he think she did this all the time?

"Upstairs," she ordered.

He didn't move. "I didn't come here for this."

"If you don't have sex with me tonight, I will hate you forever."

Probably too strong there.

His jaw worked up and down, and those inquisitive eyes demanded answers to questions she refused to acknowledge. If he turned her down, if he walked away, she'd shatter into a billion shards of brittle glass, and she'd never find normal again.

So she did the only thing a self-respecting woman on the verge of falling apart could do.

She licked his jaw while she yanked his ass, pressing his hardening shaft firmly against her.

A growl rumbled from his throat. He released her and stripped out of his jacket, dropping it right there in the doorway. She tugged him to the stairs while he nuzzled her neck and slipped his hands beneath her shirt, his knuckles grazing her skin.

She yelped.

He pulled back, eyes wide. "Sorry, I—"

"No, no." She pulled his hands back to her waist. "Startled. Ticklish. Touch me. Now."

His dark gaze searched her face again. "Pepper—"

She grabbed his cheeks and went up on tiptoe to capture his lips again.

His response was slower. She grazed his lower lip with her teeth. His fingers dug into her waist, and he deepened the kiss.

Reluctantly or eagerly, she didn't care. All she cared about was the chocolate and coffee flooding her senses, erasing her thoughts, taking her away from everything but the experience of *him*. He leisurely explored her mouth, licking and sucking, nipping and soothing. They reached the stairs, and his hard thigh angled between her legs.

This. This was what she needed.

Pure carnal escape.

"You feel so damn good," he whispered.

George jumped on her calf and wrapped his front legs around her shin. She shook him off, but he jumped right back on. "*Shoo*."

Tony straightened again.

"No, not you. The dog. You stay."

She grabbed his hand and tugged him up the stairs. When she had him in the bedroom, she shut the door in George's face, then tugged Tony's hand to her breast. The steel cords in his forearms flexed. His erection pulsed against her. Did she have condoms somewhere in here?

As if it mattered.

She couldn't get pregnant.

"If you don't want to—" he started.

"Do you not want to?"

"Oh, I want to."

"Me too."

He brushed his lips across hers, a featherlight touch of velvet skin, and squeezed her breast. "What changed your mind?"

Nope. Not going there. "I came to my senses."

Before he could respond, she kissed him again.

Because if he stopped touching her, if he stopped holding her, if he stopped kissing her, the delicate crystal web holding her together would shatter.

He growled out an approving rumble and pushed her against the door.

Too soon, he broke the kiss again, but his pirate's grin sent hot heat coursing through her blood.

"Are you ticklish anywhere else?" he murmured.

Everywhere. Her nerve endings were frayed and on fire, but if he would just keep touching her—"Try me."

He pulled back enough to sweep a lazy glance over her figure, and the first bit of apprehension slithered through her belly.

What if he was used to sleeping with more experienced women? Or kinky women? Did he want her bossy? Or compliant?

Why couldn't she simply enjoy this?

His hand slid down her side. She held her breath and fought against the quiver in her skin. *There*. So ticklish there.

Playful was good. Playful wasn't real. And she needed all of today not to be real.

"Are you?" she hissed out between clenched teeth.

"Am I...?"

"Ticklish."

His lips spread in a naughty smile that made her core pulse. She blinked, and his shirt fluttered to the ground on her soft green bedroom rug.

"Better idea," he said. "You try me."

Firm olive skin and a sprinkling of dark hair covered the rigid muscles of his chest and abdomen. His hips were cut, his collarbones thick and straight, leading to wide, sculpted shoulders and well-defined arms. A tattoo—a scroll with *vivi, ridi, ama* scripted across it —decorated his upper arm.

Her mouth went dry.

This was *hers* tonight. Hers to explore. Hers to own. Hers to lose herself in.

She had to pause and swallow. "Making pizza must be quite the workout."

His left eye crinkled tighter than his right when his smile grew. "More than dancing around with fluffy dresses all day."

"Dresses are heavy." His skin was rough satin, pebbling in goose bumps beneath her fingertips while she traced the ridges of his ribs and abs. "You might be in good enough shape to try one on."

"Keep talking, I'll tickle you on purpose."

She hooked her thumbs beneath his waistband and splayed her fingers over the denim covering his butt. "Kiss me again."

He obliged, his breath tickling her cheek while his tongue teased hers.

The needy ache grew between her legs. She pulled him closer, itching to pull her own shirt off but reluctant to break the connection, even for a moment.

"So good," he murmured against her lips.

Maybe she could just shimmy out of her pants. That was the necessary part. He'd be back for more, and she could show him *all* of the goods next time.

He *would* be back for more...wouldn't he?

The way he was licking at that spot where her neck and shoulder met—she yelped again, because *ticklish*, then quickly grabbed his head and held him in the crook of her neck before he decided to get gentle-manly. "Do that again."

He obliged. Along with suckling on her neck, he slid his hands under her shirt to cup her breasts. A rush of potent pleasure flooded her limbs when he brushed the silk covering her nipples. Her neck arched back, her breasts pushed into the solid wall of his chest, and her hips bucked.

She rocked against Tony's thigh. She had to get her shirt off. Then her pants. And his pants.

His pants definitely had to go.

She lifted a leg to wrap around his hips, but she couldn't get it high enough. Couldn't bend right.

She tried again and ended up with a charley horse in the back of her thigh. "Aah!" She bounced on one foot and grabbed at the tight muscle while Tony reared back.

"Did I...?"

"Bed," she panted while she rubbed her hamstring. "Lose the pants. We're doing this, dammit."

If Cinna or Gran came home right now, Pepper would kill them.

"Pepper—"

She tore her shirt off and glared at him.

His lips parted and his eyes glossed over. "*Damn*, you're hot," he murmured.

Right.

She and her charley horse limp and those extra ten pounds no amount of diet or exercise could shake were *so* sexy.

But his eyes were black satin, and that reverent adoration in his expression suggested his sentiment might've been the most honest thing he'd ever said aloud.

No thinking. No looking. No emotions.

She just needed to touch. That was all this was.

Touching. Physical release.

She unsnapped her jeans. "Pants off," she ordered again.

In one smooth motion, he had his pants at his ankles. His belt buckle clinked to the ground.

She hadn't seen a man standing at attention in *months*. Her greedy fingers reached for him, needing the connection, needing to *feel*, but not think. She'd forgotten the seductiveness of a well-built man. The cords of muscle in his arms. The indent of his spine. The curve of his ass.

The slight taste of anticipation mixed with fear that came from wondering if he'd fit.

He gripped her waist again. His lips settled over hers while he took his time hooking his thumbs beneath her waistband and inching her jeans down over her hips.

This was happening.

He wanted her.

She'd been poked and prodded by so many medical devices over the last year, but she hadn't felt a man's touch, a man's taste, a man's arousal in so long. *Too* long.

She needed this. Needed to remember the primal basics of coupling. Of being a woman being with a man. She needed to know she could still give and take pleasure.

No thinking.

She squeezed and stroked him harder. He bit down on her lip, another groan emanating from his throat. She pulled back with a squeak. "Did I hurt you?"

"No," he gasped, but was that pain? Or was that enjoyment?

Or...both?

Was Tony kinky? Did he think she'd want to be tied to the bed? Or blindfolded? Or licked in odd places? And what counted as *odd places* these days?

Had sex changed since the last time she'd had a real boyfriend?

He claimed her mouth again and lowered her to the bed, pausing only long enough to pull her pants off the rest of the way before settling beside her. His hard length bobbed against her hip while he cradled her head and feasted on her mouth.

Her teeth bumped his, and an odd slurping noise slipped out of her mouth.

A mortified giggle caught in her throat.

Tony lifted his head. "Is this okay?"

Oh, jeez.

There it was again. She wanted to laugh.

Had she always been this awkward?

She hadn't thought to pull the duvet cover off, and one of the buttons pushed into her left butt cheek. She jiggled and shifted, and when Tony started to pull away, she gripped the velvet skin around his shaft and gave his steel length another squeeze.

"Oh, god," he moaned into her mouth.

Oh, god. She was holding onto her jerk neighbor's dick.

Without warning, he yelped and jerked out of her grasp.

"Did I squeeze too hard? I didn't mean to, I just—"

His audible breath came quickly while he sprang off the bed and turned in a circle. "Something licked my ass."

Sadie panted happily on the floor, her big brown eyes going from Tony's erection to Pepper's boobs.

She clamped a hand to her mouth, but another giggle caught in her windpipe and nearly choked her.

He turned a flat, *so not amused* glare in her direction.

Sadie's pink tongue darted out under her dark snout, and she bunny-hopped the two feet necessary to lick Tony's calf. He stared down at the dog, his shaft losing some steam, and Pepper had to bury her face in a pillow to stifle a snort of laughter.

"Right," he said. "No sex. I get it."

She jerked upright. "No, I want to—"

"Your dog doesn't."

He sat on the edge of her forest green duvet cover, bent over toward the floor. When he stood, dimples sat on either side of his spine above the swell of his cheeks, disappearing when he yanked his pants up.

"I'll put her out," Pepper said. She started to move, but he was reaching for his shirt.

Once again, she'd been a disappointment.

She was an utter failure at being a woman.

"My place tomorrow," he said. "I'll cook you dinner."

That was the most stilted invitation she'd ever received. "I have a Knot Fest thing tomorrow night."

His lips thinned. "Thursday?"

So he was busy Wednesday. She wanted to ask with what, but it was probably none of her business.

And she didn't have much confidence he actually wanted to see her. Naked or otherwise.

She was a hell of a lot of trouble. "Sure. Thursday sounds great. Can I bring anything?"

"No, I've got it."

They sounded like two awkward horny people trying to plan a date somewhere that her dogs wouldn't care where Tony stuck his penis.

Not like two people who were friends.

Might as well just schedule a nooner.

The physical release was all sex was good for anyway, wasn't it?

And—oh, *no*.

They weren't breaking up on Thursday.

Her family would expect to see him at the wedding. Probably at the rehearsal dinner too.

Because she owed him one.

Something caught in her throat again, but her giggles were gone. She curled into the duvet and tried to cover herself, suddenly painfully aware of how naked she was. "Thanks for stopping by."

He didn't look at her. "Yeah. I'll lock the door on my way out."

Sadie wagged her tail.

And this time, when one more door shut in her life, Pepper finally let herself cry.

10

*T*ony didn't sleep Monday night.

He tried. He flung himself into bed, his face so hot he was surprised it didn't burn a hole in his pillow. He recited his family tree to take his mind off his utter failure with Pepper, but his mortification reigned supreme.

He'd had a woman throw herself at him, an attractive woman who had inspired his body to act like it could perform, but as soon as he got naked, performance anxiety had taken over.

Yeah, he'd been hard as a pipe while she'd been touching him, but it hadn't felt...right.

And as soon as she'd let go, the deflation had begun.

The dog licking his ass had been a relief, if he were being honest.

And he knew she'd seen him losing his steam.

He punched his mattress. Even if he'd been able to slide inside her, he wouldn't have lasted ten seconds.

What the fuck was wrong with him?

Lucky didn't join him on the bed. When he came down the creaky stairs Tuesday morning, she lifted her head and watched him from the lambskin cat bed he'd set up for her by the radiator in the kitchen, but she didn't move.

Big improvement from the skittish thing she'd been when he took her in three months ago. The freaked-out animal that had gone ballistic on Pepper's bunny-dog. Hell, even three weeks ago she wouldn't have let him catch her sleeping. But that little victory of knowing his cat finally trusted her home wasn't enough to break his foul mood.

He'd been getting better the last three months too. Adjusting to his new life. Finding the good. Getting back into working shape.

Until last night.

Bright sunshine and clear blue skies mocked him on his way to Pepperoni Tony's. The frigid air barely registered. Good day to check up on his Willow Glen shop.

He was in the mood for it.

Since September, he'd told everyone that getting the Bliss store up and running was taking all of his time, but he'd never been able to deny to himself that he had too many memories here in his original restaurant in Willow Glen.

He'd reconnected with Tabitha, his high school love, here. They'd had sex in the office. Planned their wedding in the corner booth.

She'd been between jobs when they were engaged, so he'd let her redecorate the dining room, moving away from his mom's vision of down-home Italian—like his store in Bliss—in favor of his wife's vision of modern sophistication, which had honestly been neither modern nor sophisticated, but it had made her happy and sales hadn't suffered, so it had made him happy.

She'd told him she was pregnant here.

And he couldn't stand being here anymore.

But he still owned the place, and he still had responsibilities to his employees, and though he trusted his manager implicitly, he wasn't fool enough not to check up on things.

He was filing receipts and double-checking inventory statements while the crew prepared for the lunch rush when his manager popped into the brick-walled office. "Your brother's here."

Tony pushed back from the built-in desk. He didn't talk much to his brothers on either side of the family, and they didn't bother with him either, which had always worked fine for them. Since he'd told his sisters he was dating someone, they'd left him alone too. Because his sisters were the ones who kept insisting they could find him someone better than Tabitha.

His sisters were the ones who were always meddling.

So why was one of his brothers here? And what did he want? "Which one?" he asked.

"Louie."

Tony hid a wince. "He order anything?"

"The Vanna special, extra jalapeños. Said to put it on his tab."

Louie's appetite was a thing of legend, as was his ability to run up tabs all over town that never seemed to get paid. Ten years ago, it had annoyed the shit out of Tony. *He* paid his debts. He didn't take advantage of family.

He wasn't his father.

A problem not shared by his older half-brother. Tony's loss in the father department had been Louie's gain.

He snagged a cup of water and sauntered out to the dining room.

"Tony, my boy." Louie grabbed him in a big hug that smelled like Lysol and ended with Louie clapping his upper arms. "Looking good. Nice to see the pizza business treating you right. You need these rugs cleaned, you know where to find me." He winked at a table of women in skirts and slid a card on their table while Tony pushed him toward a quieter booth in the back room. The red-wine paint over the wood paneling was showing wear, as were the industrial black rugs, and several lightbulbs were out back here.

He needed to pay better attention to this place.

Later.

He slid into the booth across from Louie, who grunted on his way in.

"Nancy didn't pack your lunch?" Tony asked.

"Just wanted to check on my little brother."

"Doing great."

"You tell Francie you'll be there for Bella's wedding yet?"

"Been busy."

"*Getting* busy, I hear." Louie nudged his knee. "It true you're going with one of them Aisle chicks? You looking for a way in for business? Better location? Primo spot in those crazy Knot Fest events? I got me an idea. You, me, pizza and dry cleaning. Yeah? Just need us a spot down there by that wedding cake monstrosity they got ruining the view."

That was about as likely as Tony sawing off all his own toes. "You know much about dry cleaning?"

"I know everything there is to know about every kind of cleaning. Got some money saved up. You toss in a little, I toss in a little, and we're in business."

"Appreciate the thought, but—"

"But you're too good for your family." Louie thrust a hand through his greasy hair. "Ain't told me you're coming to the bachelor party either."

The last bachelor party Tony had been to had been his own, and he wasn't excited at the prospect of hanging out with his niece's also too-young groom, watching a bunch of barely dressed women spin on poles. Bella already had enough odds stacked against her that her marriage would make it. The thought of her going through what he'd been through made him sick to his gut.

Which he couldn't say to his brother. "You got a plan for this dry-cleaning thing? Business model? Location?"

"Cleaning dresses on The Aisle, man. How much easier does it get?"

"Destination wedding town. Brides are gone before they even realize their dresses are dirty."

"Tux places need a cleaner."

"And they have a cleaner they've used for years." Tony spread his hands. "But maybe you know something I don't. Somebody going out of business down there?"

"Maybe I just want to do something nice with my baby brother."

"Joey's your baby brother."

"You're my baby brother from another mother. And Joey ain't into business. You know that."

Joey lived in Willow Glen as a banker by day, cover band rocker by night. He also made it to fewer family functions than Tony did, and was the one Tony was most likely to commiserate with over a beer at family events. "Joey turned you down." Probably didn't want to participate in the bachelor party any more than Tony did either.

"Like I said, he ain't into business. Likes working for someone else."

"You in trouble?"

"What? No. Where do you come up with this shit? You gonna tell me about this date with the chick on The Aisle, or do I have to ask Nancy when I get home?"

"You're gonna have to ask Nancy."

The server—an old friend who knew Louie too well—slid up to the table with the pizza. She added a bowl of strawberry gelato with rainbow sprinkles for Tony, because she was pretty damn awesome. "If you need anything else, get it yourself," she said cheerfully.

Louie dug into the pizza and pointed at her retreating back. "Shouldn't let her talk to customers like that, bro."

"Have to pay to be a customer."

"What? I'll pay."

Tony waved off the offer with a plastic spoon. "Any fun calls this week?"

Louie launched into a tale about a sewage problem at the courthouse while he plowed through the pizza.

And since Tony had heard it all before, he knew when to nod, when to grunt, and when to pause in eating his own ice cream.

But Louie still wouldn't take no for an answer on the bachelor party.

Maybe Pepper could help him out. Give him an excuse not to go.

If nothing else, out of pity. After his disastrous performance last night, pity was the best he could hope for.

NOTHING SAID *Sorry I can't keep it up* like flowers. Or so Tony hoped. He'd called it a day and left Pepperoni Tony's in his assistant manager's hands two hours ago, stopped for a bouquet of lilies, pink roses, and some other frippery he couldn't identify, and now he was doing his best not to pace around the island in the kitchen, checking his watch again and again while he waited for Pepper to arrive.

Homemade mac 'n' cheese was bubbling in the oven. A fresh salad with candied pecans and feta was chilling in the fridge. And there were two steaks ready for pan-searing as soon as she arrived.

Which should've been fifteen minutes ago.

Running a little late, she'd texted. *Be there ASAP.*

They hadn't talked since Monday night. He'd played basketball over lunch with Max and the crew the last two days—good people, he liked them—but she hadn't shown up again to watch.

Neither had her grandmother.

The other women watching the basketball game had all seemed to think it was normal—her sister's wedding being on Saturday and all. Which they assumed he knew, since he was going with her, wasn't he?

Hadn't been the original plan, but since they'd pointed it out... He probably was.

He hated weddings. The first one he remembered going to was his father's. And even though he'd known with all of his heart that marrying Tabitha was what he wanted to do, he hadn't enjoyed his own wedding either.

A wedding had slammed the door on his lingering hope of his parents getting back together, and no amount of logic that his mother was better off without his father could shake that taste.

Lucky slunk into the kitchen, hugging the baseboards beneath the cabinets, a green toy mouse dangling from her jaw. She deposited it in her water bowl and slunk back out.

Third toy mouse she'd drowned in the last two days.

135

He'd wonder if she had issues, but she'd picked him. Of course she did.

A knock sounded. He sprang toward the front of the house, then had to go back for the flowers. When he got back to the door and flung it open, she looked as frazzled as he felt.

"Sorry," she said as she breezed inside. "Tarra was in for her final fitting, and we were having a moment. Poor thing is *so* stressed. Weddings are supposed to be fun, but some days…"

She had another reusable shopping bag slung over her shoulder, this one black, emblazoned in pink with—he tilted his head and squinted—*Don't make me bless your heart twice.*

Huh. Didn't sound so positive.

"You like wine?" she added as she swept through his spacious living room and into the kitchen. "It's been a while since I had any, so I grabbed three bottles."

He was up for liquid courage. Might need it. Still—"Three?"

"I can't remember what I like."

"Should've brought a few more."

"Three's plenty. " She put the bag on the island with a *clink*.

He helped her out of her coat, then turned to the steak while she pulled the bottles out.

"Week get better?" he asked. Judging by the wine, probably not.

"I always forget how traumatic family weddings are when you're in the bridal business. I do this every day. You'd think it would get easier."

There was something off about her delivery, but when he glanced back at her, she was casually folding her bag. "Your cat just put a pencil in her water bowl."

"Probably trying to stab the mouse she put in there an hour ago. She's bloodthirsty."

Pepper laughed, and he decided his paranoia was acting up again. Two weeks ago, their biggest issue was that she hated his cat, and now, she was laughing at Lucky's antics. This was good. Definite progress.

He had two older sisters and a handful of half- and stepsisters, along with an ex-wife. He knew enough women to know hormonal mood swings happened. Probably all that was wrong on Monday.

She dug into his cabinets along the back wall. "Glasses in here?"

"Next to the sink."

"Bingo. Thanks." She flashed an overly bright smile. "Did I mention it smells amazing in here? Is that pizza?"

"Macaroni and cheese."

"Hope you made enough for six. I'm starving."

There was an edge to her voice again, something not quite right. He set the first filet in the cast-iron skillet on the stove. Usually, the sizzle of searing steak was enough to make him smile.

Not tonight, though.

Something was off. Again.

"Is it homemade?" she asked. "I haven't had real mac 'n' cheese in... Oh, wow. I can't even remember. Velveeta or cheddar?"

He dropped the second steak in the corner of the pan. "*Velveeta?*"

"You should see your face. Want me to tell you about my family's recipe? We call it mac and Spameeta."

"Explains so much. Corkscrew's in the drawer in the island."

While he cooked the steaks, she opened all three bottles. Two reds and a white. Should've brought some gelato home for dessert, but since she'd turned down her own cookies and refused to eat more than a single bite of the pasta the other night, he'd tried to stay on the healthier side—mac and cheese aside, which he'd made more for himself—and had a fruit bowl prepped instead.

By the time he put two full dinner plates on the island and settled on a stool across from her, she'd been sampling from two glasses. Her smiles danced with carefree mischief, and she'd peppered him with more frequent questions about his house, his cat, and his hobbies when he wasn't working the deeper she'd gotten into the wine.

"I still want to hear this polka band," she said while she cut into her steak.

"That was a test. I needed to know how serious you were."

"What? No polka band? My poor heart will never recover."

"I could try to learn. Can't be that hard to pick up the accordion."

"You better. I promised my family a performance at the wedding Saturday night." She popped the steak into her mouth, and her eyes slid closed while she moaned.

Four days ago, that moan would've prompted a party in his pants. But she'd said the w-word.

She blinked those pretty green eyes back open. He ducked his head over his own plate—one from his mother's mismatched Polish pottery set—but he could feel her watching.

"I lied. I had a date hook up with one of my cousins at my sister Ginger's wedding," she said. "I already told them I'm not bringing you, and they can just suck it up. Even Gran won't push a date on me when I'm dating someone else."

His grip tightened on his fork. "Your cousin actually stole your date at a wedding."

"And then..." She trailed off with a shrug.

"And then *married* him?" he finished for her. Sounded like something *his* family would do.

"We all get along just fine now."

"You went to their wedding."

"Without a date," she quipped.

He bent his fork.

"Seriously, it's not a big deal," she said. "If I'd married him instead, I'd be stuck in St. Louis working a corporate job with four little—" Her eyes tightened, and she took a big gulp from her glass of red. "I wouldn't have moved to Bliss, I wouldn't be half-owner in a successful boutique, and I wouldn't be enjoying this delicious meal," she finished.

She scooped a forkful of mac and cheese, lifted it to her lips with a smile, and did her moaning thing again. "Ohmigod, is this cheese or melted heaven?"

"When's the last time you took a date to a wedding?" Wedding dates were awkward. They were more awkward when relationships were new. Insane when relationships were staged. All the whispers. The bouquet and garter toss. The speculation.

She didn't answer.

He needed to quit thinking. Quit talking. Quit asking. "You've never taken another date to a wedding."

"I spent three years nursing *that* particular embarrassment, and when I was finally mature enough to be a grown-up about it, I'd had seven more successful pre-bride relationships. Didn't seem prudent to push my luck."

Nope, not touching her *pre-bride* comment. Couldn't do it. He was man enough to know his limits.

"*Pre-bride?*" he heard himself sputter, despite his best intentions.

"Oh, come on. It's funny." She switched to the white and gulped.

Not laughing at her own joke.

Had she found out another ex was getting married? Was that what her mood Monday was about?

"They were all idiots," he heard himself growl.

She blinked at him. "No, they weren't. They were smart, intelligent, normal men who simply weren't right for me."

"Like dinosaur man?"

"Gran thought giving me a different kind of date might work." She toasted him with her red. "And look. It got me you."

Him. The dysfunctional pizza man. "I'm going with you to the wedding."

She choked on the wine. "No—"

"No girlfriend of mine is spending a reception dancing with every Tom, Dick, and Harry her grandmother can find. And no girlfriend of mine is going to spend a night with her family wondering where her boyfriend is. And no girlfriend of mine—"

Her finger settled on his lips, igniting a spark that lit up his skin and burned down his neck, to his heart, through his gut and straight to his groin. "I'm not your girlfriend," she whispered.

She was the closest damn thing he had, and he was the closest damn thing to a boyfriend *she* had. That sharp ache slicing his chest suggested he'd be a smart man to remember she was right. "They don't know that."

Her lips pursed.

He could kiss her. Kiss her senseless until she forgot this wasn't real. Until instinct took over and they were clawing at each other's clothes, until he was holding her breasts again, exploring her creamy skin, tasting the wine on her tongue, thrusting into her, taking her—

Proving to her—what?

That she was valued? That she was deserving? That she was loved?

He couldn't love her. He couldn't offer her commitment. He couldn't be the kind of man she deserved, and frankly, he didn't want to be. No matter what being around her did to his sex drive.

But he couldn't stand the idea of her going to this wedding alone.

She held his gaze, her eyes wide and dark, roses blooming in her cheeks, her unsteady breathing the only sound in the room.

"I'm going with you," he repeated.

She blinked quickly. "Okay," she whispered.

"Eat your dinner."

A lopsided smile made a ghost of an appearance. She glanced down and took another swig, this time from the white wine. "Bossy."

"Damn right."

He knew a thing or two about stubborn. And he knew a thing or two about being alone.

He couldn't offer any woman much, but on this, he'd be what Pepper Blue needed.

PEPPER'S EYELIDS WERE HEAVY, her limbs like oversaturated pool noodles, and her head was swimming in a sea of wine-induced weirdness. Still darkness wrapped around her, a slow, steady drum beating beneath her ear.

She jolted upright with a gasp, her head moving more slowly than the rest of her. Green LED lights from a clock—2:10 a.m.—lit enough of the room for her to make out a cat perched at the edge of the bed, rumpled covers, and Tony.

Stubborn, reliable, sexy Tony.

One leg was kicked out from beneath the covers, one arm tossed over his head, the other flopped across beneath where she'd been lying a moment before. His breath was rhythmic and deep, issuing a subconscious invitation for her to curl back up and go back to sleep. He was still fully dressed, as was she.

How had she gotten here?

And when?

The last thing she remembered was dipping late winter strawberries in melted chocolate chips, laughing over—an elephant? Had he been telling her a story about an elephant? And a toothbrush?

She should've known better than to drink so much wine. And her belly was still full from dinner.

She'd forgotten how much she loved food.

She'd also forgotten how much she loved the scent of a sleeping man. The simple joy of snuggling in winter. The more carnal pleasures to be found in a bed.

Her hand hovered over his dark hair.

Touching him wasn't wrong. He'd touched her at dinner—held her hand while inspecting a paper cut, tucked her hair back behind her ear so it wouldn't dip in her macaroni, lined up behind her to reach around for a towel when she was rinsing dishes between dinner and dessert.

They'd been naked together just a few days ago.

The cat meowed and slunk up the bed to climb onto his chest. He stirred, and she held her breath. His shoulders rolled, his head turned against his pillow, and he tucked a hand over the cat, but he didn't open his eyes.

His breathing evened out, but the cat continued to stare at Pepper in the semidarkness.

He was coming with her to her sister's wedding. Out of pity, but he'd be touching her then too. Dancing with her. Playing the part of her boyfriend.

She shivered. Where had he been ten years ago? What if he'd never met his ex-wife? What if she'd come to Bliss sooner?

What if she'd been pregnant right now?

What if one day he wanted children?

She scrambled off the bed. His breathing stayed steady, so she fumbled in the dark, slipped out of the bedroom, found her shoes and coat, and headed home.

This wasn't real.

It wasn't real, and she had a family wedding to prepare for.

TONY COULDN'T DECIDE if the roiling in his gut was happiness or unadulterated terror.

He was going to a freaking *wedding*. Voluntarily. With a woman who had snuck out of his bed in the middle of the night.

Not that anything had happened in said bed—she'd been in the middle of telling him a story about a chicken chasing Cinna when she'd let her head droop to the island and trailed off mid-sentence, and it had seemed cruel to leave her there.

And when she'd curled into him when he picked her up to carry her to his bedroom, mumbling something incoherent that could've been *you're such a good guy*, he hadn't been strong enough to walk away after tucking her into his bed.

Never mind he could've carried her next door. Probably should've.

He'd reasoned she might've needed something—a drink, reassurance about where she was if she woke up, a bucket—but holding her was addictive.

And he still hadn't figured out how she'd gotten out of his house without him waking up.

His phone dinged. He fished it out of his pocket and smiled at the message. *Bridesmaid duties tonight. Wedding tomorrow at three, St.*

Valentine's. Reception at Twin Oaks. Remember, this was your idea.

"You know you're supposed to smile like that *all* the time when you're dating someone you like," Bella said from the office doorway.

He started at the intrusion, more so because it was his niece than because he was startled by someone being there. "If you're a helpless sap. And who says I'm not?"

"Louie says you're not. He says you're sick. Mom says you're troubled. And rumor says you're bringing a woman to my wedding, even though *you* haven't sent in your RSVP card yet. Is this a serious woman, or are you playing us again?"

His jaw worked up and down, but only for a minute.

"So you *are* playing us," she said triumphantly.

"The only playing going on here is you pretending to be Obi-Wan Bella."

"I heard you're going to a wedding with her this weekend. So you can go to a girlfriend's wedding, but you can't RSVP for mine?"

He pointed between them. "You, child. Me, grown-up. Knock it off."

She pointed between them. "Me, intelligent *grown* young woman. You, dumbass. I love you, Uncle Tony, but you haven't been *you* the last year. And that's okay. It takes time to get over these things."

He squeezed his eyes shut. "You had lunch yet? Pizza's on me." If he got food in her mouth, she couldn't talk.

Hell, what was he saying? She was part of his family. She'd talk with her mouth full.

"And you need to know we all still love you, and I don't care if you have to leave my wedding early because it's hard, and it would mean the world to me if you'd come even though I know it'll probably be super unpleasant and you're afraid I'm not old enough and you don't want anyone you love to ever hurt again," she finished softly.

When the fuck did his niece grow up and learn to say shit like this to him? "Thank you," he said gruffly.

She ruffled his hair. "And if you're serious about Pepper Blue, I approve. She's really nice."

He eyeballed her, because he wouldn't put it past his niece to have gone over to Bliss Bridal and gotten acquainted.

And dropped some of his secrets.

"What? I met her last year when my friend Sophie got married. We got our bridesmaid dresses there."

"You're all too young to get married."

"I'm old enough to know not to pass up the best man I've ever met. I hope you're not too old to realize the same."

And with that last bit of Bella wisdom, his too-smart-for-her-own-good niece kissed his cheek and pranced back out of his office.

Family.

He didn't always get them, but apparently they got him more than he thought.

---

11

*I*t had been almost two years since Pepper had sat in the cry room at St. Valentine's, waiting on Nat to arrive with an emergency repair kit to fix a tear in Saffron's veil. Funny—she'd hardly noticed Nat that day, nor had she ever dreamed she'd be living here as Nat's business partner not six months later.

Now, here she was with all of her sisters again—and Nat too, who had snuck in with the baby—getting ready for another wedding.

Tarra's gown was floor-length white silk with a flowery lace overlay. The lace extended down her arms, and instead of a tiara, she'd chosen a single lily to be tucked into the side of her updo. She was the tallest of the siblings, slender like Saffron, and today, she was glowing as she chatted with Mom and Gran about the cake and flowers.

Pepper blinked back a tear. Weddings rarely made her emotional—not after over a decade of working in the bridal industry—but she was still a hormonal wreck. She'd started her period Tuesday—of course *that* still worked—and she was still riding the roller coaster of grief.

She could've told her sisters. They were all here. They'd listen. They'd hug her, they'd comfort her, they'd promise to love her anyway.

But today was Tarra's day. A day for laughter and happiness, not a day for heartbreak. A fresh start. A beautiful beginning.

Her fertility issues weren't worth anyone ruining their makeup on Tarra's wedding day.

Maybe next week she'd tell Margie. Start with the analytical sister. Get the nonemotional response. Then Rosemary—the one most likely to cry. Sob, really. She'd help Pepper work it all out of her system at once. And then Rika—the most likely to tell the rest of the family, so Pepper didn't have to.

"Pepper, Tony's running late, but he says he's on his way." Poppy held up Pepper's phone from the pile amidst the flowers and purses on the side table.

Rika angled over and shoulder-bumped her. "Way to go, scoring the stripper."

"Worst stripper I've ever seen," Gran declared. "I've barely gotten a glimpse at the man's belly button."

"Does he know about what happened with Evan and Daisy?" Cori stage-whispered.

"He knows," Pepper confirmed. "The whole story." And no small part of her wished she hadn't told him. He wouldn't have insisted on coming if she hadn't told him.

But a larger part of her was glad he would be there. He did a good job at filling that role of *her person*. She hoped she was doing a respectable job of pretending to be his person too, but she honestly didn't know.

If he left with one of her sisters or cousins, though, she'd kill him.

An usher knocked and asked for Mom and Gran. Almost wedding time. And even though Pepper wasn't the one getting married, butterflies still swooped through her belly.

Tarra had almost given up on love too, which was heartbreaking for someone so upbeat and optimistic.

But then there had been Jack, and though his family was on the snooty side and he never quite got into the family fun, Tarra seemed happy. Was he her prince charming? Pepper didn't know. But he was still the best guy she'd ever dated, and at their age, that was enough.

"Okay, all of you, quick," Tarra said when the door shut behind Mom and Gran, who had taken Nat and the baby with them. She slid over to the table and gestured them all closer. "Sister secret. Huddle up."

They all crowded together, one big mass of Blue sisters jumbled together in matching burgundy satin. Pepper was comfortably squished between Margie and Cori, her bare arms grateful for the concentrated body heat.

"Ohmigod, are you pregnant?" Saffron hissed.

Tarra ducked, but not before her grin widened. Pepper's belly dropped, knocking on her own empty womb.

"She *is*!"

"Ohhh, this is the *best secret ever.*"

"Ten bucks says it's a girl!"

"When are you due?"

"Does Jack know? Tell me Jack knows. We love you, but you cannot tell us before you tell Jack."

She had to smile. She had to force this. No tears. No wobbles. Only sheer joy for her sister.

Tarra popped back up, cheeks flushed, her smile outshining the sun. "Yes, yes, Jack knows," she said. "He was…surprised, but it's a good thing. Really." Something squeaked, and the four sisters in front shrieked in laughter.

"I knew it!" Rika crowed.

"Told you that goat was effective," Ginger said.

"I don't ever want that thing," Cinna declared. "The cooties it'll have on it before it gets to me—gross. Just gross. And I clean the bathrooms at Suckers, so I know gross."

"Hush," Tarra said. "We only have a minute. And I know this is super unorthodox, but, well—Pepper, I want you to have the goat." She thrust the white, blow-up goat over Cinna and Rika, waving it at Pepper. "Rosemary and Ginger can't use it anymore, Saffron needs

147

some time before starting on number two, and I just have this really good feeling about you and Tony. Maybe if you have the goat, it can work in other ways too."

"If he leaves with another woman today, I'm kicking his ass," Cori said.

"Honey, you're gonna have to get in line," Rosemary answered.

"Right behind Gran," Rika added, and the whole room exploded in laughter.

Except for Pepper.

And the goat.

The goat, staring at her with its vacant black eyes. The goat that had seen things and been places Pepper didn't want to know about.

The goat that didn't have magic powers.

The goat that couldn't get her pregnant.

"No, no, don't cry." Tarra shoved through the throng of sisters to wrap Pepper in a hug. "He won't want to leave the wedding with anyone else. Don't listen to these bozos. Forget about everything in the past. You have today, and today is going to be a wonderful, beautiful day. The goat brings good things, and that's all I want for you. Just good things. They're out there, Pepper. You just have to believe."

She swallowed hard. "It's *your* wedding day, you goof," she managed. "Quit ducking the spotlight. I already have great things."

"All of you quit with the tears." Ginger whipped a handkerchief out of her cleavage. "You're going to make me start crying."

"Take the goat," Tarra whispered. "Just trust me."

No. Trusting meant hoping. Hoping had done a lot of good over the years, but when it came to husbands and babies, hope led only to disappointment. "Thank you," she forced out.

Another knock came at the door. "Tarra?" Mom poked her head in, a worried crease adding to the subtle wrinkles on her forehead. "Tarra, honey, we need you out here."

Tarra gave her one last squeeze. "I'll have Saffron deflate the goat and get it in your purse." She pulled back and gave Rika a look Rosemary had mastered about ten years ago. "Now, remember, ladies, *top secret*. Just until we announce it at the reception, okay?"

"Tarra, honey, this is really important," Mom said. "*Now*."

"Whoa, that can't be good," Poppy whispered.

Pepper dabbed at her mascara and gave a quick sniff before glancing out the door, where Basil, Jack, and Jack's mother were all in heated conversation with a man Pepper didn't recognize and who wasn't dressed for a wedding.

Tarra hesitated at the threshold, one hand slipping to her lower belly. "Mom?"

Mom looked in at all of them, grabbed Tarra, pulled her out of the room, and slammed the door shut.

Leaving Pepper and her sisters suddenly exchanging uneasy glances.

"This isn't how Saffron's wedding went," Cori whispered.

It wasn't how *any* wedding Pepper had ever been to went.

Which meant something was wrong.

And it was probably something bigger than the goat.

THIS WAS the last time Tony played hero for anyone. Weddings were bad enough, but weddings with a date were hell.

And he wasn't even there yet.

He'd cut himself shaving, one leg of his suit pants was longer than the other—a hem problem?—and he forgot to order flowers.

"Uncle Tony, you don't give your date flowers before a wedding." Bella bustled into his front door ten minutes before he was due to arrive at the church, a polka-dot zipper bag in hand, because he'd actually broken down and called his niece for help this morning after all her unwelcome wisdom yesterday. "She's a bridesmaid. She'll have her own flowers."

"Guys don't remember all this shit."

"Shush and hold still. Your hem came out." She squatted on the

149

floor in his bachelor-pad living room while Lucky spied on them from the kitchen, flat as she could get against the doorway, as though the painted trim would hide her from predators.

He stared at the weird patterns in the popcorn ceiling while Bella fiddled with his pant leg. He'd done this to himself. Pepper had given him every opportunity to bow out—the best excuse in the history of excuses, actually—and he'd ignored her. So here he was, wishing for a roll of antacids.

And wondering what color her dress would be.

How much skin it would show.

How long the dancing would go.

If she'd come back here with him after the wedding.

"Does she know how much you hate weddings?" Bella asked.

Once again, he was wondering when Bella got smart enough to know everything. He should've called one of his female servers. "Are you done yet?"

"Not just...yep. Done. Stand straight, feet together." She rose and looked down at his feet. "It'll do. If anyone notices, tell 'em to go to hell."

If his pant legs were still uneven, he couldn't tell.

Could've been a side effect of his blood pressure being too high for him to see straight.

Bella crossed her arms. She wasn't looking at his shoes anymore. Now she was giving him the mother of all *you are a stupid man* looks. "Uncle Tony."

He turned in a circle, patting his pockets. "Lost my keys."

"Give me ten minutes. I'll put a towel in the oven, and we can fake a kitchen fire."

"Not funny."

"Wedding dates are the worst dates *ever*, and you already hate weddings, and you're doing it for a woman you've known less than two weeks. You know better than this."

He damn well did. "Last time she took a date to a wedding, he left with her cousin."

"Nuh-uh."

The kitchen. He'd come in through the kitchen and tossed his keys on the counter last night. "You're right. Weddings suck. Except yours, which will be perfect." He gave her a quick hug. "Thanks for the help."

"Be careful," she called after him.

He was trying.

But fifteen minutes later, when he finally stumbled into the back of St. Valentine's church, hoping to sneak in unnoticed, it became clear *careful* wasn't exactly what he needed to worry about most.

Not for himself, anyway.

The vestibule was in chaos.

"I knew there was something wrong with that woman!" an older lady in an ice-blue dress and corsage was shrieking while she pointed at the bride, a tall, slender, semi-familiar woman who was surrounded by a sea of women in bridesmaid dresses.

"This is *not* her fault," another older lady replied, this one a little more stout with familiar green eyes. "And how *dare* you hire a private investigator to look into *my daughter*? If it were Cinna or Rika, fine, but *Tarra*? You have *no* idea what you've just done. *None*. You will *never* find another woman who could tolerate having *you* as a mother-in-law."

"Enough," a man in a tux was saying, but no one was listening.

Tony finally caught sight of Pepper marching in from the sanctuary. Her dark hair was swept up, a delicate strand of pearls around her graceful neck, her curves wrapped in dark cherry satin and her arms and shoulders bare. She wore the same fierce scowl she'd had the day he met her, the day Lucky and Sadie had their run-in.

"Everybody *shut up*," Pepper said.

Remarkably, it worked. For a moment.

"Seriously," Cinna said. "I mean, who *hasn't* gotten accidentally hitched in Vegas at least once? It's not her fault the annulment paperwork didn't get finished. Stupid fake lawyers."

Huh.

And he thought his family was dysfunctional. Somebody pass the popcorn.

"Did your *private detective* track down her supposed husband?" the mother of the bride demanded. "So we can at least get this mess cleared up *now?*"

"I'll have silence in this church or I'll call the police, and I frankly don't care that I'm related to half of you," a new voice behind Pepper intoned, and this time, the silence stayed. Father Basil, Tony was almost certain. Apparently being a priest—and the brother of the bride —came with some privileges. "Tarra—"

"I know," the bride whispered.

"Jack—" Father Basil started.

The man in the tux—nowhere near the bride, Tony noted—held up a hand and walked off. "Right. Wedding's off."

"Asshole," one of the sisters whispered.

"Shut up, she loved him," another whispered back.

"Don't use those damn curse words in Father McStuffy's church," Pepper's other brother said. He, Tony noted, was also standing back from the women, but he was watching the groom as though he were deciding if the asshole walking away from his bride needed to have his ass kicked.

Pepper turned, and she spotted him. Her lips curved up in a soft, half-lost, *sorry and thank you for coming* smile and he didn't know if he was supposed to smile back, given the circumstances, but his pulse stalled, his mouth went dry, and rational thought fled his brain.

He didn't know if he wanted to be here, or if he even *should* be here, but he knew one thing: he wasn't leaving.

12

*P*epper had known there was a danger she'd be the center of attention today, but she hadn't expected to feel an obligation to stay in the limelight.

With Tarra's wedding falling apart, though, she figured her sister would appreciate the distraction that Tony brought. Even though she wanted to be among the sisters comforting Tarra at the hotel. So at the reception—was it still called a reception when the wedding was canceled because the bride was apparently technically still married to her accidental Vegas fling?—she made the rounds, introducing Tony to anyone who seemed to be a little too jolly in their whispers about the drama.

Good *gravy*. Pregnant and dumped at the altar.

Poor Tarra.

And how terrible was she that she was glad there was so much focus on Tony, that no one had noticed she wasn't in the normal fight to hold the babies? She made sure to slip Noah and her nieces Hershey's Kisses all afternoon and into the evening though.

If all she'd ever be was Aunt Pepper, she'd be the best damn Aunt Pepper in the history of aunts. And she'd kick out Gran and Cinna and let Tarra move in with her, and they could raise Tarra's baby together since Jack was being a jackhole about Tarra still being married, as if he didn't know her at all, or possibly as if he were glad to have the excuse not to go through with the wedding.

What was *wrong* with men these days?

No matter. She had cake, she had a date, and she had a plan for her and Tarra and the baby. During a rare down moment in the awkward reception, she licked the last of the frosting off her fork and set it aside. She'd forgotten how much she loved cake.

And handsome men.

Tony had shaved, gotten a haircut, and shown up in a navy suit, white shirt, and black tie that had made her mouth go dry. Everyday Tony was sexy, but dolled-up Tony was lethal.

And that he was here for *her* was helping her forget she had the goat of fertility in her purse.

"Pepper, I haven't met your boyfriend yet." Aunt Lavender, mother of the boyfriend-stealer, stopped at their table. She was a foot taller than Gran, though her hairstyle was the same. Not quite as white, but just as tightly curled. And Pepper was eighty percent certain Aunt Lavender wasn't consciously checking Tony out for one of her other daughters, though she was definitely giving him the once-over. "Is it finally your turn?"

"Gran used to ask me that all the time," she replied, "until I asked her the same at a funeral."

Tony coughed into his fist.

She put a possessive hand on his thigh. His hot, hard thigh. "This is Tony. Tony, my aunt Lavender."

He held out a hand. "Pleasure, ma'am. I'm leaving with Pepper tonight."

Aunt Lavender's handshake visibly stumbled. "Oh, my goodness, you're a funny one, aren't you? Whoops, Blossom needs something. Nice meeting you, Tony."

She tripped away, and Pepper smiled at him. "That wasn't subtle at all."

"Subtle is for the birds. Your aunts all named after flowers?"

"Aunt Lavender's girls are all named after flowers. Or flower parts. My mom and aunts are named for shades of purple."

"So much is beginning to make sense."

She squeezed his thigh again, mostly because she could. "Shush."

Nat slipped to her side, TJ resting his adorable little head on a burp rag on her shoulder, Noah tagging along, probably looking for another Kiss. "Your family does *not* do normal weddings, do they?"

Pepper shook her head and forced a smile. "Never."

"Have you heard from anyone about Tarra?"

"Update fifteen minutes ago said she and Jack were finally talking, but Rosemary didn't think it looked good."

Gran plopped down at the table with them. "Where's the goat?"

Pepper's shoulders hitched up to her ears.

"Is this the goat of fertility?" Nat said. "Why haven't I seen this goat yet?"

Pepper eyed the sweet little bundle on her shoulder. "You didn't need it."

"Goat of fertility?" Tony repeated. A muscle ticked in his jaw, his face blanched, and his distinct lack of a smile made her wonder if she were looking in a mirror, or if he were truly opposed to a goat of fertility.

"It's a blow-up goat," Nat supplied. "Or so I hear. I haven't actually seen it, but I heard Tarra got it at—oh. *Oh* no. Tell me they didn't—"

"Who's got the goat?" Gran demanded again. "I need to make sure it doesn't do something we're all going to regret."

"I took it away from her," Margie said. She, too, plopped down at the table. God bless her.

"No, you didn't," Rika said, also invading their party. "She gave it to Pepper after—*mmph*."

While Margie tried to suffocate the more disposable of the twins, dozens and dozens of eyeballs swiveled her way.

Or possibly only three or four sets of eyeballs, but it felt like a dozen.

"What does Pepper need with the goat?" Gran asked. "Little early for that, even for my tastes."

Tony shifted away.

"The goat's protecting her from having anyone steal her date tonight," Rika lied around Margie's mouth. "Its powers have grown."

Didn't have to be a mind reader to know what Tony was thinking. *They're batshit crazy.*

"What if you break up?" Gran asked. "There are six more girls after you. What if they break up and curse the goat? Where will the family's fertility come from then?"

"The same place fertility *actually* comes from," Margie said. "This is why you get kicked out of your homes."

Pepper stilled. "Margie—"

Margie swung around. "I'm not a robot, and neither are you, and this whole ridiculous goat baloney has gone far enough. We don't need babies and husbands to complete us, and the patriarchal bullshit surrounding the institution of marriage makes me ill."

Her breath caught. Did Margie have issues too? Did she really not want children because she didn't want children, or did she know she couldn't have them either?

"Hey, music man," Margie yelled. "Light it up. We need to celebrate our sister's freedom."

The first strains of Marvin Gaye's "Let's Get It On" filled the air. A hand touched her back. Pepper jerked in her chair and found Tony behind her, wary and unamused.

He extended his hand, palm up. "Care for a dance?"

It was just a hand, but it looked like so much more. Touching him, letting him close, after he'd just heard she was packing a goat of fertility, was too much. Too much pressure. Too many expectations. Too many assumptions.

She didn't want to be here anymore.

She didn't want Tarra's heart to be broken. She didn't want to be surrounded by family. She didn't want her family to know she'd failed. More, she couldn't turn Tony down.

He'd come to this canceled wedding, stayed, met her entire family, aunts, cousins, and he was staying to ask her to dance.

To help her escape. To be her rock. To be the first man not to leave her and go on to marry the next woman he dated after her.

If she took his hand, she wasn't sure she could hold in the tears anymore.

She'd never be able to pretend she was fine again.

———

BOTH OF TONY'S parents had remarried within two years of the divorce—Dad to the woman he'd been seeing on the side for eight of his ten-year marriage to Mom and the mother of his other children, Mom to a nice man from church who didn't drink, didn't smoke, didn't gamble, and didn't cheat. His first wife had died in a car accident, and he'd been raising his son and daughter by himself.

He'd been faithful, he'd treated Tony and his older sisters the same as his own children, and Mom had seemed content enough to pop out one more kid. Until he passed away five years ago, he'd reached out to check on Tony every few weeks, see if he needed anything or if he was free to get together for coffee and solve all the world's problems.

When Tony had gotten married, he'd wanted to follow his stepfather's example of the kind of husband he wanted to be. Dependable. Trustworthy. Faithful.

He was determined to do better than the rest of his family had. To marry one woman, have children with her and her alone, and love her until the day he died.

He'd had it, too.

A wife he adored.

A dog they walked together every night.

A baby on the way.

Until that awful moment in the maternity ward when all of his hopes and dreams and beliefs had shattered, spraying shards of glass over his entire life.

Now here he was, pretending to date another woman, a woman with an insane family with horrible traditions, who needed a friend. A woman who had too much pride to admit she needed a friend. He'd never seen a smile so determined to be happy when it obviously wasn't, and he couldn't help wondering if it was something more than the stress of her sister's canceled wedding.

He should've asked her if she wanted some cake at his place instead of having seconds of cake here. Gotten both of them out of here ten minutes ago.

Hell, he could've snuck away two minutes ago, as soon as Natalie had said *goat of fertility.*

A week ago, he would've.

But he couldn't abandon Pepper.

No matter how much his chest hurt and his pride stung and his stomach burned.

She blinked quickly, then settled her chilled fingers in his.

He wrapped his other arm around her waist and pulled her to him on the dance floor before she could retreat. She dropped her forehead to his shoulder, and he tucked their hands over his heart while they shifted into an easy sway to the music. Who put bridesmaids in sleeveless dresses in February? She was freezing.

Gorgeous—that dress had been giving him ideas all evening—but still so cold.

Her breath heaved out irregularly, and he pulled her tighter.

She had secrets. He'd seen too many emotions he couldn't explain flash across her face today. Whatever those secrets were, she was keeping them from her family too.

Was she seeing someone—a professional—about her dating history? Had a shrink recommended she not date for a while, and she was too proud to tell her grandmother? Or was Pepper having problems with *her* equipment working?

Was that even an issue for women?

Did she want to get married? Have kids? Did she *want* that goat?

He could picture her with a family as easily as he used to picture a family for himself, and his heart squeezed tight. She had three sisters and a brother with families of their own, and she worked in this crazy love-obsessed town. Her grandmother probably wasn't the only one who had introduced her to men in the last few months.

"You okay?" he murmured.

"You're very warm," she replied quietly.

Four of her sisters were watching them as they all moved around the dance floor. Margie—the one with the glasses, the smart one, Pepper's defender, stood to the side of the dance floor, not even trying to be subtle about sending him a *hurt her and die* message.

He swallowed a smile. It wasn't funny—Pepper's sisters threatening him, her grandmother being utterly insane—but if he didn't laugh at the insanity of all of this, he'd toss her over his shoulder and march them both the hell out of here.

And then her whole family would wonder if that stupid goat of fertility was working.

He snorted softly to himself.

No fucking way he should've been within spitting distance of a goat of fertility.

Who believed in that bullshit anyway? Pepper was bright. He'd thought her family would be the same. CJ seemed decent. Cinna was mildly annoying, but she was quick-witted and funny. And Gran—yeah, Gran was a special case.

A privilege that came with age.

She shifted against him, and he could feel the tension leave her body. She slipped her free arm around his waist. "Thank you for being here today. I had no idea it would go down like this."

Was she kidding? If he hadn't been here, if he'd let her go Monday like she suggested instead of coming up with a lame-ass excuse to keep her around longer, this whole goat mess that had upset her even more than the canceled wedding wouldn't have happened.

Or maybe they would've found something different. If they had a blow-up goat of fertility, they probably had something equally insane like a blow-up camel of commitment. Or one of her sisters would've found her a last-minute date, or they'd do a rain dance for men.

She lifted her head, eyes tired, her face mere inches from his. "I don't know what you're thinking, but that's not a pretty smile."

No, it wasn't.

But she didn't need to know that.

She needed to know he was here for her.

Today.

That he was here for her today. As promised.

He leaned into her and touched his lips to hers. Nothing chaste about his thoughts or where he wanted to put his hands—not because he wanted to get laid, not because he was sexually deprived and would've taken any woman, but because Pepper was that special combination of hot-as-hell, too-good-for-him, and needed-him-anyway.

There wasn't a man on earth good enough for her.

Her arms tightened around his ribs, her fingers dancing across his back while she tilted her mouth to his and turned a soft kiss into a third-date, come-back-to-my-place suggestion. Her lips were hot satin, her mouth heaven, her touch irresistible.

He wanted to go back to her place. Kiss her without wolf whistles and cheers in the background. Unwrap her, savor her, slide into her.

Not screw it up like he had on Monday. Lose himself. Push her to lose herself. Let instinct take over. Forget the world.

Her lips left his, but the taste of her, the imprint of her lingered.

"Thank you," she whispered before pulling back with a shy drop of her gaze.

No, thank you.

"How long do we have to stay?" he murmured into her hair.

"Not much longer. I think most of the guests left are just family now, and we don't need to entertain them."

He squeezed his eyes and his jaw shut.

This was supposed to be pretend. A trade-off with his too-perfect neighbor to get his pizza place up and running with a solid local customer base.

But he had an overwhelming need to take care of her for real.

———

WHEN PEPPER LEFT Tarra's non-wedding, her date was still at her side.

Holding her hand, in fact, after insisting her matching wrap for her dress was ridiculous and that she needed to use his coat instead.

It smelled like him—spicy and warm and male—and she was rapidly falling under a spell of almost believing this was real.

At her car, she tried to give him the coat back.

"Keep it."

Stubborn man. "I have a coat of my own at home."

"Which is right next door to my house, so I can get this easily enough tomorrow."

The stars glittered overhead, diamonds in the abyss, but the real gem was right in front of her. "Come back to my place?" she said quietly.

He was going to decline. She could see it in the way he glanced to the side, the uncertain hand he ran through his neatly trimmed hair.

"Please?" she added.

His dark gaze slid back to her, deep and wary and searching. He'd been hurt. By his ex-wife, by his family, by *someone*. Life had disappointed him. Robbed him of something irreplaceable.

She didn't know what, but she *felt* it. Felt it in the tension of the invisible string pulling her closer to him, in the imaginary monster claws trying to keep them apart.

He dipped his head in a single nod. "Sure."

Wings sprouted in her heart. Before she could think better of it, she pushed up on her tiptoes to brush a kiss to his cheek. "Thank you."

His arms came around her, and once more, she found herself in the safe cocoon of his embrace. Warm. Safe. Loved.

Loved? No. Not *love*-loved. Affectioned? Friended? Just—he was there.

For her.

Not because he owed her anything. Not because he was related to her.

Simply because he wanted to be.

Such a little thing.

But tonight, it was everything.

———

THE LAST TIME Tony had walked a dog, he hadn't known his marriage was already over. Tabitha had been almost nine months along. He'd thought she'd been miserable and cranky because she'd been as big as a whale, and the late November weather had been crazy warm, which made it impossible for her to get comfortable. She was too warm or too cold, wearing too much clothing or too little.

Turned out her problem was him. Or rather, who he wasn't.

Taking a stroll with Pepper and Sadie and George wasn't the same, and he pushed away the ugly memories in favor of enjoying what he could of subfreezing temperatures and a dog who thought his leg made a good girlfriend.

"Knock it off, George," Pepper said sternly after the third time they had to stop so Tony could disentangle the horny pup. They'd also stopped six times for text message updates about the post-non-wedding drama. Her family was tight. "This isn't how we earn treats."

Sadie plopped back on her haunches and cocked her head, her cute little black ears tilting up.

Pepper pulled a doggie snack from her pocket and held it out to her own dog. "Good girl," she murmured.

George lunged on his leash, going up on his back legs and straining against his collar.

"Sit," Pepper said.

George barked.

She shrugged. "Your loss. C'mon. Two more blocks, and we're home."

George barked again, then flopped to the ground, back legs splayed.

"Obviously your grandmother's dog," Tony mused.

She laughed, then treated George to a little snack too. "Now behave yourself."

George lifted his head and pranced down the sidewalk. They all continued along their way, Sadie on Pepper's other side, giving the poodle a wide berth.

Pepper slipped her hand into Tony's. "Was it horrible?" she asked quietly.

"Having my leg humped by your grandmother's dog?"

"The reception."

"Been to worse."

"Worse receptions? Or worse events in general?"

He squeezed her hand. "Both."

"I locked myself in the bathroom at my aunt Wisty's wedding when I was four. The manager had to physically remove the doorknob to get me out. Gran introduced the family to the Chicken Dance that year, and she accidentally gave the family priest a bloody nose with her elbow—he was sitting too close to the dance floor, and she got a little exuberant. The mother of the groom had too much to drink and flashed the entire dance floor. Rosemary was getting over the chicken pox, and nobody knew Ginger was coming down with them, so five days later, *all* of us were down with it. So pretty much every family wedding is measured against that one, and none have ever been as bad —or as memorable. Until possibly tonight."

"This was pre-goat?" he asked.

She sighed. "Pre-goat."

"You want a family?"

Her fingers twitched. "I want...not to be alone when I'm old." She blew out a slow breath, her gaze shifting upward, but not at him. "You?"

"Used to." There would always be a part of him that still did. He'd learned to minimize the desire, to rationalize away the need, but watching Pepper whisper with her nieces and dance with her nephew hadn't helped. "Not part of the life plan anymore."

"Life has its own plans sometimes."

Wasn't that the truth.

They turned onto her street, George still prancing proudly, Sadie doing her funny bunny-hop walk. Pepper didn't say any more the rest of the way to her house, but she paused on her porch.

"Mom and Dad are driving Gran to look at a retirement home over in Willow Glen early tomorrow," she said. "They're keeping her at the hotel tonight."

Interest stirred below his belt. "Yeah?"

George made a circle around him, wrapping his leash around Tony's calves.

"Cinna and the twins are hitting the karaoke bar," she added. "Since Tarra's camped out in the honeymoon suite with Margie playing guard dog."

He swallowed. "You gonna be okay here alone?"

Those beautiful emerald eyes had turned into shimmery pools of uncertainty and hope. "Maybe not just yet," she whispered.

Sadie scratched at the door. George kept circling.

And Tony couldn't believe he was actually giving this any thought. "Lucky likes having the house to herself."

A smile blossomed on her pretty lips. "So she wouldn't miss you if you stayed for a while?"

He shook his head.

Pepper settled her hands at his waist. "Would you like to come in?"

"If you insist."

"I definitely insist."

Her smile grew wider. "Good. Because I have something to show you."

Yep.

He was all in.

———

INSIDE, Tony didn't ask why Pepper wanted to take him downstairs.

He was too busy trying to tamp down his expectations at being invited in, and then having to wait while she slipped upstairs to change. But when he got downstairs, his hesitations changed to sheer happiness. "You have a Skee-Ball table."

She smiled. Her basement smelled freshly painted, and the walls looked relatively new. A brown suede couch sat against one wall, a TV on a second, and the Skee-Ball table was against the wall beside the stairs. The chill of the linoleum floor seeped through his socks, but given the potential for water problems in this part of town, he wouldn't have wanted to see carpet down here.

"And now you now know the real reason my sisters always want to stay with me when they come to town."

He angled closer to the machine. "That's vintage."

"I have a thing about spotting good deals. It came from a ShowBiz Pizza that shut down when I was in high school. Haven't had much time to play it in—well, months."

"It's beautiful."

"And I can still set it up to make you have to pay a quarter to play." Light had come back into her eyes, and there was nothing forced about her smile.

She was simply a woman happy to be showing him her toys.

Made him feel like a sixteen-year-old kid again. Hiding in the basement. Wanting to kiss a girl. Afraid he'd get it wrong.

She stepped beside him, still smiling. Scents of cookies and that unique floral bouquet she carried with her tickled his nose. He wrapped an arm around her, and she cuddled in close.

The feel of her breasts pressed against him caused more stirring below the belt.

Slow, he reminded himself. Easy. They had time.

He rubbed at the goose bumps trailing down her arms. Crazy woman should've put on a sweatshirt.

"I couldn't date because I was doing a...project," she whispered. "I failed."

He frowned. Maybe she hadn't been seeing a therapist. People didn't usually say therapy *failed*, did they? She didn't strike him as the type to try magic or old wives' tales to change her love life, but then, normal people did weird things sometimes.

Although, if she'd been trying to change her love life with some kind of witch doctor, she probably wouldn't be sitting on the couch with him right now.

Maybe she'd been working on something professionally.

Or maybe she'd been waiting for a man to leave his girlfriend or wife, and she really had just needed him as a decoy.

His fingers curled.

She wouldn't. Not Pepper.

But he'd thought the same thing about Tabitha, hadn't he?

He forced his jaw to unclench and made his shoulders relax. "Anything I can do to help?"

"Just...stay," she whispered. "My family doesn't know. The wedding—they've been busy. And I—I don't fail. My love life might be awkward, but it's not a *failure*. Not like...not like this is."

He pulled her all the way against him. "So try again."

She shivered. "I *can't*. It doesn't work that way. I know it's supposed to make us stronger, but I don't feel strong. I feel broken."

She was so warm, so comfortable. And she needed him. She couldn't be bad for him.

Could she?

The last woman he'd blindly trusted with his life had put his heart through the meat grinder. But Pepper wasn't Tabitha. She was *more*.

The last week or so, he'd wondered if he could be more again. If he could still remember how.

Maybe, just for tonight, he could try.

IF PEPPER DIDN'T PULL AWAY from Tony, she was going to kiss him again.

Not a friendly peck on the cheek either.

And if she kissed him again, where she wanted to kiss him, she'd probably crawl into his lap and straddle him, and then who knew what creature would try to lick him, or which of her family members would decide to crash in and interrupt, or what body part of her own would malfunction.

Today had been fairly awful. And she didn't want to make it worse with another awkward attempt at reacquainting herself with sex. But a kiss—a kiss could only make today better, couldn't it?

Her heart bobbed.

Just being near him, with him holding her tight and warm and safe, was pretty fantastic. Why risk it?

She was about to pull away when his arms tightened around her. "Pepper?"

"Hm?"

"You're the first friend I've trusted in a very long time. Those other women—they were decoys. Not *friends*."

Her heart swelled and glowed even as a skitter of nerves shot through her body.

Finding out she couldn't have babies had been devastating. But he'd been hurt too. Badly. When was the last time *he* had had meaningful human contact?

Did he crave it as much as she did?

"Close your eyes," she whispered.

He held her gaze with big, dark orbs of uncertainty. As if he were asking her to be gentle. Not to betray him. To understand what this was costing him after everything else he'd already done for her today.

His dark lashes slowly lowered. She touched hesitant fingers to the sandpaper darkening his jaw, then traced a small scar on his cheekbone. His lips were firm, not too thin, not too full, and when her fingers brushed over his mouth, his Adam's apple bobbed.

Her breath quickened as his chest rose and fell rapidly. Was his heart thundering as fast as hers? As hard as hers?

When had a simple kiss become such a monumental task?

Just one kiss.

No pressure. No expectations. No need for them to go any further.

She just wanted to know that she could have one perfect kiss. She wanted *him* to have one perfect kiss.

She was going to screw this up.

His lashes fluttered open, and his eyes connected with hers again.

Could he see her overthinking this? Or did he not want her to kiss him?

"I—" she started.

His solid, capable hand hooked around her neck. His thumb touched that sensitive spot behind her ear, and with the same fluid grace that he'd cooked her dinner the other night, he slanted his mouth over hers.

But unlike that first kiss, this kiss wasn't desperate.

It was slow. Leisurely, even. A journey more important than the destination.

His lips were firm but gentle, sucking, teasing, exploring, gentle murmurs coming from him as they sank into the kiss. She gripped his forearm and let herself go. Just be. She parted her lips, letting him in more while her body hummed to life. Her toes wiggled and stretched. She arched her back, pushing her pelvis against his, never breaking contact with him, tasting his lips, learning the texture of his skin, falling into his kiss as easily as if she were falling into a dream.

His fingers threaded into her hair, massaging her scalp, holding her exactly where she wanted to be.

With him.

Not the Tony who made smart-ass comments to her sisters. Not the Tony who had a revolving string of women coming to his door and a crazy cat that scared her dog. But this Tony, the man who had gone to a wedding with her, the man who made her laugh, the man who cooked her dinner, the man who'd been hurt, but still wanted to be here.

Kissing her.

She licked his bottom lip. He groaned into her mouth and pressed closer to her. Not pushing her back, but holding her against him, deepening the kiss, exploring her mouth as though they had all the time in the world.

And they did, didn't they?

The world was dark and frozen outside, and they were safe and warm and together here.

She drew her hands over his shoulders and down his back, the stiff fabric of his shirt too much of a barrier between her palms and his hot skin.

"More?" he whispered against her lips.

"More." She tugged on him and pulled him across the room to the couch, kissing softly as they went. He followed her down, covering her with his solid body. Through his pants and her leggings, she felt his hard length settle between her thighs.

He lowered his mouth to hers again, caressing her cheek, holding her tight, safe, protected.

Whole.

His kisses, his touch, his body were all a salve to her wounds. More than the joy of knowing she could be physically intimate—that her body could still crave physical intimacy—was the joy of blossoming arousal. Being seduced with a kiss.

Being wanted.

She tilted her hips into him, and his breathing hitched even as he strained back against her. "Pepper—"

"Sshh. More kissing."

"More everything."

Everything.

Yes, tonight, she wanted everything.

He was bolder when he recaptured her lips. More frantic. Deeper. Rougher.

She tugged his shirt loose and stroked her hands up his back, the heat from his skin making her fingers tingle almost as much as the ridges of his muscles made her core ache.

His tongue slid against hers, and a rough, needy sound came from deep within in him. She matched him stroke for stroke. Her hips thrust against him, and she couldn't have stopped herself if she'd wanted to.

Going slow was no longer an option. He pulled back and yanked his button-down off. She twisted on the couch and tugged at her own shirt, but ended up with her arms all cockamamie and caught in the fabric.

She groaned. "Not again."

Sure, capable hands slid up her sides. "We've got this," he said, and the amusement in his voice settled that momentary panic. "But wait. What's this I see?"

She was still tangled in her sleeves when hot air penetrated her bra a moment before his mouth came down on the fabric over her nipple. A needy whimper swelled in her throat, and she thrust her breast higher for him.

"Delicious," he murmured, and then he moved to her other nipple.

She dropped her arms over her head and panted. "You—can do—that more," she panted. His teeth, the wet silk, his hot breath were all building waves in her core, pulling dormant, primal needs out of hibernation.

"Tell me when to stop," he murmured.

"Never."

He cupped her breasts through the bra and licked the sensitive skin between them.

Then he slowly licked a path lower, all the while turning her into a whimpering, needy, thrashing mess. Her arms were going numb, still tied up in her shirt, and she didn't care, because the rest of her body was on fire. Alive. Perfect.

"I'm going to take your pants off," he said.

"Thank God."

She lifted her hips while he hooked his thumbs beneath her waistband and pulled. Cool air rushed around her hips and thighs. He'd taken her panties too.

She closed her eyes and breathed through the temporary panic at being laid bare. This hadn't gone so well last time.

"Beautiful," he murmured. And then his tongue touched her center, and she forgot she was naked. She forgot where she was. She almost forgot *who* she was.

All she knew was that her nerve endings were on fire all across her body, and he had the most talented mouth she'd ever met. He found that perfect spot. She gasped and moaned his name. Her arms finally came free, and she gripped his hair, holding him in place, there, *right there*, as the pressure mounted deep inside her, pulsing, aching, building. He slipped a finger inside her, and the dam broke, sending pleasure crashing through her veins and shattering her into a million satisfied pieces.

She couldn't catch her breath, and she honestly didn't care. Tony kissed his way up her belly, pausing on her still-covered breasts. His pants brushed her inner thighs, and she whimpered again. "Your pants have to go."

His smile was half ego, half adorable. "Not satisfied yet?"

"*You're* not satisfied yet."

"Wouldn't say that."

But he reached for his button, and when he pushed his pants down, his stiff shaft suggested otherwise. Desire flared deep in her center again, colliding with her already overheated, satisfied cells. She reached for him with lazy hands and squeezed the silky skin over his hard length. He hissed out a breath while his eyes squeezed shut.

"Too much?" she whispered.

"Too long."

"Too—*oh*."

He pulled a condom from his wallet—no sense in telling him it

171

wasn't necessary—and his grin was decidedly less cocky this time. "Go easy on me."

She crooked a finger at him. "Dream on, pizza man."

He settled over her again, brushing her entrance, but not taking any liberties while he pressed a kiss to her collarbone. "You were sexy all tied up," he whispered.

She raked her fingers down his chest and angled her hips toward him. "And you weren't very gentlemanly to not help me."

Still, he didn't take the hint and penetrate her. "I thought I was very gentlemanly."

"Well, maybe a little."

His smile made her heart swell again. He slowly pushed into her, and her breath caught at the feel of him filling her. She arched into him, wanting more, deeper, craving all of him, but he stilled.

"No laughing if I make a fool of myself here," he said.

This man. Couldn't he feel how badly she wanted him? Not just for her, but for him too? "Tony, take me. *Now*."

He lifted a brow.

"Please," she added on a laugh.

He slid in deeper, all the way, until he hit her other magic spot, and slowly pulled nearly all the way out, leaving her empty and needy and desperate. "More," she said.

He obliged, his gaze fixed on her face, steady concentration drawing his brows together while he pushed in.

"You feel so good," she whispered.

He didn't feel *good*. He felt *perfect*. He fit as though he was meant to be hers. As if she'd been made to hold him. As if they'd been born for each other.

As if he could've been her *one*.

Except she couldn't give him everything a woman should give a man.

Her breath caught, and that unwelcome intruder clawed up her ribs to clog her throat again.

No. No, not now. Not with Tony. Not after everything he'd done for her.

She shut her eyes and gripped his ass. "*More*," she said.

He thrust faster, but it wasn't enough to reach past the grief, to recapture the desire, to find that place where she could still enjoy being a woman.

"Pepper," he ground out.

She squeezed. She squeezed her eyes tighter, she squeezed his ass harder, she squeezed her inner walls around him. "Yes, Tony, *yes*."

He shuddered and called her name again, then groaned from deep, deep within before collapsing on her.

She wrapped her arms around him and held on.

Because he was all she had.

13

"*U*h, boss man, you gotta come see this."

He glanced up from the chicken avocado pizza he was taste-testing Sunday morning to find his busboy looking like he was about to swallow his tongue. The kid wordlessly pointed toward the dining room, so Tony wiped his hands and headed to check it out.

They weren't open for another fifteen minutes, but there were three people standing expectantly outside his front door.

Two very important people and one big guy who looked like he knew how to take care of things.

He flipped the locks and ushered them in. "Lindsey, looking lovely as always."

His former divorce lawyer gave him a quick hug. "And you're looking quite happy yourself."

Damn right he was. All his equipment was back in full working order, and he'd left Pepper satisfied from her roots to her toenails. Or so she'd mumbled when he'd kissed her goodbye in her bed just after midnight.

"Will, have you and Tony met?" She pulled her belly out of the way so he could shake hands with her husband, the legendary Billy Brenton. *Will*, apparently, when he wasn't on stage.

"Not yet, lawyer lady, but I got high hopes," Billy replied. His grasp was warm and friendly. "You get that avocado yet? I can't even spell the stuff."

Lindsey laughed. "Hush. You can too. And if he doesn't have avocado, I'm leaving."

"Bunch of hipster brides cleaned us out yesterday," Tony said while he grabbed two menus. "Clean out of kale and leeks too."

"Now you're mocking me."

He grinned. Before she'd been his divorce lawyer, she'd been a good customer. He gestured to the wide-open dining room. "Take your pick. I've got avocado. Just for you and the eighty other pregnant women in town. What kind of horrible concoction can I whip up for you today?"

"She really just wants a dessert pizza," Billy said. "You got that cinnamon kind?"

"Avocado, artichoke, and anchovies," Lindsey corrected.

Even Billy and their bodyguard looked repulsed. "You ain't feedin' my baby that."

"While they work that out, get you anything?" Tony asked the bodyguard.

"Bruno wants three live chickens and a lemon chiffon cupcake," Billy said.

"Sure, *he* can eat live chickens," Lindsey grumbled.

Bruno's lips hitched up a millimeter. "Chicken and artichoke," he said. "And Billy's taking me to Kimmie Cakes later."

"Need me to delay opening here?" Tony asked. If the famous man wanted privacy, he could provide.

"Ain't no fun in that," Billy said with a wink.

"You're going to have to quit saying *ain't* when the baby's born," Lindsey teased.

"Ain't no fun in that neither," Billy drawled.

Tony knew a good bit about *no fun*, but today was starting with all the fun.

And for the first time since he'd opened this place in September, the rest of the day saw packed tables, good tips for his crew, and happy local customers.

He was nearly dead on his feet by eight, but not so dead he couldn't send a quick note of thanks to Lindsey. Billy had taken a selfie outside Pepperoni Tony's on their way home.

Tony wasn't stupid.

He knew where his customers were coming from.

Our pleasure, she'd replied. *Now do your part.*

Wasn't sure what that meant, but he intended to keep serving good pizza and fitting into this crazy town.

And having a damn good time with his neighbor for a while too.

GRIEF REARED up and sent Pepper back into anger mid-afternoon Tuesday. She'd been cheerfully helping a sweet bride about her age when the woman touched her belly in that intimate way newly pregnant women did, and she'd nearly doubled over in pain and come back up wanting to hit something.

She'd left one of her managers in charge and called it a day early. Her staff had given her the sympathetic look of women, assuming she was still drained from Tarra's wedding drama.

As if she was the one hurting there.

Jack was damn lucky he'd left the state.

And talking to Tarra should've been a good reminder that her sister had bigger issues to worry about, but she couldn't talk to her sister without contemplating that little baby growing in her belly, which sent her down a bad path all over again.

When she walked into the house, George was doing the potty dance. Gran and Cinna were bent over the kitchen table, and based on their piles of pennies at the side of the game board, they were gambling over Ticket To Ride.

Gran's tour of the new seniors' home—delayed until yesterday thanks to the wedding drama—hadn't gone well. But she'd come back with caramel corn from a specialty shop in Willow Glen, cupcakes from Kimmie Cakes, and a tin of gourmet hot chocolate from the chocolateria on The Aisle to go along with her massive hug, and her inquisition over the goat at the wedding was forgiven.

Wasn't her fault she didn't know what Pepper had been trying.

Didn't make it easy to keep her temper with Gran and Cinna though. "Did either of you walk the dogs today?"

"Pulled a long shift this afternoon after closing last night," Cinna said. "So, no."

"Too cold for my princess bones," Gran added. "Storm's coming too. I can feel it in my left knee. By the way, I called Tony. He's meeting you and me and Elmer at Suckers in an hour."

Her pulse leapt at the mention of Tony's name. They'd texted a few times since Saturday night, but he hadn't asked to see her again.

Nor had she asked to see him, if she were being fair about it. But what were the rules of sleeping with a guy you were only supposed to be pretending to date, when said pretend boyfriend was beginning to feel entirely too real?

"Elmer?" she said.

"This nice gentleman I met last night at the seniors' center. He used to train tigers but had to retire on account of a misunderstanding with his circus bosses."

"I have a Knot Fest meeting, Gran."

"Not until eight. I checked your calendar."

"How—never mind. I'm taking the dogs out." And texting Tony. Maybe he'd have an emergency come up at work and be unable to make it.

A girl could hope, anyway. Goodness knew what Gran would be up to tonight.

But she was grateful for the excuse to talk to Tony.

She snagged the leashes from their hook near the back door. Sadie crept around the corner, doing her little bunny shuffle while George attacked Pepper's tights. "Down, or you're staying home," she said.

He eyeballed her with those dark marbles of his, but his wiggly

177

butt slowed and he sat back on his haunches. "And if you terrorize my sweet Sadie, you're sleeping outside tonight."

"Sixteen points!" Gran crowed. "Hand over those pennies."

"You haven't won yet, old lady," Cinna countered.

She left the two of them to their game and took the dogs out for a walk in the rapidly darkening evening. She tried calling Tony, whose truck wasn't in his driveway, but his phone went straight to voicemail.

Probably just as well. Much easier to meet him at Suckers with other people around. They'd pretend to be dating, pretend they hadn't had sex, pretend they were both normal.

Grief snuck into her chest again, another wave of agony squeezing her lungs and trying to suffocate her heart.

Nope.

She wouldn't let it win.

Miracles happened every day. She'd been trying too hard, and the doctors were wrong. She could have babies. Women had babies later and later all the time. Forty wasn't too old to be a mom. Her body would work out its own kinks, and she'd be a mother when she was supposed to be a mother.

Wouldn't she?

She was surrounded by death out here in the twilight. The grass in her neighbors' yards was dead. The trees were dead. That streetlight ahead was dead. The blow-up goat, still crinkled and airless and now shoved deep in her closet, was dead. The inky sky seemed dead.

And her ovaries and uterus were dead.

That thick knot of pain clogged her throat again. She forced it down and tried to count her blessings.

Hot chocolate. She could have all the hot chocolate she wanted now. An entire strawberry cake. Ice cream. As much pizza as she could eat.

Pizza.

Sex.

More sex with Tony. At least until it was his turn to call things off. Three weeks and five days until his niece's wedding.

She pulled on George's leash when he tried to sneak around her to jump Sadie. "Keep that thing to yourself," she growled at him. "Didn't Gran have you fixed?"

George turned an injured doggie pout up at her, and her shoulders sagged. Yes, the dog was a terror, but he couldn't help himself. He'd been trained by Gran. And it wasn't his fault Pepper was...broken.

More streetlights flickered awake down the street. A hint of smoke hung in the air, and bare branches rustled in the winter wind.

Two blocks down, she turned a corner. George lunged, yipping his head off at the silhouette of a couple approaching with a dog even smaller than he was.

"*Down*," Pepper ordered. She held the leash firmly and stepped aside, poor Sadie cowering behind her again. "Sorry," she called.

A familiar laugh bubbled out of the darkness. "Don't mistake silence for weakness," Dahlia called. "Ringo here can take it. Mikey's been teaching him self-defense. We need to get him a job."

"Mikey, or the dog?" Pepper called. There. That was normal.

"Both." Dahlia stepped under a streetlight, and her massive pregnant belly took all the light. Pepper's breath caught again.

"I *have* a job," Mikey said. "I take care of you and help you invent ice cream flavors. How's it hanging, Pepper?"

The couple owned the ice cream shop around the corner from Bliss Bridal, and they lived on the block behind Pepper. Mikey had grown up with Will, played drums in the Billy Brenton band, and still wrote songs with his old pal, as far as Pepper knew. Usually, she would've been happy to see her friends.

"Perfect as always. How about you two?" The words left a trail of acid in her mouth, but she forced a smile anyway.

All of her friends had taken all the fertility in Bliss and left none for her.

"Waiting for this to be over." Dahlia was a cute girl, shorter, with brown hair that she'd stopped dyeing with streaks of red during pregnancy. She rubbed a gloved hand over her belly, still smiling, her eyes enlarged by her glasses. "But I'll miss the excuse to sample so many more of the goods at work."

Ringo growled low and slunk toward George. Mikey bent his long frame to pick up the rat terrier. "Eat all you want, baby," he said to Dahlia. "Kid still has to eat after he's born."

Pepper tugged on her own dogs' leashes. "Let me know if you need anything," she said to Dahlia. "I should get these two home." And find her happy place before this date with Gran and Tony and Elmer the tiger trainer.

Maybe she could move up the Knot Fest meeting.

Or maybe she could simply enjoy the distraction of keeping Gran out of trouble for one more night.

TONY HADN'T BEEN to Suckers much since moving to town—once for a take-out dinner while he was getting Pepperoni Tony's set up, and then again on Super Bowl Sunday. Bars weren't really his scene, but since Gran had made a point of coming by at lunch and threatening not to leave until he agreed to meet her and Pepper for a double date tonight, here he was.

Eagerly looking forward to seeing Pepper again. Hoping for a chance to touch her. Kiss her. Invite her over to his place after her Knot Fest meeting tonight.

And the raw nerves eating at his stomach could go fuck themselves.

He might not have believed in casual relationships before getting married, but that didn't mean he couldn't figure out how they worked now.

Inside, the crowd was so-so. Neither Cinna nor CJ appeared to be working tonight. Pepper was seated near the end of the curved bar, sipping on a pink drink in a fancy cocktail glass, complete with a pineapple slice on the rim.

Her thick, dark hair was pulled up off her neck, and she was in an emerald green, shimmery top that made her complexion glow. She didn't wear heavy makeup. Her jewelry was simple and elegant, much like her wardrobe. Her lips were pursed, her gaze somewhere off in the distance as though she were lost in her own head.

And she took his breath away.

If she'd been nothing more than elegant grace and intelligent determination, he would've admired her, but she was more. She was warmth. She was strength. And she was vulnerability.

She wouldn't admit it—she was stubborn too—but he recognized the chink in her armor, because he'd worn the same chink for so long.

How had all those other men left her? How could *any* man?

He pulled up the stool beside her.

"Is that an umbrella in your drink, or are you just happy to see me?"

She turned startled green eyes on him. Her eyes went shiny and her chin trembled, and a chorus of profanity lit his brain.

She was going to call off their deal. He *hadn't* left her satisfied Saturday night. She'd been faking. He was broken.

This fake-dating shit was for the birds. He didn't want to fake date her.

He wanted to *real* date her. To see if this interest could be something more. He hadn't been interested in a woman in over a year. Letting her go would be like ripping a bandage off a scab that hadn't quite healed yet.

"Uh, if I told you that you have a nice body, would you hold it against me?" He forced a grin, though he knew it probably looked panicked, because *let's do this for real* wasn't an option. Not when she looked ready to bolt. "It's National Bad Pick-up Line Day. Didn't you hear?"

"I—" She shook her head, visibly bucking up and willing back her normal confidence. She took a swig of her drink before meeting his gaze head-on. "If you were a fruit, you'd be a fineapple."

"Nice, but your Gran already used that on me today. Try again."

Her jaw slipped. He grinned—*gotcha*—and his heart lit up when she tipped her head back and laughed.

A real laugh that ended with a playful shove to his shoulder. "You are so obnoxious."

"About a lot of things," he agreed.

Her amusement faded, and it didn't take a brain surgeon to see what was coming.

She wanted to talk about Saturday night.

"Speaking of Gran," he said, "where is she?"

Apparently she was willing to not talk about it too, because she turned her attention to sliding the pineapple around the rim of her glass. "She and Cinna are picking up Elmer."

"Cinna's coming?" Could be good or bad. He liked Pepper—that wasn't an act, and he wasn't worried Cinna would see through him. But he didn't know how much Pepper confided in any of her sisters about her love life.

Or the disasters therein.

"Long story," she said. "Which is pretty much any story involving my family, dates, weddings, baptisms, birthdays, holidays, reunions, or who's driving whom. Don't ever get involved in joint gifts. The money is a nightmare, Rika always 'forgets' to pay, and Ginger will spend the next two months complaining that she should've gotten three more dollars back."

"Add in remembering who's related to whom, and you've just described my family too."

She smiled. Not a fake smile, not a placating smile, but a wide, honest, you-get-it-and-I-dig-that smile. "Ever wish you were an only child?"

"Still do most days."

Her sympathetic laugh settled some of the acid nipping at his nerves. "I'm rethinking having Cinna and Gran both live with me."

"We'd miss them if they weren't here."

"Maybe not *all* of them," she said with a wink.

True enough.

"You okay with your gran?" he asked quietly.

"She got over boundaries about two decades ago, which I know and accept and love about her. Also, she brought me presents."

"Good presents?"

"The best."

The door swung open, and Gran's entourage paraded in. Gran in her massive winter coat and curls that appeared freshly tightened, Cinna swinging her hips with a grin that spelled trouble, and a relatively young older gentleman in jeans, a button-down plaid shirt beneath an open winter coat, full head of gray hair, and a scar bisecting his left eyebrow.

Pepper tilted a wry smile at him. "You ready for this?"

"Ready for time with my favorite ladies? Always."

"Better not let your own sisters hear that."

"You kidding? Might inspire them to be nicer." The lady was digging for information. This was good. Interest was good.

She slid off her stool and squeezed his shoulder. A *thanks for being here*? An *I like you*? Or simply a friendly gesture to keep up the charade?

She pulled her coat and a bright green scarf off the back of her stool and draped it over her arm. But when she reached for her drink, she suddenly froze.

He glanced back in the direction of her gaze.

The door had opened again, and Kimmie Kincaid—owner of the best cupcake shop in all of Bliss, he had now confirmed for himself— and her husband were wandering in.

When he turned back to Pepper, a simple smile adorned her lips. Not fake, but not much warmer than simply pleasant either, which was odd. Tony hadn't been trying to fit in long, but even he knew only the evilest of the evil people in the world could dislike Kimmie.

Pepper gestured to the bartender and waved toward Gran before picking up her drink and nudging him to two square tables being pushed together near the door.

"Pepper! Hey!" Kimmie waved at them.

Pepper steered around the tables to lean over Kimmie's pregnant belly for a hug. "Hey. Coconut cream pie craving?"

"Always. Pretty sure at least one of them is going to be a dreamer." She eyed Tony. "Are we interrupting a date?"

"Not if you join us," Gran announced. She put her hands on Kimmie's belly. "Maybe you could spread some of this fertility to these two. If she gets knocked up, he'll have to marry her."

Tony's gut reared up and kicked like a caged stallion.

"If we were living in nineteen fifty," Pepper said. "Quit giving Tony heart attacks, and quit saying things you need to apologize for." She hooked her arm through his elbow and put on her professional smile again, but this one didn't even approach mildly pleasant. "You've met Kimmie and Josh, right?"

"Got my ass kicked by him on the basketball court once or twice." Tony shook hands with both of them.

"How did you two meet again?" Kimmie asked.

"His cat terrorized my dog," Pepper said lightly. "I forgave him when he delivered a delicious pizza."

Kimmie pointed to her belly. "Josh delivered me a pizza once, and now look where we are. Just be careful."

Kimmie laughed. Josh laughed. Gran and Cinna laughed, and Elmer joined in too.

Tony forced a laugh. But it caught in his throat when he realized he wasn't the only one faking it.

Pepper's eyes had lost their light. She blinked quickly, but not before he'd caught the sheen of moisture and the quiver in her lips. And once again, she seemed to summon her steel. "We should order."

Or he should grab her hand and drag her out of here.

Forget the double date. Forget the friends.

Something was wrong. He couldn't fix it if he didn't know what it was.

"I haven't had cheese fries in ages," Pepper announced. She draped her coat over a chair and took a seat. "And I'd give my left hand for a bacon cheeseburger."

"Elmer almost gave his left hand to a tiger once," Gran said. "Or was that your left foot?"

Josh pulled out a seat for Kimmie, and Elmer helped Gran sit as well.

"My left knee," Elmer said. "Almost lost the whole leg. Can tell the weather by it. We got a doozy coming this weekend. Can tell because it aches like a bitch. Want to see the scar?"

"Maybe after dinner," Pepper said quickly, as easily as if nothing was wrong.

He took the seat beside her and draped his arm over the back of her chair.

Maybe nothing was wrong. Maybe he was making it up.

Even if he was right, he wasn't really her boyfriend.

Yet.

So he'd be here for now, and later, when the time was right, he'd feel out the waters and see if it was time to take a swim.

*F*riday morning, Pepper was slipping into her boots and debating the perfect reply to Tony's text message about dinner tonight when George erupted in yips and charged down the stairs.

A knock sounded a moment later. Sadie peeked out from beneath the bed. "Have to come out and face him sooner or later, pup," Pepper said. "Mom's running out of seniors' homes to call for Gran."

Sadie whimpered.

"I know, I know, but he's trying. He's used to being a single child. Show him you can't be bossed around, and you'll be fine."

She grabbed a pair of emerald earrings off her dresser and put them in while she made her way down the stairs. Gran and Elmer had been right—a blizzard was forecasted to descend on Bliss tonight, which had put the town into a frenzy the last couple of days and interrupted Pepper's idea to go visit Tarra this weekend. Most appointments were canceled at Bliss Bridal today, but she still wanted to get in and check on things before they closed up.

And probably tell Tony dinner was a bad idea, given the forecast.

Dammit.

She hadn't seen him since Tuesday. Just more texts here and there while they both prepped for the storm.

The knock sounded again as she reached the bottom.

Tony stood on the porch in a leather bomber jacket, ice skates hanging off his shoulders. Her heart gave a hiccup.

Was it the thicker scruff on his chin and cheeks that set off the fireworks in her belly, or was it a trick of the morning light that he seemed more virile this morning?

George leapt for his calf like a long-lost lover. So he'd noticed how delicious Tony seemed this morning too.

"Hey," Pepper said.

He snagged the little white pain in the ass and held him while he wiggled. "I called in sick. For both of us. Go get changed. We're going skating."

"What? No."

"When's the last time you took a day off?"

"Nat's on maternity leave. I told most of the bridal consultants to stay home and get ready for the storm. *You* should be getting ready for the storm."

"Your manager said you've left with a headache every day this week. She's glad to see you're taking care of yourself, and there's only one bride—a local girl—coming in today. Had a good week, so I could afford to put my assistant manager in charge of closing things up at one at Pepperoni Tony's. Go get your coat. Open skate starts in fifteen minutes and is closing early because of the storm. If you can't do it for you, do it for me. I haven't taken a full day off in a year. Maybe more."

She opened her mouth to argue.

But he was right. She'd had a long week—a rough week—and she hadn't taken a single sick day since she'd moved to Bliss.

Nor had she ever ice skated. "Okay."

He drew back. "Okay?"

"Yes, okay. As soon as I call Bliss Bridal and confirm, *okay*. You don't want to go now?"

"I do, but Cinna said—" He snapped his jaw shut and pushed into the house. Once the door was shut, he released George. "Go on. Change."

"Cinna told you to take me ice skating?"

"No. She said you're stubborn as a goat and peckish as a chicken and that I'd need to carry you up the stairs and change your clothes for you."

That was a happy tingle in a very pleasant place. "She might be right."

"I'll be loud enough for your grandmother to hear. And you know she'll want to come with us."

Right. This was all an act.

It was also the closest thing to a real relationship she'd had in forever. "Give me five minutes. Ten if you're lying about already calling me in sick."

She raced upstairs and found Gran leaning out her bedroom door and shoving her dentures in, white flowered nightgown billowed to her toes. "Tony's taking us ice skating?"

"Gran—"

"Don't you go pulling that *you're too old* baloney. Besides, you two need a chaperone. There wasn't enough kissy-kissy going on at Suckers the other night." She teetered to the top of the stairs. "Young man, don't even think about leaving without me," she called.

He stepped into view down in the living room. "Wouldn't dream of it, Gran." He tilted a wry smile at Pepper. *Should've worn pants*, that grin said. *If you hadn't had to change, we could've gotten out without her.*

Fine for him to suggest. He could've texted and asked her to meet him at the rink.

Which she would've ignored.

And which he apparently knew.

"Ticktock, ladies. Gonna miss all the good ice."

Sadie bunny-hopped out of the bedroom. When she spotted Tony, her tongue dipped out in a happy doggy pant, and she took the stairs like a normal canine.

"Don't let George push her around," Pepper called.

"My George would do no such thing. He's a good boy. Tony, be a sweetheart and pop a can of tuna for him if you can make Pepper's newfangled can opener work. Can openers shouldn't need smart-phones to work. They're make-you-dumb phones, you ask me."

"Yes, ma'am."

"You see those manners?" Gran said to Pepper. "We gotta get you hitched to this one before some other woman sneaks in and snags him. Especially if he knows how to work a can opener. A man who can cook is a man worth marrying. That goat's really working, isn't it?"

"You know what Mom would say about you going ice skating?"

"Probably the same thing she says about me and skydiving. When did my girls get to be such fuddy-duds?"

Probably around the time Gran broke her hip. Or maybe when she got arrested for goosing a policeman who was investigating a rash of thefts at her first senior citizens' home. Or it might've been when she disappeared to Vegas for a week without telling anyone she was going, and came back claiming she'd gotten hitched to Elvis's ghost.

Cinna might've been right about that Vegas-accidental-marriage thing.

The only way to discourage Gran from skating would've been to offer her something better, but shuffleboard at the seniors' center wouldn't have the same appeal. Plus, the seniors' center probably wasn't open this morning.

And honestly? Spending a morning with Gran, on a day she didn't need to be at work, held almost as much appeal as spending it with Tony. Because while she lived with Gran, she never got to have *fun* with Gran.

Thirty minutes later, they were inside the Bliss Civic Center. Gran had convinced one of the young whippersnappers who worked at the arena to help her skate behind a folding chair, and he'd been warned to make sure she kept both hands on the chair. But Pepper cared less that Gran kept her hands to herself and more that she stayed safe and didn't break anything.

There was a good possibility Pepper should've used a chair for balance too. Her arms windmilled while she tried to steady herself and keep her feet pointed straight ahead.

"Relax," Tony told her. His hands settled at her waist while he skated backward in front of her, that amused grin teasing his lips. "Trust your skates."

She latched onto his shoulders with her mittened hands. She loved that smile—so easy, so uncomplicated, so handsome.

"I haven't done this since I was a little girl," she confessed.

"Doing great." He guided her into a curve while some eight-year-olds lapped them, laughing and shouting. "Not as good as you throw a softball, but you can't be perfect."

"You saw me play?"

"Saw video. One of your sisters sent me a link. Killed 'em out there. That grand slam you hit was a thing of beauty."

She tipped her head back and laughed, and her feet slipped.

He gripped her tighter. Even before noon, he smelled like woodsy male and pizza sauce. Shouldn't have been nearly as good a combination as it was.

"That was a total fluke. Do you play?" The Bliss softball league was hardly the stuff of legends, but they had fun. Her grand slam had happened because of a couple of misthrows.

"Like a boss."

He grinned again, she laughed again, and she almost slipped again.

Which meant Tony gripped her tighter again.

Maybe there was something to playing the helpless female every now and again.

A mother and a toddler bundled up in a blue snowsuit skated past them. Pepper's womb gave another pang at the same time her pride told her to pick up her speed.

Getting passed by a *toddler*?

But if she went any faster, she'd have to let go of Tony. And she very much didn't want to let go of Tony.

Not today. Not in three weeks. "Tell me about your family."

"Ah, my second least favorite topic in the world. I'll bet you played softball in high school. Any other sports? You strike me as the wrestling type. Down on the mat, twisting arrogant assholes up like pretzels…" His thick, dark brows wiggled. "You can twist me up like a pretzel."

"That went okay Saturday night, didn't it?" Oh, *crap*. There went her mouth.

But he chuckled, and interest sparked deep in his eyes. "It did."

Did he want to sleep with her again?

She wanted to sleep with him again. "Did I ever tell you that my sister Ginger told her first boyfriend that she was an orphan being raised by the nuns at our local parish? Want to guess what happened when some of my older siblings found out?"

"Does it involve wedgies?"

"No, that was Rosemary's husband and CJ before he bulked up. Ginger's boyfriend got the pig incident."

"What's with your family and farm animals?"

"We raised them." And collected blow-up versions that Pepper didn't want to talk about. "Your turn. Tell me something to make my family seem normal."

Being bossy wasn't unusual in her relationships. But what *was* unusual was that she felt lighthearted about it today. She'd never have children. She didn't need a husband. Hanging with Tony, getting to know him better, was just…fun.

"Really not much to tell," he said.

"Liar."

"I'm the best of the bunch."

She laughed. "That ego. You are such a guy."

"You have no idea, princess peach."

That twinkle-eyed grin promised things that made her core clench. She wobbled on her skates and gripped his shoulders tighter.

His legs widened and shifted, taking on her weight and steadying them both.

Would it be wrong to lure him under the stands and talk him out of his pants?

They approached Gran and her chair. Her feet were wobbly, but her dashing twentysomething assistant was right there to catch her.

"Looking good, Gran. You'll be doing double axels before you know it," Tony said to her.

"Triple or nothing," Gran replied. "What's with this distance between you two? Get closer. Act like you like each other. Make it uncomfortable for the Holy Ghost to fit in there."

"I can't decide if she wants us to go at it like rabbits right here on the ice, or if she's trying to turn me celibate for life," Tony murmured.

Gran's left hand left her chair and headed in the direction of her assistant's rear end. "Hands on the chair," Pepper ordered.

"Just trying to set a good example," she replied. "Oh, look, honey. That little infant is passing all of us. Is he old enough to walk?"

Yep, there went that three-year-old, lapping them again.

Tony's dark eyes were dancing with amusement, his grin bright and easy.

Apparently they'd both needed this.

"You okay if we go faster, Pepper?"

"Can't go any slower," Gran said. "Sneak a kiss. Use some tongue. The boys like that. I won't tell your mother."

"Yep. Scarred for life," Tony murmured.

"She's an inspiration. Wouldn't you like to have that much enthusiasm for life when you're eighty-seven?"

He opened his jaw, then closed it. "Not helping erase those mental images."

Pepper laughed again. There was something different about him today. She couldn't quite put her finger on it, but she liked it.

"Softball, volleyball, and basketball," she said.

"Pardon?"

"You asked what I played in high school. Softball, volleyball, and basketball."

"Overachiever much?"

Once upon a time, her achievements and drive had been a source of pride. "In some things. Obviously not in skating. What about you? Play anything in high school?"

"Football. Surefire way to get the ladies." He added an exaggerated wink that had her laughing again, but this time, her feet didn't slip.

Because this time, he skated closer to her, pressing his body against hers while they went into another curve.

Gran would be so proud.

She blinked up into his eyes, much closer than they'd been before she stumbled. "I don't believe for a minute that you were a football jock just out to score with the ladies," she whispered.

"Them's fighting words, Miss Blue."

"Have you dated since your divorce? Really dated, or just taken a woman here and there to make people *think* you're dating?"

"And she hits below the belt too."

"We're *friends*, aren't we? Friends talk. Friends share. Here. I'll go first. I've been to three ex-boyfriends' weddings, one as bridesmaid—that was my cousin's wedding—and I haven't dated anyone seriously since I got to Bliss. Your turn. Have you honestly dated anyone since your divorce?"

His dark eyes twitched every time she said *date*, but it was the hitch in his breath when she'd said *ex-boyfriends* that made a shiver skitter over her skin.

"Your cheeks are pink," he said. "Getting cold? We can stop."

"How many of your sisters and brothers have you told that we're dating? Shouldn't I know these things if they ambush me while I'm having lunch one day?"

"Like your family ambushed me? They'd be disappointed if they got a single straight answer out of you." He flashed a seductive smile that warmed her from her neck to her knees. "I know you're up for the challenge."

"Don't give me that male sex kitten look. I'm immune."

He laughed. "Sex kitten? You mean sex lion."

"Pushing it, delivery boy."

When *was* the last time she'd had this much fun? Not just with a man, but with anyone?

The toddler who'd passed them went down. He flopped onto his back and wailed while they slid past.

"You're okay," his mom told him. "Everybody falls. Come on, bud. Up and at 'em. You've got this."

Pepper blinked. A pang seared her midsection, but it wasn't until she noticed Tony watching that she realized they'd slowed. His lips were pinched, the lines around them tight and white. Grief deepened the set of his eyes.

An intimately familiar grief.

He'd lost someone.

A child?

Was that why he was divorced? Was that what he'd meant when he'd said a family wasn't in his life plan anymore?

She reached for his cheek. He blinked, and easygoing, goofball Tony returned. "Getting better on those skates, Miss Blue. Think you can beat me to the door? Loser buys hot chocolate for all of us, including Gran's new boyfriend. I'll even skate backward to keep it even. And *go!*"

He released her. Her legs wobbled, but she kept her balance.

And because she was a Blue, she set her sights on the entrance to the rink, and she did her dang best to win.

THE DARK CLOUDS gathering overhead gave Tony pause when Pepper pulled into her driveway. After a thoroughly enjoyable round of hot chocolate, they'd stopped at the grocery store for a few last essentials before the storm hit.

Like a normal couple.

He wasn't a fan of the weather bearing down so ominously now, casting a literal cloud over the most enjoyable morning he'd had in over a year.

Not a bad sign, he told himself. Just normal winter weather.

But the chill felt heavier when he pulled himself out of the car and opened Gran's door. Her grip was firm, and like her granddaughter, her hands were cold.

Unlike her granddaughter, though, as soon as she stepped out of the car, she sneezed a massive sneeze that could've come from someone twice her size and should've propelled her onto her ass.

"Okay there, Gran?"

"Just a sneeze, young man. Not like my nose is going to fall off."

"She always sneezes like that," Pepper said. She tilted her head toward the house, an invitation for him to follow. "Family lore suggests Grandpa was half-deaf in his right ear after twenty-something years of having Gran sneezing on his right."

"He had selective hearing," Gran said. "Couldn't hear a single one of the kids asking for anything, but he could hear his paper land on the doorstep every morning. God rest his soul. Tony, you coming in? Pepper makes the best chocolate chip cookies in the world, and she shouldn't be left alone right now."

Pepper froze with her key in the lock, some caught-with-a-hand-in-the-cookie-jar guilt making her eyes wide. "I shouldn't?"

"Not if you have a handsome, virile man willing to sit with you on a day when you were too sick to go into work, dear."

"You know what I love about you, Gran?" Tony said.

"My dashing good looks and sparkling personality?"

"That, and your remarkable gift for subtlety."

Pepper laughed. "Don't encourage her." She pushed the door open. "You two coming?"

As if there were anywhere else he wanted to be.

"I'M TAKING my hearing aid out, so if you and Tony want to do something with the goat, I won't hear a thing," Gran said in her bedroom after a delicious lunch of peanut butter and jelly sandwiches. She sat on the quilted bedspread and winked, though her voice was deeper and leaning more toward the nasal side than usual. "And I'll be napping for a good hour at least."

"Tony probably needs to go check on things at Pepperoni Tony's, Gran." Pepper squinted at the dark clouds rolling in before she closed the blinds. "And I need to make sure the girls close the shop early. Weather reports are getting worse."

Which meant there was no reason for her to leave home either, provided her employees had closed up already.

An entire afternoon all to herself. It had been so long since Pepper had taken a weekday off, she wasn't entirely certain what she was supposed to do.

"Can't make babies if he leaves," Gran said.

For a few hours, she'd almost forgotten about babies. "Maybe I don't want kids."

"Margie might not want kids, but you—you've always wanted kids. Don't try that baloney with me. I'm still your grandmother, and I still know a thing or two about you."

Did she?

Pepper leaned over and kissed Gran's forehead. She was unusually warm. Coupled with the sneezing and the froggy voice, she might've been coming down with something. "You feeling okay, Gran?"

"I always nap in the afternoon. Perk of being old."

As if Gran would admit to anything holding her back. She was a tough old lady, and she didn't like to let anything slow her down.

Except afternoon naptime, apparently. Which she didn't indulge in every day, and which Pepper knew because she was usually at Bliss Bridal every day now.

"If you need anything, I'll be downstairs."

"Go on. Shoo. Have fun with Tony." Gran flopped onto her back, closed her eyes, and let out a fake snore.

Pepper suppressed her smile, but only until she'd closed Gran's door.

Downstairs, she caught Tony checking his phone in the kitchen. He pushed off the counter and shoved it in his pocket. His dark hair was growing out already after his haircut before the non-wedding last weekend, curling at the ends, and she had a flash of two little boys with his dark hair and green eyes running through the kitchen, flinging meatballs at one another.

Her throat clogged. *Dammit.* "Thank you. I had fun this morning."

"My pleasure. You still free for dinner?"

"The weather—and Gran. She's—"

A sneeze from upstairs rattled the window over the sink.

"That," Pepper finished.

"Hmm. That." He angled closer to her and settled his hands on her hips. "Is that sonic sneeze genetic?"

"Margie has it, and Cinna fakes it, but the rest of us are much more dignified and subtle about sneezing."

His laughter rumbled low and warm, and it was so easy to let her head drop to his shoulder.

His hugs were the best of everything—warm and comforting like hugs were supposed to be, but spiced with his unique, tantalizing scent and the hard planes of his body.

If he got married when they were done with this fake dating—which oddly no longer felt fake at all—she'd be talking to Basil about what it would take to go to nun school.

Forget Bliss. Forget the boutique. Forget a career.

She was done watching men she cared about marry other women and have babies.

His hands were innocently rubbing up and down her back and inspiring not-so-innocent thoughts and feelings that she refused to act on today.

"You going into Bliss Bridal this afternoon?" he asked.

"Nope. They're closing early. You?"

"Thought about it, but you didn't have any dresses in my size last time."

"Smart-ass. It's like fake-dating my sisters."

His arms tightened around her. "Yeah, but I've got something your sisters don't have."

"If you're talking about your penis—"

"Actually, I was talking about all-you-can-eat pizza. And I'll throw down with any one of them in a chili cook-off too."

The back door banged open. Pepper didn't let go of Tony, but she did glance over at her baby sister and the two dogs tromping inside. George lunged for them, but Cinna hadn't unclipped his leash yet.

"You two are so disgusting." She stomped her boots on the mat and let Sadie off her leash first. "Can't you save the PDA until after coffee?"

"It's two in the afternoon," Pepper said.

"Which is my morning. And we're out of cold pizza. Hint, hint."

Another sneeze shook the house. All three of them looked toward the ceiling.

"Not a Gran-cold," Cinna whispered.

"Don't say it out loud," Pepper hissed. "She probably just got some dust caught in her nose when we were skating."

Tony disentangled himself, and cool air swirled through her shirt where his body heat had been. "I need to run over to the shop," he said. "Make sure it's closed up tight."

Cinna let George off his leash, and he leaped for Tony's leg.

"Whoops," she said. "Looks like George doesn't want you to go."

George wasn't the only one.

Which was silly. This wasn't a for-real relationship.

No matter how real it had felt today.

Pepper rescued him from the dog and held the toy poodle tight.

"CJ's closing Suckers too," Cinna said. "But if there's a Gran cold in the house, I'm begging to sleep there instead."

And if there was as much snow on the way as the weatherman was predicting, Pepper wouldn't be having dinner with Tony tonight. He'd be locked up with Lucky. She'd be here with Gran and George and Sadie.

Which was probably for the best.

Because if he cooked for her again, and if they were alone in his house, there would be far fewer reasons not to kiss him. Persuade him to make love to her again.

Or talk to him. Get to know him better.

Learn his secrets.

Forget again that this wasn't real. Lose herself in a fake relationship so she didn't have to deal with the realities of her life.

"Be safe out there," she told him.

He pressed a kiss to her cheek. "I'll call you."

She'd be waiting.

15

The snow started just after four. Pepper, Cinna, and Gran—who was trying to hack up a lung—kept drifting to the windows to watch the large white flakes swirl in the unnaturally dim afternoon light. Pepper had texted Tony to ask if he was hunkered down yet.

He hadn't replied. Probably taking care of final storm preparations. He'd posted on Pepperoni Tony's Facebook page that they were closed tonight due to the snowy forecast, but his truck wasn't next door.

She hoped he wasn't planning on riding out the storm down at his pizza place.

A not-so-small part of her was relieved he wasn't home though. She'd barely begun to process that she couldn't have children. She didn't need to get wrapped up in a man right now. Especially a man she wasn't dating for real.

She tried for a while to read the latest Mae Daniels book, but the story—a secret baby romance—had hurt her heart. So she'd tried for a while to read *Phoebe Moon and the Missing Sunshine*, but reading a book for middle schoolers had also made her heart hurt. So instead, she tossed her e-reader aside and went into the kitchen to bake.

She was pulling the first batch of chocolate chip cookies from the oven when someone knocked on the door.

George yipped and charged the door.

"Back, you little spawn of Satan," Cinna said. "Gran, this dog needs obedience training. If you don't sign him up, I'm going to."

"Hush and get that door," Gran said. "I'm waiting on a package."

Not today, she wasn't. Sadie pulled herself out of her doggy bed in the corner of the dining room and hopped her little doggy-hop behind George, close enough to see what all the excitement was, far enough away not to draw the other dog's attention.

"You really need to put him in his place," Pepper said to her pet while she slid the next tray of cookie dough into the oven.

Sadie nodded, but she still hung back. The door clicked in the other room, and her tail went wild.

"Hey, pizza man," Cinna said. "Please tell me you're not here with a package for Gran. Because *ew*."

Pepper leaned out of the kitchen. "Hey."

Thick snowflakes dusted Tony's dark hair. He had at least a half-dozen plastic grocery bags in hand, a streak of marinara sauce on his dark jeans, and a warm smile on his lips. He kicked his shoes off beside the door. Her useless feminine parts stirred to life.

"I brought dinner," he said.

Yep.

She was a goner.

She stood gaping a second too long. "Cinna, help the man with the groceries. Gran, if you can't cough in your elbow, cough in a tissue." She hustled into the room and took two bags from him, but he shooed her away when she tried to take more, sidestepping her on his way to the kitchen.

"You didn't have to—"

Her objection died on her tongue when he cast a silent, *yes, I did* at her.

"Thank you," she amended.

He deposited the groceries on her kitchen table. "Been too long since I had anyone to cook for."

Her heart squeezed, but before she could reply, he added, "Beautiful cookies. You remembered chocolate chip is my favorite."

"I thought cannoli was your favorite."

He flashed a pirate grin that made her belly clench, and while she tried to hide the flush in her cheeks by busying herself with preparing the next pan of cookies, he went to work pulling groceries out of the bags.

———

TONY HAD NEVER MET a kitchen he couldn't work in, and Pepper's was nearly perfect.

Wasn't her counter space doing the trick—she had about as much room as he did. And while her kitchen itself was more modern than his, her stockpot wasn't as nice as his, nor was her rolling pin. But she had a stand mixer, sharp knives, and a big kitchen table he could work at.

She also had an easy way of keeping him company while he worked, telling stories about her family and some of the more outrageous brides she'd worked with, both here in Bliss and back when she worked for a big bridal chain in St. Louis. By the time he added the diced onion, carrots, and celery to the chicken in the stockpot and set it to boil, he was more relaxed than he'd been in at least a year.

Probably two.

A swirling sheet of snowflakes danced in the backyard. Gran and Cinna were curled up in the living room, watching pro wrestling with George. Pepper's dog snored softly at her feet beneath the table. And Tony was doing what he loved—cooking for people he cared about, in a home that felt like a home.

Wondering at his chances of getting his favorite woman naked again.

"Flour?" he asked Pepper.

"Big mushroom."

She smiled when he glanced back at her, catching her reaching for another cookie. "On the counter. The mushroom crock."

He'd noticed the four crocks of various sizes, each with orange mushroom cap lids and little doors and windows painted on the stems, but he hadn't given much thought to anything being in them. He peeked in each.

Tea bags in the smallest, playing cards in the next biggest, then sugar, then flour.

"Stylish," he said.

"Gran had them in her kitchen for years before she downsized and went into a senior living facility. I had to arm wrestle Ginger for them, and that was back when she was picking up toddlers all day long and had guns of steel. So you know I had to want them badly."

There went that stirring in his pants again.

He couldn't decide if Pepper was good or bad for him. Probably both. "Video evidence?" he asked.

"You wish. What's the flour for?"

"Noodles."

"You're making us homemade noodles?"

"No, I'm making Gran homemade noodles. You're going to have to suffer through salmon, bacon-wrapped asparagus, and a Tony special treat." He dumped two cups of flour in the mixer and topped it with a healthy dose of salt. Pepper was watching him with an intensity that made him squirm.

"You really love to cook," she said softly.

A foreign heat crept up his neck. Because her statement struck him as a question. *Do you love to cook for me?*

She hadn't asked that, of course. Probably wouldn't have occurred to her to ask if he was doing this for himself or for her.

"Just compensating for what I'm not good at," he said with a rueful shrug.

"I'm struggling to imagine anything you're not good at."

He kept his head ducked down while he cracked the two eggs into the mixer and turned it on. The noise made talking impossible, and he needed to pay attention to the dough to make sure he added the right amount of milk.

When he shut the mixer off a minute later, Pepper was eyeing the chocolate chip cookies again. "Gonna ruin your appetite," he murmured.

"No chocolate chip cookies for you," she replied.

"That's not the way to a man's heart," Cinna called.

Gran coughed.

Worry lines creased Pepper's forehead. She reached for her phone. "I know it's probably just a normal cold," she said quietly, "but she's eighty-seven. And her brain is stronger than her body."

His mom had been too. Especially the last few weeks. "She's too feisty to let this get her down for long."

"Let's hope." She typed something on her phone, then plunked it on the table. "Screw it. I want another cookie."

He wanted to lean over the table and kiss her. Pull her hair out of that ponytail, take his time, and learn what she liked. Everywhere she was ticklish. Her secret, sensitive places that would make her breath hitch and her heart pound.

His own heart thumped harder.

He didn't even want to kiss her to prove to himself that he wasn't broken anymore. He just wanted her to know she wasn't alone.

But she thought he was here because she was doing him a favor in pretending to date him so he could avoid blind dates from his sisters.

Not because he couldn't resist her.

Tonight, as soon as Gran was settled, as long as Cinna took a hint and left them alone, he'd ask her if they could date for real.

———

"You should marry this one, Pepper," Gran said over her chicken noodle soup two hours later.

"I find men are more likely to want to be involved with women whose grandmothers don't bring up marriage while they're sniffling into their soup," Pepper replied.

Not that she honestly disagreed with the basics of Gran's sentiment. She had salmon, bacon-wrapped asparagus, and Brazilian cheese rolls waiting for her once Gran was in bed, and this soup was utterly divine.

But she had too many complications in her life to work through to even consider marriage.

And her primary motivation for wanting it was gone.

Besides, Tony had heard Gran's suggestion, and he'd shoveled another spoonful of soup into his own mouth before turning back to the rest of his cooking.

"Tony, how long have you been divorced?" Cinna asked.

"*Cinna*," Pepper hissed.

"Little over a year," Tony replied.

"Plenty of time to move on," Gran announced. "So? Will you marry Pepper?"

"You can't make that judgment call, Gran," Cinna said. "What if she was the love of his life? What if he'll never love another woman again? What if she looked just like Pepper, and he's trying to make her fit into a box she doesn't actually belong in?"

Maybe it hadn't been Pepper's fault she'd never been able to seal the deal with a man. Maybe the problem was in her genes. "What if you all quit talking and mind your own business before I drag you out in the snow and lock you out for the rest of the night?"

"I'll walk to CJ and Nat's place. And Mom would skin you alive if you mistreat Gran, even when she deserves it. Besides, we *should* know Tony's history if he's going to date you."

"No, *I* should know Tony's history. It's none of *your* business."

Huh. That came out pretty easily. Too easily.

Almost as if this were real.

"You know what would make this soup better?" Gran said.

"If you'd eat it without talking?" Pepper muttered.

Tony coughed, and she caught a hint of a smile before he ducked his head.

"If *I* had a man to eat it with tonight."

"Talk to Mother Nature, Gran," Tony said. He was effortlessly slicing the ends off a bunch of asparagus, and though she'd watched him slice, dice, and prep all of the chicken noodle soup, she still was fascinated by his dexterity in the kitchen.

By the way his shoulders curved, and the way his muscles flexed and bunched beneath his simple blue T-shirt. By the way his ass filled out his jeans. His easy grace. The way his face gave her subtle clues to the emotions playing beneath the surface.

His ex-wife had hurt him. She was as sure of that as she was of her own name. And he'd lost his mother—that might've been what his grief was about this morning at the skating rink.

Or maybe there was something more.

He had a wicked sense of humor. Not new knowledge, but that spark of amusement had lit his eyes or quirked his lips more often than not all afternoon.

All day, even.

"Good thing you live next door, Tony," Cinna said. "Not sure how you'd get home if you weren't so close."

Pepper kicked her under the table, because that was rude.

"Or you can stay here," Pepper said. All night. With her. In her bed.

"That's a horrible example to set for your baby sister," Cinna said.

"So is sending someone out to walk home in the freezing cold during a blizzard. Even just next door. Quit being a brat."

Cinna was still eyeing Tony. "You packed an overnight bag, didn't you?"

"No need. I sleep naked."

Ah, right. He had a big family of his own. He could handle himself. "Wow, those carrots are so uniform," Pepper said. "You really know how to handle a knife."

"Useful skill for so many reasons," he said.

SPICED

They shared a smile while Cinna snorted and Gran sneezed into her soup bowl.

Gran eyed her soup, then lifted bloodshot eyes to glance around the table. "George," she called, "come have some soup."

The poodle was already dancing around the room. He charged straight to Gran's side. Her hand wobbled when she picked up the bowl, but before Pepper could reach her, Tony was there, gently lowering the soup for the dog. "Hold tight," he said. "I'll get you another bowl."

"That's sweet of you, and it was delicious, but I'd really like to just go to bed," she said. "Help me up the stairs?"

She was either feeling way worse than she was admitting, or she was planning to slip Tony some condoms.

It was odd to hope it was the condoms.

"My pleasure," he said. He took her hand and helped her out of the seat while George slurped his homemade soup.

As soon as the stairs stopped creaking, Pepper turned a glare on Cinna. "Can you please be a little nicer?" she whispered. "He came over here *in a snowstorm* and made Gran homemade soup, and you throw his divorce in his face? What's wrong with you?"

"He has a secret," Cinna hissed back. "His brother was in Suckers last night, and as soon as I mentioned you two dating, he clammed up. Like, you should probably make sure Tony's actually divorced. And that his ex-wife is still alive."

"First of all, *some* families actually respect each other's privacy. Second of all, you're hardly the most trustworthy person to gossip with. And third of all, why can't you just trust me?" And fourth, why did Cinna get to meet Tony's family, and Pepper didn't?

Cinna pressed her lips together and looked away.

She had a light dusting of freckles on her nose year-round, her red hair tied up in a messy bun, and pajamas on. Looking every bit the baby of the family. The one who didn't want to go to college, who had moved here on a whim two years ago to tend bar for CJ because it was easier to let family coddle her than to figure out what she wanted to do with her life.

But there was something perceptive about her tonight. More intelligent. More grown-up.

More mature.

More knowledgeable.

"What do you know that you're not telling me?" Pepper asked.

Cinna stood and carried her bowl to the sink.

"Cinna?"

She flipped the water on, still not answering. Pepper's heart rattled out an uneven beat. Regardless of everything else, Tony had been her friend. The last three weeks, he'd become a *good* friend.

"I know in my heart he's a decent guy," Pepper said.

"One of you is going to get hurt, but I don't know which one."

A chill raced down her arms. "Nothing new for my relationships," she said, aiming for light and funny, but missing the mark.

She'd had enough of getting hurt.

And she didn't like to hurt other people, intentionally or accidentally.

"I just—" Cinna dropped her bowl and slammed the faucet off. "Never mind. It's all in my head. I get bored at work and make up stories about my customers, and I'm sure I'm overreacting. Have fun. Date him. Sleep with him. Whatever. But don't—"

She cut herself off with a head shake.

"Don't what?" Pepper said.

A host of emotions danced over Cinna's smooth face. Worry. Compassion. Frustration.

Did she *know?*

A wave of fear crashed through her veins. Did Cinna know about Pepper's fertility treatments? She'd gone out of her way to keep all of her medicines locked up. She'd listed her doctor appointments as phone calls with vendors on her calendar. Not a single document had come through the mail at home. She'd even put her doctor's office in her phone as *Smith, V*—a random name that wouldn't mean anything if Cinna went snooping.

Cinna finally snorted and rolled her eyes. "Don't go psycho if he marries someone else next year."

"You are such a brat," Pepper said to her retreating backside.

"That's my job," she replied.

She disappeared up the stairs, and Pepper dropped her head to the table.

Life was never easy.

FOR SEVEN DAYS, Tony had thought of little else besides Pepper. And now that he had her alone again, in her basement again, she was killing him, one slow bite of dinner at a time.

Her lips closed around a forkful of salmon, and the moan that followed left him light-headed.

"Is there anything you can't cook?" she said.

Her grandmother and sister had been complimentary about his soup, but their praise didn't warm the chilly edges of his soul the way Pepper's did. "Wait until you try the rolls."

She plucked one of the round, cheesy rolls from her plate. "These are going to kill me, aren't they?"

"Yeah, but it'll be worth it."

Her eyes slid shut as she sank her teeth into the roll. More of Tony's blood rushed south. Another moan emanated from her throat.

"Good?" he asked.

"*So* good."

He'd done that to her. He'd made her cheeks flush, made her moan. He'd given her a foodgasm.

He slowly cut into his own salmon, holding his utensils too tight. Felt like a sixteen-year-old kid again. Hiding in the basement. Wanting to kiss a girl.

Wanting to shove her up against the wall and take her.

"I'm sorry about Cinna being so nosy," she said.

He forced himself to unclench his fingers around his fork and knife. "My sisters would've done the same."

"One of those sisters I haven't met?" she teased.

"That's the one."

"I could take her."

She probably could. "But what evil secrets do *you* have lurking in your past?"

"I tried to take CJ out with a tailpipe once."

"Was this before or after he outweighed you by seventy pounds?"

"He was big enough to handle himself then." She set her fork down and turned to face him. "Gran didn't give you any trouble, did she?"

"Define trouble."

"I really don't want to know," she murmured. "I'll talk to her tomorrow and remind her to behave."

He squeezed her knee and let his hand linger. "She wanted a selfie of a hot guy in her bedroom to show all her friends at the seniors' center. All perfectly innocent fun." And then she'd said Pepper was very driven when she had a goal, and not to let that intimidate him like the "other pussies she dated before" did, but the way he'd handled everything so far suggested he was a champ.

"Did she grab your butt again?"

"Is she a one-and-done grabber, or a repeat offender? Because if she's a repeat grabber, I'm starting to get a complex about why she hasn't tried again."

A rueful smile lit her pretty eyes. "Don't tell Gran that unless you're serious."

"She's a remarkable woman."

"One in a hundred billion."

She went back to her plate, and her eyes slid shut again on her next bite of salmon. He liked food, and he'd done a bang-up job on dinner tonight, if he did say so himself. The salmon was perfect, the bacon was crisp, the asparagus delicious, and the rolls were cheesy heaven.

But much as he liked this meal, he liked watching her eat it more.

Every smile, every moan, every little compliment settled into the bucket of his self-worth that Tabitha had knocked over for him. And while he'd never admit to needing validation from another human being—especially a woman—he couldn't deny the relief at knowing he still had the ability to make someone else happy.

It made him want to cook for her again.

Every night.

Dangerous territory there.

But, hell, *being* here was dangerous territory. He could've spent the night home alone with Lucky. Probably should've. Could bolt any minute to wade over there and get home. But since the moment Pepper had offered her trade with him being her pretend boyfriend, he'd had something more to live for.

Even if he hadn't realized it at the time.

"Is yours okay?" she asked. "Or are you full of soup?"

The basement air held a chill. She was wrapped in a thick maroon sweater and black leggings, with mismatched socks—one red and white stripes, the other yellow with ducks. Her hair was tied at her nape, and as he sat there, holding her gaze, her eyes went dark.

"*Oh,*" she whispered.

"Eat your dinner," he rasped out. "It's getting cold."

She glanced at her plate on the spindle-legged coffee table, then back at him. "It's really good food. But you're pretty spectacular too."

He could work with this.

He scooted closer to her and pulled her plate across the dark wood surface until he could reach her utensils. When he lifted a bite to her lips, she leaned into him, her hand igniting sparks as she rested it on his thigh, her fingers tickling the inside of his leg.

"You let me know when you're done," he said.

She lasted three bites before she launched herself at him, hands roaming, shoving his clothes aside, lips clashing, her tongue seeking his. He was standing at attention below the belt, straining against his jeans, healthy and strong and ready to be tapped into the game. He tugged her hair loose, and the feathery softness surrounded him, teasing him with hints of orange and flowers on top of the sweet sugary scent of her skin.

"We should do this more often," she gasped as his fingers found her bra strap.

"Every fucking night," he agreed.

Her skin—like silk. Her moans—music. Her touch—heaven.

She cradled his hips between her thighs and kissed him, hot and frantic and desperate, on his lips, his jaw, his neck. *This* was what he craved.

Being wanted.

Being needed.

He grabbed the hem of her sweater and pulled it off. She tugged his shirt over his head, and then her hands were on his chest, rubbing, circling, tweaking his nipples and making his groin pulse. He palmed her breasts, perfect, just the right size for his hands, with those beautiful, delicious rosy tips, while her hungry eyes watched him.

Her fingers attacked his button, then his zipper. She tugged his pants down. He sprang free, and she wrapped both hands around him. He arched back, his head rolling on the couch arm while he thrust into her grip, his breath hissing out, her touch hot and cold, soft and hard, *everything*.

"Pepper—"

"I love how you feel." Her lashes lowered, and she stroked him again.

"Slow, baby," he whispered.

She dipped her head over him, her hair a curtain closing out the world. "I need you inside me."

A man didn't need a second invitation.

He fumbled for a condom and rolled it on. She pulled herself off the couch and peeled her lush hips and long legs out of her pants, that gorgeous, curvy body, full breasts, creamy skin—all his.

SPICED

Tonight, she was completely, unquestionably his.

He'd lost the ability to speak, to think, to breathe.

He had to be in her. To claim her. To own her.

Now.

He rose from the couch, hooked her by the waist, and spun her against the wall. Her eyes lit up, and when he crashed his lips to hers, she was smiling. She hooked one leg around his waist. He grabbed her other leg and lifted, and when he slid into her, they both breathed out the same hot moan.

"So good—" he gasped.

"More," she demanded.

He pulled back, then thrust into her, deep, full, desperate. Her moans and cries spurred him harder, faster, deeper, until her walls clenched around him, coaxing his own release.

She bit his shoulder. He pressed her hard against the wall, heart throbbing, cock twitching, stars dancing in his vision, bone-deep satisfaction settling in his soul.

"Definitely every night," she whispered into his neck, her breath tickling, but her body so warm and pliant and perfect.

"My place. Bed. Every night."

She giggled—Pepper Blue, *giggling* for him—and he slowly pulled out and lowered her back to the ground.

And that was when reality hit.

His condom had broken.

"*P*epper?"

"Hm?" She blinked sleepy eyes up at Tony, her body sated, her limbs loose, happiness radiating from a point so deep inside her, she finally understood true bliss.

"It broke."

She blinked again.

He wasn't smiling. His brown eyes weren't warm, and he'd gone pale as a ghost. "What—" she started, but a trickle between her legs answered the question.

The condom.

The condom had broken.

"It was new," he said. "Swear to god, a week old." He backed up, scrambled for a tissue, then grabbed his pants.

"Tony—"

"Are you—are you on birth control? When was your last period? This wasn't—it was brand new. I can't—are you?"

She tried to breathe, but the air was hiding in little bubbles around the room, unevenly scattered, making her search for it while a burn in her eyelids betrayed her.

Birth control?

What the hell for?

"Tony," she tried again.

He scrambled into his pants, not looking at her. "I'll do the right thing," he muttered. "I'll do the right thing."

Do the right thing for *who*?

"Tony," she whispered, "I can't get pregnant."

God. Saying it aloud was so—so final.

So real.

So *wrong*.

Why? Why did her body have to not work? Why did the condom have to break? Why did she have to say it? *Why?*

"Don't look at me like that." She squeezed her eyes shut and slid down the wall. Who cared if her body was naked?

She'd just bared her soul.

The linoleum was like ice on her butt cheeks, but her shaking came from the cold inside.

The emptiness inside.

Footsteps shuffled across the linoleum.

She gripped her knees tighter and buried her head. *Don't touch me. Don't touch me. Don't touch me.*

He didn't.

But she still felt the heat radiating off his body when he slid to the floor beside her.

"My wife was pregnant." His voice was thick and low. Raw. Hurt. Broken.

She shook her head. "I'm so—"

"It wasn't mine."

Her gasp caught her off guard. She lifted her head.

He was staring straight ahead, but she doubted he was seeing the Skee-Ball table.

"Don't look at me like that either," he said.

She shifted closer. Wrapped her hand around his bicep, right beneath his tattoo—*live, laugh, love*, she'd discovered it meant—and leaned into his body. "We're a mess, aren't we?"

215

"We are." His lips pressed her temple, hot and hard, and he covered her hand with his. "But we're not alone."

"Do you two dingbats realize it's two in the morning?"

Tony glanced at his watch, then at Cinna in a bathrobe and Pokémon slippers. He'd been too busy trying to beat the pants off Pepper in Skee-Ball to pay attention to the time.

"I didn't." He glanced at Pepper. "You?"

"Yes, but I didn't care." Pepper tossed another ball up the Skee-Ball table, and she did a happy butt-wiggle that made his groin twitch when she hit the top hole. "Ha! Beat *that*, pizza man."

"Is she drunk?" Cinna asked.

"This is called a natural high. Or possibly a second wind."

Or relief, Tony guessed. She'd told him a little more—her doctors had been testing her for a disease called PCOS, and she had it bad enough that they'd told her she'd never have children—and he'd confessed to meeting Tabitha's boy toy and father of her child when he burst into the delivery room to meet his daughter.

When Pepper had asked him to hand over her pants so she could pretend their conversation hadn't happened—and could he please forget it, seriously, because she hadn't told her family yet either—he'd been happy to oblige. They'd played Skee-Ball and watched movies most of the night.

She'd pause to squeeze his hand every now and again. He made excuses to kiss her.

And a peace he hadn't felt in years was slowly settling into his bones.

Was this what second chances felt like?

"Is Gran sleeping okay?" Pepper asked.

"She's snoring like a lumberjack, so I know she's still breathing. George is refusing to go out in the snow, but he's doing the potty dance upstairs. Thought you'd want to know."

"You came down here to tell me to take the dog out?"

"Actually, I was hoping to catch you passed out on the couch and drooling so I could post the picture to Facebook, but, yeah, this works too."

"I'll get him." Tony smelled a catfight coming, and the snow seemed a safer bet than staying in the basement.

Cinna looked him up and down. "She's got you whipped already, huh?"

"This is why we don't feed her after midnight." Pepper let one more ball fly and scowled when it landed lazily in the bottom tier. "I'll get the dog."

Which would probably entail shoveling a foot of snow at this point just to get the door open. He headed for the stairs. "No trouble."

He left the ladies downstairs, whispering like only women could, and retrieved his boots and coat from the front closet. Pepper had left a shovel by the back door, so he grabbed it and pushed his way out, George on his heels but not his leg for once.

Poor dog must've had to go bad.

Outside, a flurry of white was still swirling about the night sky. The snow was close to a foot deep already, a pristine sheet shimmering under the back porch light. Felt good to thrust the shovel into the thick, heavy wall and heft it off the patio.

Let his mind drift back to the way Pepper's body felt against his. Her mouth. Her skin. Her womanhood.

Two weeks ago, he would've been high-fiving his junk for finally performing. Celebrating being able to not just get it up, but follow through without embarrassing himself.

He'd forgotten his first rule of sex though.

It was never *just* sex.

It hadn't been when first he'd slept with his girlfriend his junior year of high school. It hadn't been with Tabitha before she'd claimed pregnancy made her not interested. And it hadn't been tonight.

And that was before he'd shared the worst moment of his life with her.

She was more than a warm body. She was a friend. A confidante. She was the moment he'd begun to come back to life, to live instead of just giving off the appearance of it. That little blip the night he'd delivered her pizza, then staking his claim during her date with the dinosaur-puppet man—she'd reminded him that the world still held little joys.

The back door opened behind him. Sadie hopped out and headed to the darkest cleared corner, and Pepper stepped out in a coat, mittens, scarf, and hat.

He couldn't suppress a smile. "Didn't have to get all bundled up for me."

She plunked a second shovel to the concrete. "I can shovel snow too, thank you very much."

Even in the dark, he knew that look. It was the same stubborn *I will own you* look her grandmother used when she was working up to an ornery idea. His smile turned to a laugh. "You *like* shoveling snow."

"I like being productive."

He propped his hands on the top of his shovel. "You want me to take a break so you can catch up?"

Her laughter mixed with the big wet snowflakes, and that spot in his chest right behind his breastbone went warm and squishy.

"Notice you're not denying a competitive streak," he said.

"No point." She dug her own shovel into the snowdrift and tossed the load up. "We're both going to pay for this tomorrow, aren't we?"

"Only if you're out of coffee."

"Pretty sure we're stocked. I don't drink it much. Cinna mainlines it though."

She shoveled snow like she lived life. Determined, mind over matter, sexy as hell.

She didn't fail, she'd said. Not willingly. She'd had a few crushing blows in her life, and she was fresh off another, but she was still standing.

How would she take a snowball fight?

"Don't do it," she said as though she'd read his mind. "I will take you *down*."

"Them's fighting words, Miss Blue."

Her gaze swung back to connect with his. Her lips parted and her brows went up. "I was talking to the dog. What, exactly, were you contemplating, pizza man?"

Getting in trouble, apparently.

She stood there, watching him, a slow smile growing on her lips.

He could beat her. He was bigger, stronger, faster. And closer to the snow. She had a four-foot swath cleared on all sides, but there was a big pile right behind him. He widened his stance.

She dropped her shovel and dove for the snow. He lunged and scooped up a handful into a snowball, then came up firing.

Her shriek of laughter lit up the night and made the falling snow sparkle. And it was just enough of a distraction for him to move too slowly to duck the snowball she lobbed at him.

Direct hit. Right to the chest.

In more ways than one.

PEPPER PEELED her eyelids open to bright sunshine streaming in her window and the explosive sound of Gran sneezing downstairs.

Eleven a.m. She'd almost slept through the morning after. Was Tony still here? Or had he gone home to check on his cat?

She threw off her covers and bolted out of bed. Her foot landed on something furry. Sadie yelped and bolted, and she stumbled over her own two feet, arms windmilling. Pain shot from her neck to her heels. She braced herself, arms out, and collided with the wall. "*Ouch!*"

Every single muscle in her body ached. Her calves. Her thighs. Her shoulders.

Even her pinky muscles ached, and she didn't think her pinkies had muscles.

"Finally up, sleeping beauty?" Tony pushed into her room, a steaming mug in hand, worry lines etched around his eyes.

"Debatable. You okay?"

"Gran lost her hearing aid. Need to go see how Pepperoni Tony's fared, but I didn't want to leave her alone."

"Cinna's gone?"

"Called in to Suckers for the early shift."

"Roads?"

"Getting there."

She took the mug from him and inhaled. Sweet chocolate tickled her nose. "You're good."

"You said you don't drink coffee."

She'd given it up when she'd started her fertility treatments.

For all the good it had done.

He slipped an arm around her waist. "Ask you something?" he said quietly.

She nodded against his shoulder.

"Can I take you out on a date?"

The mug bobbled.

A date.

A *real* date. With Tony. Who knew everything she could never give him. Who had his own demons.

Ten years ago, he would've been her last choice to fit into her life plan. Divorced, scarred, and overly private. Even one year ago, she would've weighed the pros and cons, the risks and the rewards, and she would've walked away.

But she wasn't that woman anymore.

And for once, she was damn glad.

"I'd love to go on a date with you," she whispered.

His smile wasn't a charmer smile. It wasn't big, but it also wasn't fake.

It was hope.

He cupped her ears and touched his lips to hers. "And then come back to my place," he added.

"I do like all those things you do in your kitchen."

"Have a bed to show you too."

She laughed a wobbly laugh. "I'd love to see it."

"Are you molesting my granddaughter in her bedroom?" Gran shoved in, her hair in pink curlers, still wrapped in her pink flowered bathrobe, bunny slippers flopping beneath her support socks. Her voice was froggy, her complexion too pale, but she didn't seem much worse than she'd been yesterday morning.

"Just looking for your hearing aid, Gran," Tony said easily.

"This man has been through every inch of trash in the house, lifted every couch, and even dug out beneath the fridge and oven for me," she said proudly.

Pepper frowned even as her heart squealed *and he's mine*. "Has he?"

"Sure has," Gran said.

Pepper quirked a brow at Tony. "Did you check her ear when you were looking?"

He blinked at her, then shifted a glance at Gran.

Gran smiled broadly at both of them, her hearing aid visible in her left ear.

He rubbed the dark stubble making him look like a pirate. "She only has one?"

"She only has one," Pepper confirmed.

"But I'm feeling a lot better," Gran announced.

She sneezed, and her top denture shot across the room.

Tony lifted his hands. "I'm out," he said. "You get to search for that one."

But he was smiling, and he kissed her again before beating a retreat.

"Call me," she said.

"Yes, ma'am," he replied from the stairwell.

Did she need a man in her life?

No.

But she was damn grateful to have Tony.

Tuesday evening found Tony whistling to himself as he double-checked that everything was locked up tight. He had two last pizzas in the oven. Dishes were done, the till was closed out, dough was proofing in the fridge overnight for tomorrow, and he had a beautiful woman due at his back door any minute now.

Hadn't been his first choice for a date, but he'd been short-staffed tonight, and since she'd texted that she was starving and in a mood for pizza fifteen minutes ago, having her here made sense. Quicker than fixing something at his house.

Plus, he liked watching her eat his food.

He checked his watch again. She'd said she was leaving her Knot Fest thing when she texted. Even if she'd walked, she should've been here by now. He headed to the back door to see if she was in the parking lot yet just as a knock came, and his heart went light-headed.

He opened the door, and there she was.

The pretty lady who'd offered to make sure his cat had enough food and water since he had to work late.

He pulled her in for a deep, lingering kiss while the door shut behind her. Her arm looped around his neck, her body melded to his, and for the first time since he'd left her place Saturday morning, the world was right.

She touched his cheek as they eased out of the kiss. "Hi," she whispered.

"Hi, yourself." He felt like an idiot, but he couldn't stop smiling. She was here. Smiling just as broadly back at him. Blushing? Or were her cheeks pink from the cold? "Hungry?"

"Starving. It smells amazing in here."

It smelled like her pizza needed to come out of the oven before it burned. He released her to grab a pizza paddle and opened the top oven. "One custom smoggy bacon special coming up."

"Is this your secret?" she asked. "The brick oven?"

"That and the dough. And the sauce. And the cheese."

"The cheese?"

"Top-secret supplier. Can't say any more than that."

She laughed. He was still smiling when he put her pizza on a pan. He pulled out the second pizza and slid it into a box, then sliced them both.

"Avocado?"

"Lindsey Truitt's having cravings. Billy called in a take-out order."

"Ah."

The sad he'd seen so much in her smile made sense now. Couldn't go ten feet in Bliss without running into a pregnant woman.

"You know them very well?" he asked.

"My sister Saffron used to play in Billy's band. And I basically bought Lindsey's half of Bliss Bridal. She's Nat's sister."

He flipped the box shut. "Lindsey told me about this place going up for sale."

"She said she loves your pizza."

"The respect is mutual."

Pepper's brow furrowed. "I didn't think anyone in Nat's family cooked."

"Wouldn't know."

"But you—oh. She handled your…got it."

He nodded and held out her pizza—sausage, mushroom, onion, green pepper, and extra bacon. "Powdered cheese?"

"I don't need to ruin perfection." She snagged a piece, still hot enough that the melted mozzarella stretched when she pulled it away. The crust was fluffy perfection, the cheese just starting to toast, and when her eyes slid closed and that delicious *mmm* slipped from her lips, not only did blood rush south of the border, but a peace settled in his chest.

He took compliments on his pizza every day, but watching Pepper enjoy it was bigger.

She was a woman who didn't need anyone to take care of her, but she was letting him feed her and enjoying every morsel.

"You are a pizza god," she declared.

"Just a guy with a gift."

"You still like pizza as much as you did when you were a kid?"

"I'll love pizza till my dying day."

She held out her slice, and he took a bite. The lady had a point. This one was perfect.

And she was within kissing distance again, propped against his prep table, her coat unzipped to let his hands settle around her waist with just a thin silk blouse between his fingers and her skin.

"Do you clean and do laundry too?" she whispered as he lowered his lips to hers.

"I do it all."

She tasted like pizza and perfection and felt like heaven. They were locked in. He could have her right here. Right now.

Her tongue touched his, and *could* became *would*. He went hard as granite in an instant. She pressed closer to him, her mouth eager, her fingers exploring and igniting his nerve endings, her breasts pressed to his chest.

He could've kissed her for making him feel whole again—not just physically, but emotionally—but he was already kissing her.

He'd just have to kiss her more.

Those whimpery noises she made, the way her fingers curled into his shirt and pulled it taut, the taste of her lips and tongue were driving him mad. Too many clothes. Too many barriers.

Too many—*shit*.

Too many knocks on the back door.

Pepper pulled back with a gasp. "Is that important?"

"Billy." He pointed to the box.

Damn well better have been Billy, anyway.

Pepper rubbed her hands over her bright pink cheeks. Her eyes were dark emeralds, glittery and bright, her breath ragged. Tony adjusted himself and headed to the door.

Sure enough, there was a happily grinning Billy Brenton, ball cap covering his hair, hunched into a thick coat against the backdrop of last weekend's snow piles. "You ever fall for a lady from the South,

jump at the chance to move down there with her," he said. "Colder'n a
—oh, hey, Pepper."

"I'm telling Lindsey you said that."

"Shoot, told her myself before I left to get her a pizza. The lady
thinks I'm funny."

Tony handed him the pizza box. Billy held out a bill with too
many zeroes on it, and Tony waved it away. "On the house."

"After-hours fee," Billy countered.

Pepper slid between them and plucked the Benjamin from Billy.
"Knot Fest thanks you both for your generous contribution," she said.
"Rule number one," she added to Tony, "arguing with Billy is pointless
unless you're married to him." She turned to Billy. "Rule number two,
don't make people uncomfortable. Do we need a group hug?"

"We're good," Tony said.

Billy laughed. "Like having Saffron back on the road." He tipped
his hat. "Y'all enjoy your evening."

"Oh, hey, wait." Pepper snagged his arm. "Does Lindsey know
what Nat and CJ named the baby?"

"Reckon so," he said, "but since she doesn't know CJ's real name,
don't think she's planning on sharing. Might be up for trading some
information though."

Tony didn't know what that all was about, but he could see
Pepper's wheels turning. "The baby's far more adorable than CJ. Does
she *really* need to know his name?"

"What I know about your family, information's gold. Never know
when it might come in handy." He rocked back on his heels and
grinned. "Don't let me keep y'all. Many thanks for the special order."

Pepper was still frowning at the door after he left. "Do you think
they really know, or is he pulling my leg?"

"Think your pizza's getting cold." He double-checked that he'd
turned off the oven, then flipped the lock on the back door. "Five
minutes to finish up, and we can head out." Go back to his place. Eat
more pizza. Grab a beer, get Pepper a glass of wine.

Show her his bedroom. This time while she was awake.

She picked up her half-eaten slice and studied it. "Does it bother you?"

"Pizza?"

"All the babies."

That stopped him as effectively as if he'd run into a brick wall. Babies. Weddings. Happy ever after.

It all bothered him.

"Never would've guessed it bothered you," he ventured.

Her wry smile didn't reach her eyes. "I've been an aunt a lot longer than I've been a failure."

"You're not—"

"I keep trying to tell myself that, but I'm not listening yet."

He eased closer to her. His arms ached to hold her, and his heart hurt for her. "Your family know yet?"

She shook her head. "Not ready for the inquisition and suggestions. Plus, things with Tarra and her breakup have gotten complicated. It's not my turn to be an attention hog, and I don't want the attention they'd want to give anyway."

"Family sucks sometimes."

"They mean well. They just... They think there's nothing I can't do. And I *like* that. I don't want to be like Ginger, always needing validation. I don't want to be like Cinna, bouncing around and mooching. But I don't know how *not* to be me with them. Even though I'm not feeling all that much like I'm good ol' Pepper Super Star right now."

"You're still standing."

"I'm faking it."

He pinned her against the prep table. Not touching her wasn't an option. "Know what you need?"

"Somehow, I doubt you're going to suggest a hug."

"Not even three weeks, and you already know me so well."

A smile broke through the clouds. A smile, and a spark of interest. Her fingers trailed down his chest. "What do I need?"

"Pizza." He snagged a piece behind her and brought it to her lips. "Pizza cures everything. Especially if you eat it while it's hot."

Her surprised laugh brought more sunshine into the kitchen. "And here I thought you were offering something else."

"Yeah, and you're going to need your energy."

He fed her two slices of pizza, teasing her and touching her and laughing with her. Then he locked up, took her home, and showed her his bedroom. Kicked Lucky out. Turned that laughter to gasps and moans.

And he lost himself in being with a woman who couldn't ever hurt him the way Tabitha had.

a week later, Pepper was unexpectedly alone after work. Cinna was tending bar at Suckers, and Mom had picked up Gran and George to take them to check out a new senior living facility. Sadie was asleep on the floor, and Pepper was trying to read a book.

But the house was too quiet.

She'd almost texted Tony eighteen times in the last twenty minutes, but she'd sent him some variation of *Want to come over?* or *Want company?* every night the last week. And every time, he'd cooked for her, entertained her with stories of life in the food industry, listened to her tales from the bridal industry, and in general, acted the part of the perfect boyfriend.

He *was* the perfect boyfriend. Her perfect boyfriend.

And the anxiety was settling in.

What if she was being too clingy? Wanting to see him too much? Stifling him?

What if she was getting boring?

Dating without the pressure of settling down, getting married, and having kids was amazing. She'd never had this much fun with another person, just talking and cooking and playing Skee-Ball. Ice skating. Snowball fighting. Making love.

But not having an end goal was weird.

Or was this the end goal? It didn't have a date, a milestone, or a way of measuring.

They simply...were.

But they could be more.

He knew she couldn't have kids. After his experience with his ex-wife, she had no idea if he wanted kids or not, but if he did, maybe he'd be open to adopting. In another few months, or maybe a few weeks if everything kept going well—

No.

No, this was about *today*. About no expectations. About fun and food and laughter.

She dropped her knitting needles and grabbed her phone.

Screw it. She liked him, he liked her, and if she wanted to text him, she would.

As her thumbs hovered over the screen, debating if she should send him the nonsensical joke Noah had told her at lunch today about ninjas crossing the road, or if she should simply ask if he was busy, a message popped up.

Chocolate bacon pizza—yes or no?

Her thumbs answered for her. *Will you marry me?*

"Oh, *shit*," she whispered to herself.

A bark of laughter outside her door answered.

Sadie lifted her head and sniffed at the door while Pepper tossed aside her knitting needles—one more thing she was proving incredibly inept at—and lunged for the door.

There he was, tall, dark, and drool-worthy in his red Pepperoni Tony's jacket, a square pizza box in hand, phone in the other. "Somebody call for a stripper?" His eyes were twinkling, his lips spread in a wide, amused smile.

"Gran's not here," she replied. "You'll have to strip just for me. While you feed me chocolate bacon pizza."

"It's messy." He stepped inside and kicked the door shut. "You should probably strip too."

"Tony Cross, are you trying to get me naked?" she asked.

"I'm trying to *keep* you naked."

If you don't quit feeding me like this, I'm going to balloon up like a house, she'd told him two nights ago after he made an amazing shrimp alfredo.

He'd snorted, rolled his eyes, and threw her over his shoulder to take her to his bedroom and kiss every last inch of her. And here he was again tonight, still touching her, nuzzling her neck, bringing her dessert—*all* the desserts—as though she were the sexiest woman on the planet.

Fun. Food. Laughter.

With kisses. And his hot hands sliding down her hips. Scents of garlic and onions and yeasty pizza crust, along with something sweet, tickled her nose. She pressed closer to the solid planes of his body, a thrill growing low in her belly where his hard length bulged against her.

She'd never enjoyed sex for the sheer pleasure of it. It had always been with a purpose, another step in trying out a potential mate. Was he good? Did she enjoy him as much in bed as she did out of bed? Would she want to sleep with him for the rest of her life?

A month ago, he would've been out of contention after their first mishap.

Now, she wished he'd toss her over his shoulder and carry her up the stairs to have his way with her.

"Delicious," he whispered as he pulled out of the kiss. A spark of mischief that he hadn't had two weeks ago lit his eyes. "Not sure you're as good as my pizza though."

"You lookin' for a fight, pizza man?"

"Your eyes turn the prettiest green when you jut your chin out like that." He bent to ruffle Sadie's fur and tugged her toward the kitchen. "C'mon. I need an opinion."

"Are you riling me up so that I won't go easy on you?"

"Depends. Is it working?"

"Not at all."

He laughed again.

Something was working. Because she couldn't stop smiling, and she couldn't let go of his hand either. The man was wiggling into those cracks in her soul, filling them and making her feel whole.

In the kitchen, he set the box on the table and filled a glass with tap water. She settled into a chair, peeked in the pizza box and discovered two different halves of Tony's puffy-crusted pizza. One half looked like a s'more had melted over it, with bacon bits sprinkled over the marshmallow, and the other looked like it was smeared with Nutella, then topped with bacon and a drizzle of frosting.

"What's the difference?" she asked.

"One's going on the menu. One isn't."

He took a seat beside her, his knee brushing hers while he lifted a slice of the Nutella side and held it to her lips. Chocolate and sweetness coated her tongue, with the salty bacon lingering as she chewed. Definitely Nutella. And real bacon. And that delicious brick-oven pizza crust.

He was marriage material. Without a doubt.

"Good?" he asked.

"Ohmygod," she replied.

"I'll take that as a yes." His shoulders, she realized. His shoulders didn't ride as high as they had when she'd met him. They were still broad, but not so close to his ears.

Warmth spread in her chest as well as her belly. Had she been good for him the same way he'd been good for her?

"Scale of one to ten?" he asked.

"Definitely an eleven."

"Your bias is showing, Miss Blue."

"If you weren't so stingy with the bacon," she added quickly.

He handed her the water, amusement dancing across his features. "Noted."

She took a sip while he lifted a slice of the second kind. "It's not marshmallow," he said. "No expectations, just taste."

Intriguing.

He held the pizza to her lips again, his hand resting casually on her knee, and this time, chocolate once again flooded her mouth, along with bacon, and...something creamy.

"Mmm," she breathed.

"Better or worse?"

"I'm going to have to try both again."

He leaned into her and captured her lips, and she giggled while she threaded her fingers through his thick hair and opened her mouth to him.

So fun. So easy.

"You're right," he said softly against her lips. "We need to try them both again."

"Several times," she breathed.

His eyes slid closed, and he tilted his forehead against hers. "I needed this," he whispered.

This?

Or her?

Because she was pretty sure she'd needed *him*.

She hadn't realized how badly she'd needed to put the *fun* back in her life. And he was fun in all the best ways.

"Me too," she whispered back.

This wasn't how she'd pictured her life going, but if she couldn't have kids, having Tony was a pretty damn good second.

———

Two hours later, every limb in Tony's body was sated and happy. Pepper was nestled in his arms, her curvy rear tucked against him, her bare skin warm and flushed in the low light cast by the lamp on her bed stand. Her fingers trailed lightly down his forearm. "I could get used to this," she said softly.

So could he. "The food or the company?"

"Both." She twisted in his arms until she faced him, and her fingers went to his cheeks. "You should offer both."

"At the shop? I didn't think Bliss was that kind of town."

Her sleepy smile set his heart beating a different beat—not racing, not dragging, just...happy.

"The chocolate bacon pizzas," she said. "You should offer both for a limited time, and take votes on social media about which one should stay."

"You give the best pillow talk."

"Would you rather have sweet nothings?"

"No, it's hot when you give me business advice."

She narrowed her eyes at him. He pulled her tight to him by the hips, pressing his once-again growing erection against her soft belly, and the suspicion turned to interest. "You *do* like it when I talk business to you."

"I like it when you talk anything to me," he said before he could think better of it.

Her delectable lips spread in a wide smile, a soft light lit her pretty green eyes, and his heart went deeper into its satisfied beat. She closed the distance between their mouths, licking and sucking and teasing, her fingers igniting a trail of need along his arms and chest.

He could almost pretend he didn't hear his phone buzzing in his pocket on the floor.

Nothing good ever came of buzzing.

Especially when he was losing himself in a woman, all his parts working, his brain on board, his heart almost whole.

"Is that your phone?" Pepper whispered.

"Probably a bug." He grazed his teeth over her shoulder, hands sliding lower to the sweet curve of her rear end.

"Ssh." She pushed him back. "Is that *my* phone?"

"It's mine. Ignore it."

"It's been buzzing for five minutes."

It had not, but she had that look. That stern librarian of his fantasies look. "You know you're incredibly sexy when you're being bossy?"

"They've called at least four times."

"If I answer it, will you do that thing with your tongue again?"

"*Tony.*"

Right. Could be something wrong at Pepperoni Tony's. Four calls was probably worth checking. He rolled off the bed and snagged his pants.

When he pulled his phone out, the buzzing stopped. His sister's name flashed over the screen, along with a list of four missed calls.

From her.

In the span of half a heartbeat, the worst-case scenarios flashed through his head. His nephew in a car accident. His niece thrown off a horse at one of her riding competitions. Francie with a cancer diagnosis.

His father with a heart attack.

The phone immediately rang again, again with Francie's name popping up. His thumb slipped when he tried to swipe to answer the first time, and he had to swipe again. "Hey, what's wrong?"

"Other than having a brother who won't pick up the phone? Having a brother who *still* hasn't sent in his RSVP card for his niece's wedding."

The teasing note in Francie's voice set his nerves at ease, but her message sparked his irritation instead. "That's all?"

"I could add that my children have forgotten your name since you never call, and I've had to talk to Louie six times myself this week, but instead, I suppose I'll let you off at *that's all.*"

He eased back to sit on the floor against the side of the bed. Pepper's fingers laced through his hair, her short nails giving his scalp a light scratch.

"Like I told Bella, I'll be there," he said begrudgingly to Francie.

"Alone? Or are you bringing someone?"

He glanced back at Pepper. She tilted a brow.

"Put me down for two," he told his sister.

"Officially? This counts as sending in your card, and I will hunt you down and *end* you if you don't show up."

So dramatic. "Officially."

"Praise be, the man's making a commitment."

If he didn't know his sister so well, he might've been offended. "You're hilarious. I'm hanging up now."

"Love you, brat."

"Love you too, bossy-face."

He hung up and let the phone slip through his fingers to the carpet. Pepper's fingers trailed down his neck. "Everything okay?" she whispered.

No. No, it wasn't okay. "Yeah. All good."

"You're a terrible liar."

He grunted. "My family's not quite as awesome as yours."

The mattress banged his shoulders. Her hands left his scalp and neck, but came back wrapped around him, her fingers lingering on his chest.

"I didn't talk to Basil for three years once," she said. "I'd just started dating, and he was home from seminary for a little break. My boyfriend and I were going to go to a movie, but Basil answered the door, had a two-minute conversation with him, and the next thing I knew, he was leaving without me. I didn't have a car, so I couldn't follow him. He wouldn't talk to me at school, and finally sent a note through a friend that my family was, quote, *fucked up* and we were done. As far as I knew, he didn't date anyone else until after he graduated high school the next spring, and I heard he met his wife his first week in college."

"So it's Basil's fault you have this little curse?"

"Yes. Let's go with that. Always blame the priest."

He smiled. "You two get along now?"

"Sure. A few months before he took Holy Orders, he came to see me and apologized. An apology from Basil is more rare than being struck by lightning and seeing a tyrannosaurus rex on the same day.

Just in case you haven't picked up on why CJ calls him His Holy Obnoxiousness."

"You must've really liked the guy."

"I don't know if I liked him, or if he fit the mold of what I wanted in a boyfriend. I actually forgave Basil well before the three years was over, but I deserved an apology, and I knew it. Time can wash away a lot, but time passing isn't the same as everything being *right*."

He gripped her forearm and rubbed her cool skin. "I hate weddings."

"For obvious reasons, or...?"

"When my dad married his mistress, Mom made me go. It was the worst day of my life. Came home and told her I hated her. She made me chocolate chip cookies. Only time I ever got away with giving her lip."

Pepper pressed a kiss to his cheek. "Because you picked her."

Huh. Hadn't considered that. "All the men in my family get divorced. And my sisters are all married, but I don't know that I'd say happily. Except maybe my mom's later kids. You know how hard it is to sit there on what's supposed to be the happiest day of someone's life and wonder how long it'll be before your niece's heart is broken?"

"Maybe her generation will be different."

"She's nineteen. She acts eighty-five, but she'll always be three to me. Definitely not old enough. Hell, I was in my thirties, and *I* wasn't old enough."

She dipped her head to rest on his shoulder, hanging over the edge of the bed, still wrapped in covers. "Your divorce wasn't your fault, Tony."

Wasn't it? He might not have cheated, and he might've done everything in his power to make Tabitha happy, but he'd chosen to marry her. Maybe that was where he'd gone wrong. "You only say that because you don't know my deep dark secrets."

"That's okay. You don't know about that thing I keep under my bed either."

It took every ounce of self-control not to lean over and look. "Can't be worse than a dead blow-up goat."

"You're trying not to peek under there, aren't you?"

He twisted to face her, and her bright, mischief-tinted smile, coupled with the come-hither crook of her finger, topped off with the hint of bare shoulders and breasts, put him solidly back in his own happy zone. "There's somewhere else I want to peek," he said.

Her brow suddenly furrowed. "Why did you need a pretend girl-friend to a wedding you hadn't committed to going to?"

Oops. He'd used that, hadn't he? A rare heat rose up his neck. *Because you made me sprout wood* had been the answer a few weeks ago. "Just in case."

She studied him, lips pursed.

"And I was enjoying myself for the first time in ages," he added, though the admission put some heat in his neck and cheeks. He tucked a lock of hair behind her ear. "I wanted a little more time."

She pulled him back onto the bed. "I'm glad one of us was smart that day," she whispered. Her arm hooked around his neck, and she pulled him in for a kiss, and then another, and for the rest of the night, Tony was finally, absolutely, unquestionably living in bliss.

*a*n early March heat wave had zapped the last of the blizzard snow and put Pepper in linen pants, a short-sleeve tunic, and a light jacket as she and Gran walked into Pepperoni Tony's behind Max and Merry for lunch two weeks later.

"I never should've told Max to get a garage right next to this place," Merry said. "It smells *so* good in there all day long, I can't help coming here for lunch every day."

Marinara sauce, melted cheese, and baking crust tickled Pepper's nose, and her mouth watered. "You're working at the garage too?"

"Have laptop, will travel. But I might have to start writing something else on the side, because I do *not* have kid-appropriate thoughts when I'm watching Max with a wrench." She fanned herself. "And Tony's not helping. Have you tried his gourmet cheese pizza?"

"Does it have aphrodisiacs in it?" Gran asked.

"Depends on how much you like cheese," Max told her. "You found yourself someone special here in Bliss?"

"Sonny, everyone's someone special. But I'm still looking for the one good enough to peek under my knickers."

"Party of four?" one of the servers that Pepper didn't recognize asked.

"You go on back there and tell the boss his lady's here," Gran said. "And that I want some of this gourmet aphrodisiac cheese pizza."

"Yes," Pepper said quickly when the poor girl's eyeballs threatened to fall out. "Table for four, please."

"Your life must be so very interesting right now," Merry murmured.

"That's one word for it."

The server led them to the back room, where someone called her name. Lindsey and Will were tucked into a quiet corner in the back room, along with Mikey and Dahlia.

And a baby.

An unwelcome, surprised swell of grief pinched her heart.

"Come settle a tie." Mikey lifted the baby bundle with a big grin. "Lindsey says TJ is cuter than Evelyn."

"He is," Lindsey said.

The server pointed to the table next to the happy fivesome. Max and Merry settled in with a wave at the happy parents, but Gran followed Pepper to look at the baby.

Evelyn was wrapped in a pink baby blanket with cartoon guitars all over it, her little head covered with a pink knit teddy bear cap, and she was sucking on her fist, big blue eyes staring intently up at Mikey.

She had to swallow twice before she could speak. "She's beautiful. Congratulations. I didn't realize you'd had her."

"Six hours of labor, three pushes, and boom! My girl's the rock star in this house." Mikey beamed at Dahlia. "And her boobs got bigger too."

"Always with the boobs." Dahlia sighed, but she was smiling just as big.

"It pains me to say this," Pepper said to Lindsey, "but Evelyn is definitely cuter. And what an adorable name."

"This is because you don't know TJ's real name, isn't it?"

Pepper smiled sweetly. "Of course not."

"I agree," Gran declared. "And it *is* because I know Evelyn's name."

A familiar hand slid over Pepper's back. "Hey," Tony said. His eyes slid toward the table, then back to Pepper, and it was a little thing, but the slight tightening of his lips and softening of his eyes said it all. *You okay? Babies shouldn't be this hard.*

"Hey, yourself." She smiled as he kissed her cheek.

"My turn," Gran announced, and he obliged her with a peck to her cheek too. Gran went up on her toes. "And to think your waitress didn't believe you might have the hots for me."

"I'd apologize," Pepper murmured as both tables laughed, "but I think we're past that."

"We are," he agreed.

She congratulated Mikey and Dahlia again, then pulled Gran back to the table with Max and Merry. But Tony snagged her arm before she could sit. "Borrow you a minute?"

"What for?" Gran demanded.

"A quickie in the kitchen."

"Oh, by all means then." Gran waved them away. "I'll just tell this kind young couple about how awful people get when an elderly woman accidentally pulls a fire alarm at a senior living facility."

Pepper's eye twitched. Tony was chuckling as he pulled her back into the front dining room. "Good thing she's cute," he said.

"She's actually been an angel at home. I think she's afraid I'll kick her out if George pees in my plants like he did at that facility Mom took them to last week. And she knows she has to clean up any food fights she starts in my house."

He was smiling as he pulled her through the kitchen to his little office, where he slammed the door, pulled her close, and kissed her.

"Wow," she said a few minutes later when they came up for air.

He grinned. "You should stop by for lunch more often."

Someone knocked at the door. "Hey, boss, that old lady in the back room's causing some trouble."

Pepper sighed.

Of course she was.

They returned to the dining room, where Gran had squirted honey mustard dressing all over the ceiling. Evelyn was crying, and

Mikey was eyeing Gran as though he wanted to hang her by her toes from the ceiling fan. Will, Lindsey, Max, and Merry were all sucking in their cheeks, and the rest of the customers were gawking with undisguised glee.

Tony put his fists on his hips, sent a look at the ceiling, and then pinned Gran in his sights. "This one's gonna cost you."

She clapped. "Are you gonna spank me?"

Lindsey choked on her water, most of the men grimaced, and a few people snickered behind them.

And Tony?

First his lips twitched on the left. Then the right. "You win this round," he said to Gran. "But I know where you sleep."

"Hot diggity." Gran pumped a fist in the air. "Better watch out, Pepper. I told you your boyfriend has the hots for me."

Tony was staring at the yellow glob on the ceiling. Head tilted back, lips straight, a five o'clock shadow starting already. He rubbed his chin, then tucked his hands under his arms, thinking.

And unless she was way off base, he was contemplating clearing the room out and letting Gran finish her mustard-dressing master-piece on the ceiling.

"The health department wouldn't like that," she said.

He blinked down at her, surprise and then amusement dancing in his dark eyes. "Wouldn't like what?"

"Salad-dressing art. And I'll kill you with my own two hands if you help her ego get any bigger."

"How did you—" he started, but he stopped himself with a shake of his head and a wry laugh.

How did she know?

The same way he knew babies were her weakness. The same way he'd known she played sports in high school. The same way he knew she'd never kick her grandmother out.

She just knew. Because she knew *him*. His strengths. His weaknesses. His sense of humor. His heart.

She'd thought she was done with men.

Now she couldn't imagine her life without Tony in it.

Ever.

And that might've been the scariest situation she'd faced all year.

PEPPER DIDN'T KNOW exactly what to expect of Tony's family, but big, loud, and boisterous—much like her own—pretty much covered the reality.

Tony had been stiffer than his sister's hairdo, and Pepper hadn't been entirely certain he wasn't going to object to the wedding when the priest asked, but they'd made it through Bella's wedding and were now seated at a round table in the back banquet hall of the biggest Italian restaurant in Willow Glen.

"A *month*?" one of his sisters—the one with the dress that made her look like a spotted apple and a beauty mark just below her ear—was saying. "You've been dating a *month* and we haven't met you yet? He usually brings his bimbos by as first dates."

The teenage girl beside her rolled her eyes. "Don't call Uncle Tony's dates *bimbos*, Ma. Most of them are smarter than you are. Do we have to stay for the dancing? I told Logan I'd go to the movies with him tonight."

Tony's eye twitched. His sister's eye twitched. Their aunt Josefina —seated on Tony's other side—stared at the teenager as though she were silently working an old family curse in the girl's direction. Either that, or the antipasto appetizer had given her gas.

"This is why you should never have children," Tony's sister declared with a pointed jab in his direction.

Pepper reached into her purse. "Hershey's Kiss?" she asked the table at large.

The teenager lunged. So did her little brother and Aunt Josefina.

"What is it you do?" the teenager asked Pepper.

"She runs half of Bliss," Tony answered for her.

His sister's eye twitched again, which seemed to make Tony's eye twitch again.

"My uncle's second wedding was in Bliss," the teenager said.

"I threw up," her little brother volunteered. He was probably eight, maybe nine. "It was *epic*. Like even better than that scene in *Phoebe Moon and the Sneeze Snatchers* when—"

"That book is *so* for babies," his sister interrupted.

"I love Phoebe Moon," Pepper told the boy. "And did you know Amber Finch lives in Bliss?"

His eyes went round. "Nuh-uh."

"Yep. And she comes into your uncle Tony's place for lunch almost every day."

Tony sent her a curious look.

"Loves cheese pizza," she supplied. "Practically lives in the garage next door."

"Huh. Didn't know that."

"Mom, can I go to Uncle Tony's for lunch tomorrow?" the boy asked.

"We're helping Bella sort presents tomorrow."

"Awww, *Moooooom*," he groaned.

"Tony, my boy," a big voice boomed behind them. "You planning on introducing us to your beautiful date, or do I have to steal her away?"

And there went his shoulders, dancing with his earlobes.

Pepper turned in her seat and stuck a hand out. "Hi. I'm Pepper."

The man was Tony thirty or forty years into the future. Silver streaked his dark hair, distinguished wrinkles carved into all the right places, his belly about the size Pepper expected her own to be soon after all the food she'd been eating lately. He took her hand, bent over it, and pressed a kiss to her knuckles. "Such a beautiful name for a beautiful woman."

"She's a little old for you, Dad."

His sister cracked up. That was something. Pepper extracted her hand and kept a bland smile on her face.

"You make sure you get out there for the bouquet toss," Tony's dad said with a wink. "We love our weddings. And save a dance for me."

So maybe his family wasn't *entirely* like hers.

But it was big. And loud. And boisterous.

And when she squeezed Tony's hand under the table, his lips settled into a resigned line.

For today, that close to a smile was practically a miracle.

TONY WAS BEING AN ASS TODAY, and he knew it. He *wanted* to be happy for Bella, but even she'd seemed to sense that his heart wasn't in the hug and congratulations he'd offered in the receiving line. Pepper had covered for him—how had she become his better half so quickly? —and then endured a so-so pasta dinner and a thinly veiled, suspicious inquisition with cheerful grace.

While Tony had barely refrained from taking an entire bottle of wine all for himself.

This wedding was worse than Pepper's sister's non-wedding, because *this* wedding was full of all the people who knew where his life had gone off track. They knew about Tabitha. They knew about the baby. If Bella knew, then they probably all knew he'd been faking his way through dating women the last year, and they almost certainly knew his pizza location in Bliss hadn't taken off as quickly as it should've.

And here he was, supposed to be happy for his niece, when all he could see was bleakness in her future.

Pepper had excused herself after cake to hit the ladies' room, so he'd followed suit. Now, he was walking out of the men's room between the restaurant's main dining room and their banquet hall, wondering if he could talk her into cutting out early, when a toddler streaked by him.

"Destiny, *stop!*"

The little girl didn't stop, but Tony did.

Froze, actually. Rooted right there, his heart suddenly spinning up into his throat, pulse launching like a rocket, knees tingling.

Turn around, his brain ordered. *Back into the bathroom.*

But his body was in lockdown mode.

And that was before he smelled the gardenia perfume.

"Destiny, I said—"

The little girl—the little girl who should've been *his*—was suddenly yanked before she reached the banquet hall. Her mother hadn't spotted him yet. He could turn, duck back into the men's room, ignore this, pretend he hadn't seen her, except his feet were cemented to the ground.

She turned and made eye contact, her eyes flared, and she visibly tightened her grip on the squirming child. "Tony."

He could barely nod in response. A giant diamond glittered on her left hand, and the little girl was staring at him with her mother's eyes.

The door to the ladies' room swung open, and Pepper stepped out. She looked left, started to smile at him, and then she, too, stopped.

"Lookin' good," Tabitha said.

He couldn't feel his face, but he suspected *good* wasn't the right word.

That little girl should've been his.

The ladies' room door swung open again, and Francie nearly collided with Pepper. But where Pepper was suddenly moving to Tony's side, hand extended to grab his, clearly uncertain as to what was going on, Francie took one look and went into screeching harpy mode.

"Tabitha? Oh. My. God. What the *fuck* are you doing here, you *bitch*?"

A cool hand settled in his. "Hey." Pepper nudged him. "You okay?"

Tabitha picked the little girl up and put her on her hip. "Don't you use that language in front of my daughter."

"How *dare* you come into *my* daughter's wedding after what you did to our family?"

Tony wasn't seeing red. Not like Francie was.

No, he was seeing his future.

A future where Tabitha got to have a family with a husband and kids. Where his siblings and nieces and nephews would have weddings he wouldn't want to be at. Where he was married to his work and where one day, Pepper would recover after her own personal struggles and realize he wasn't all that and move on.

Because he wasn't forever material.

It wasn't in his genes.

The proof was right there. Right there with the two women about to launch into a fistfight despite an innocent little babe being between them. The restaurant's staff and a few patrons were gathering to watch from the main dining room. His family had noticed the commotion from the banquet hall.

This would be all anyone talked about whenever Bella's wedding came up.

For years.

"Oh, for pity's sake," Pepper said on a sigh.

She pulled her hand away, stuck her fingers in her mouth and whistled. "You." She pointed at Francie. "Go back to the wedding, *right now*. And you." She turned her finger to Tabitha. "I have half a clue who you are. And if you don't want me to get the full clue— which, I highly suspect you don't—you're going to take that innocent child and leave. Aah-ah." She wiggled her finger in a *no-no* gesture when Tabitha opened her mouth. "You want to be a good mother, you're going to take that baby out of here before this gets ugly. And you're not going to like *my* brand of ugly, because I don't have a single thing to lose. Understood?"

Tabitha went white as a ghost.

Which Tony didn't appreciate nearly as much as he should've. His equipment might've started working again, but he obviously still didn't have full possession of his man card, or his girlfriend wouldn't have to come riding to his rescue just because his ex-wife was standing there.

He didn't wait to see if Tabitha left.

Instead, he shouldered past all of them and made his way to the bar.

This kind of day called for a drink.

———

TONY HADN'T SAID MORE than four words in the last two hours, but he'd had about six shots of bourbon, and Pepper was starting to worry about him. His sister—the one they'd had dinner with, Joella, she thought—finally helped her get him out of the wedding and into his truck.

"I'm sorry I called you a bimbo," she said sheepishly once they had Tony closed in the truck.

"I have twelve siblings. I've been called worse."

"He just…hasn't been himself the last year."

"Who would be?"

Joella paused with one hand on the truck. "I miss him. He never comes back to visit, and when he does, he's always bringing some girl who tries too hard, like she thinks she's going to be the one who heals him. He's a really great guy."

Was that what they thought of Pepper? That she was trying to heal him? "Bliss isn't that far away, and he *does* run a pizza place open to the public. Go see him. He'd probably appreciate the visit."

The other woman looked back toward the restaurant. The raucous sounds of laughter and music were still carrying out into the night. "He's not like our brothers. We all thought he'd be the one to make it. And now—now, I don't think he'll ever get married again. Just so you know."

Pepper had no idea if she'd ever get married, but for today, she didn't need to be. "Go on back in there and enjoy the rest of the reception. I'll take good care of him."

Joella nodded. "Thank you."

Tony didn't sleep most of the way back to Bliss, but he didn't say much either. Pepper couldn't tell if he was mellow from the alcohol, sleeping with his eyes open, or just contemplating how life looked through bourbon goggles. When she helped him through the front door, Lucky greeted them with a plaintive yowl.

Tony threw himself face-first onto the couch. "I fucking hate weddings."

She smiled and settled on her knees beside him. "You okay?"

"Shoulda moved to Canada. I'd be a good Canadian."

She ran her fingers through his hair. "You'd be the best," she agreed.

He tilted his head to look at her. "But I like your boobs. All four of them."

"They like you too," she said on a laugh. Poor man would hurt tomorrow.

"I was off boobs before I met you."

"I was off dicks before I met you."

He snorted a sloppy laugh. "Mine didn't work."

"Your boobs?"

"My dick. It was dead. Ding-dong dead. Until you. You made my dick work again."

Yep, he would definitely hurt tomorrow if he was far enough gone to tell stories about his penis not working. "You're very funny."

"Mean it. No wood. No boners. Ever. Tabitcha broke me. You fixed me. Mmm. Boobs."

He rubbed a hand over her chest. Her nipples pebbled to attention, and she ordered them to behave. "You need water."

"Just need you. You make all of me work again."

Her heart swelled to twice its size. "You make me work again too."

She didn't believe for a minute that he'd had equipment problems, and he couldn't fix *her* equipment problems, but he was everything else. Her friend. Her lover. Her partner.

Her everything.

She didn't care if he never wanted to get married. If he could never say he loved her.

So long as he didn't leave her.

A snore slipped out of his lips, and his head settled deeper into the couch. "Hey, it's bedtime."

"I love going to bed with you."

She loved him.

The realization hit with enough force to jolt her back. She loved him.

"Tony, wake up. Just enough to walk to the bedroom, okay?"

He grunted, another snore emanating from his chest, and her heart swelled again. She'd always expected love to come with a shower of hearts, bouquets of flowers, fancy dinners, long walks around a lake. Not creep up on her while she was fooling herself into thinking she was just indulging in a mutually beneficial friends-with-benefits relationship.

But she did.

She loved him.

She loved the way his eyes twinkled when he was teasing her. She loved the way he hovered his fork over his own dinner when he cooked for her, waiting to see if she liked it before he dove in. She loved the way he slept with one hand curled around his rescue cat. She loved the way he appreciated Gran and her siblings, and the way he got along with her friends, and the way he'd come to treat Sadie as if she were a normal dog.

She loved that he wasn't perfect, that he had baggage, and that he might never be whole.

Because she was pretty much the same.

"Let's go." She disentangled herself from him and pulled him upright. Not exactly an easy feat, but he snore-snorted and startled himself awake. "You'll be more comfortable in your bed."

A glassy-eyed, goofy smile crossed his face. "Pretty lady come to see me."

How could she *not* love him? "Stand up, studmuffin. I'm not strong enough to carry you."

"You're strong enough for both of us."

Finally, she got him to his feet and to the bedroom. He stripped along the way and face-planted across the bed, showcasing his perfect butt cheeks in his suit. Lucky hopped up on the bed beside him. Pepper got a glass of water, rummaged through his medicine cabinet for Tylenol, borrowed a shirt for pajamas, and pushed him to the side as best she could.

He probably didn't need her.

But she'd be there if he did.

*S*omeone had wedged a pizza slicer into Tony's brain. That bourbon needed a warning label. Or perhaps his family did.

He followed the scent of coffee into the too-bright kitchen.

"Morning, sleepyhead." Pepper's cheerful voice should've been as grating as the sunshine. Instead, it put a warmth in his chest. She was here. He hadn't dreamed her being next to him last night. Details of when and how they'd gotten home—and what he'd said and all the horrific glory of the wedding—were fuzzy, but she was here.

She slid him his favorite mug—an oversize number with *Pizza is life* scrawled in red over the white porcelain—and touched cool fingers to his forehead to brush his hair back. "Feeling okay?"

He grunted and lifted the steaming coffee to his lips. She held out two Tylenol, and he almost asked her to marry him.

Toast popped out of his toaster. She snagged a plate from the cabinet, slid out the silverware drawer for a knife, and turned to the fridge, bustling about fixing breakfast as though she'd done it in his kitchen every morning of her life.

That warmth in his chest swelled almost as big as the pain behind his eyeballs.

She slathered strawberry jam on the toast. "Belly okay?"

It rumbled in response.

Her laugh almost undid him. She was so bright. So happy.

So good for him. "Thanks."

She put the toast on the island behind him and reached up to rub his temples. His eyes dropped closed, and the pain put up a good fight, but it was no match for her cool fingertips.

"You gonna be okay today?" she asked softly.

"Gonna live." His phone dinged somewhere, and he winced without opening his eyes. Probably one of his brothers or sisters checking on him. "Don't usually drink like that."

And he shouldn't have let Tabitha get to him last night. He needed to buck up and be a man about it.

Be a man.

Oh, *fuck*. He pried his eyelids open.

Pepper was still rubbing away the pain at his temples, standing close enough to suggest either her sense of smell was dead, or she was a freaking goddess. Her smile was soft. Not mocking, not laughing. Just caring. Warm. Sympathetic.

To his state this morning?

Or to his drunken confession?

"I'm never drinking again," he muttered.

"Oh, I don't know. You were pretty funny last night."

Teasing. Definite teasing. He swallowed hard. "Did I compliment you on having four breasts?"

"Yep." The extra sparkle in her bright eyes wasn't good. "We'll have to work on you being nicer to yourself though."

He should've laughed. Said something sarcastic. Changed the subject.

But his brain was moving at the speed of frozen sludge, and his face was getting hotter than the coffee.

He'd told Pepper he'd been impotent.

"Yeah," he said belatedly. Toast. He needed toast. And for her to leave.

Twisting out of her reach felt wrong, but he had to. Before she realized—

"You were serious," she said softly.

"Go away."

"Tony."

Her hand settled on his back. He jerked away. Jackhammers exploded in his head, and he had to grip the island countertop for balance.

Soft arms wrapped around him from behind. She pressed a kiss to his spine. "It's okay."

"No, it's not." He looked down at the toast, and his stomach lurched. One more thing he didn't need anyone else to see. One more way he'd broken himself. "Let go."

She ignored him and held him tighter.

As though she were holding him up. Offering to be his rock. His stability. Patching him back together and keeping him from falling to pieces.

How could she not know that relying on her would break him? He didn't need anyone else. He didn't *want* anyone else. Not like this.

Not if it meant giving her the power to crush him.

"Go—" he started again.

"Don't," she whispered. "Please don't push me away."

Push her away. Reject her. Protect himself from her.

Do to her what he was afraid she'd do to him.

His heart thumped under her hand. He didn't want to hurt her. Hell, he didn't want her to go. But he didn't know if he could let her all the way in.

He licked his lips. Swallowed hard. Set his pulse hammering harder. He'd spent over a year burying himself in work, pretending he was dating woman after woman, he was fine, that he didn't need anything else in his life.

Lying to himself.

The lies were comfortable. But they hadn't made him happy. Not like she had.

"Found out the baby wasn't mine in the delivery room a week or so after Thanksgiving," he said. "Mom was diagnosed with cancer at Christmas. Died mid-January. I lost my daughter. I lost my wife. I lost my mother. Pepperoni Tony's was all I had left. It was the only thing that understood me. Nothing else mattered."

She rubbed his racing heart. "Lot to go through alone."

He pushed the plate across the countertop. "You're going to be late to work." Hell, it was Sunday. Did she work on Sundays? He didn't know.

"Close your eyes."

"For what?"

"Shush. Close your eyes."

He obeyed. Mostly because he didn't want her to let go.

"Are they closed?"

"Yes."

"Good. What do you see?"

"The backs of my eyelids."

"Imagine it's a pile of dirt."

"Pepper—"

"Do it or I'm telling Lucky to pee on you."

"My cat doesn't take orders."

"I'll bring George over."

He didn't mean to shudder, but she'd caught him off guard. "My cat could take him."

"As good as that would be for George, right now, we're talking about you. Can you see a pile of dirt?"

Sure. He was picturing it on top of the last of the melting snow in his small backyard, piled waist high. A nice, brown, muddy stack of dirt. "Are we getting dirty, Miss Blue?"

"Imagine every speck of dirt is something someone you love did to hurt you."

His teeth clenched together, and the mound grew like a mountain rising out of the ground. "This is stupid."

She pinched his nipple.

"Ow!"

"Close your eyes. Picture the dirt. Now get a shovel, or a backhoe, or whatever, and shovel it into a box. It's a Mary Poppins box—it'll hold way more dirt than you think it will."

He grunted, but he pictured it. A massive pile of disappointment and heartbreak, starting with finding out his father was leaving them for his other family and ending with Tabitha leaving him for her other family. The pain. The outrage. The blackness. The impotence. All of it in a big, massive, shitty heap of dirt.

Him driving a big old yellow backhoe, feeling the power, thrusting the machine into that pile of shit and dropping it into a box. A small box—smaller than his oven—but since Pepper said it would fit, it did. The magic cardboard box took eight scoopfuls of dirt, and even when he tried to miss, the dirt went in the box.

"Can you drive a backhoe?" he asked.

"No talking until your pile is gone."

"It's half gone. Box is full."

"All right. We can work with that. Put your backhoe away and grab a torch."

He started to grin. The backhoe disappeared like magic, and he was suddenly holding a massive flaming torch, the kind they used in post-apocalyptic movies to light dark caves.

"You've got the torch?" Pepper asked.

"Mm-hmm."

"Light the box on fire."

"Dirt doesn't burn."

"Your brain is a magical place, Tony. Light the box of dirt on fire."

He imagined himself touching the torch to the box. The cardboard lit and flamed, and the dirt inside it lit on fire too. Sparks shot off it as though the dirt were made of sparklers. Firecrackers shot out of the box. The dirt pile burped, and lava launched into the sky.

He let out a satisfied chuckle.

"Burning good?" she asked.

"One hell of a show," he said. And one hell of a good time. He hadn't shot off firecrackers in years.

"Feeling better?"

He blinked his eyes open.

The untouched toast still sat on Mom's old china plate, Lucky was slinking toward the back door to drop a play mouse in her water again, and Pepper was once again rubbing his chest right over his heart.

And he felt twenty pounds lighter. "Yeah," he said.

But as realization settled in, tension crawled back into his shoulders.

"Relax," she said. "This is about *you*. Nobody else has to know how you feel inside. Just you. You deserve some peace. Let yourself have it."

He closed his eyes again and imagined the burning box. It was a low, hot fire now, embers burning to the ground, the other half of the dirt pile still there. He climbed back into the backhoe, found a new box, and tackled the rest of his baggage. He knew he was standing in his kitchen, Pepper still behind him with her arms wrapped around his waist and chest, but he could feel the rumble of the backhoe's engine, see the pile of dirt getting smaller, the box bulging as he finished dropping all of his problems into it. Tabitha went into that box. His father's betrayal. The wedding. The moment his mom told him she was sick. Her funeral. All the women he'd brought over so he could say he was dating. His family's expectations. His brothers laughing, his father too—*guess it was your turn for the divorce, Tony boy.*

He grabbed his torch again—now a light saber with fire glowing on the tip, because he was apparently still a kid at heart—and this time, when he lit the box, flames shot a hundred feet high into a dark night sky. Then a thousand. Reaching all the way up to the heavens, pulling the sun to the horizon to chase away the shadows.

His breathing slowed. So did his heart. Time ceased to exist.

In his mind, he saw the sun lighting the backyard. Daisies and tulips pushing through the two smoldering piles of dirt. A big maple tree sprouting. A hammock hung between the tree and the house. Cold lemonade. Hot pizza. Classic rock on the radio.

Happiness.

His eyes flickered open again, and he realized he was rubbing Pepper's hand over his heart. He sucked a big breath through his nose, and he let go.

Let go of the hurt. Let go of the walls. Let go of the darkness.

"Thank you," he said.

"Helped?"

"Yeah."

"I struggled to make friends when I was growing up. I wasn't entirely normal, and I took a lot of things personally. My mom taught me that trick. It got me through my teenage years until I figured out most people are inherently nice, and they weren't out to keep me from my dreams. Even if they were, though, I didn't have to let them into my mental space. You don't have to either."

He twisted around to wrap his arms around her. "I like you in my mental space."

In his mental space, in his house, in his heart.

She squeezed tight. "Me too." Her arms relaxed, and she slid out of his grasp.

Not back.

Down.

"And I like that you work for me," she whispered as she reached for the waistband of his sweatpants.

Her hands brushed him, and there he went, showing off for her.

And then she showed off for him.

And he wondered how he would ever survive without her.

PEPPER SLIPPED into her house early Sunday afternoon after a lazy morning of just enjoying being with Tony. Sadie bunny-hopped to her, tongue lolling, and she bent to love on her dog. "Hey, sweet girl."

"See?" Cinna said. "She's glowing."

Pepper glanced up to find not just Cinna, but also Margie—on a video call on Cinna's phone—scrutinizing her.

"She's practically nuclear," Margie intoned.

"Time for a plan." Gran bustled into the living room too, arms laden with candles, a framed eight-by-ten picture of Elvis, and the dead blow-up goat. "She's got herself a good one, and we're not gonna let him go without a fight."

"What are you talking about?" The glow, she couldn't deny. Tony did it to her. But a plan? For what?

"We're pulling out all the stops to get Tony to elope. With you. Getting engaged isn't enough. Not with your track record."

"I thought we were here for an intervention," Margie said over the video chat.

"Definitely an intervention," Cinna agreed.

"I'm not eloping." She shot a *what the hell?* look at her sisters. "And I don't need an intervention."

Margie didn't blink. "You're sleeping with him and you're attached. You need an intervention."

"I do not—"

Cinna glared at her. "We know a lot more than you think we do. And we like Tony. So, yes, you're getting an intervention."

Unease slithered into Pepper's spine. "Again, what are you talking about?"

"Not in front of the troublemaker," Cinna hissed to Margie.

"She's making an elopement ritual," Margie hissed back. "*With the goat.*"

Gran dropped the candle and a rubber chicken she'd pulled from Pepper didn't want to know where. Then she plopped onto the couch and blew into the goat's air nozzle. George trotted into the room and growled at the growing white atrocity.

Pepper lifted Sadie. "You do whatever you need to do. We're going for a walk." Back to Tony's house, where she hoped Sadie and Lucky could find a way to get along.

Sadie approved. Her butt wiggled, and she twisted to lick Pepper's chin.

"Good girl," she murmured.

"Pepper, are you sure you know what you're doing?"

Margie wasn't one to dance around a subject, but something in her tone gave Pepper pause. As though Margie knew things Pepper still hadn't wanted to talk to her family about. As though Margie knew she was broken.

And if Margie knew, did Cinna know too?

"Yes, I know what I'm doing," she said. "For the first time in my life, I don't know what's going to happen, and I don't have any plans for tomorrow, but I know he makes me happy. And that's enough."

"See?" Cinna thrust the phone closer to Pepper, pushing Margie closer. "She's crazy."

"She does appear to be missing a few key parts of her normal personality," Margie agreed.

"It's called *love*, you goobers," Gran crowed. She huffed out a breath. "Dang. This goat needs a lot of air." The nozzle was in its left thigh, which made Gran look like she was kissing the goat's rear end. "Here. Somebody else blow the goat for a while."

"She doesn't get the goat, Gran," Margie said.

"Listen here, missy. You might have some fancy degree, but I'm still your grandmother, and I'm still the boss of the goat."

Pepper stepped around Cinna and phone-Margie to snag Sadie's leash. "We'll do the goat another time, Gran. I need to walk Sadie and go into work for a few hours."

"Not getting any younger," Gran chirped. "Go see Tony. Take the goat with you."

"Don't think she needs the *goat*'s help," Cinna muttered.

Every muscle in Pepper's body went tense. But she pursed her lips together, clipped Sadie's leash to her collar, and forced herself to turn back to walk out the door. "Margie, miss you, hope to see you soon. Cinna, don't let Gran go out alone. I have a Knot Fest meeting, and I'm not missing it again to go pick her up at the strip club in Willow

Glen. Gran, be good, or I'll find a new seniors' home for you myself, and I know you ate the last of my M&Ms last week, so you're already on my list."

Her sisters were acting as though they knew about her fertility treatments.

As if they disapproved.

Just as she thought they would.

She'd deal with them later. For today, she was going to enjoy the good things in her life.

ANOTHER EARLY SPRING warm spell had brought temperatures nice enough to leave the windows open. Tony took his time getting going Thursday morning. Sales were up, he'd spent half of last night at Pepper's house with her and Gran, binge-watching old *Supernatural* episodes with one dog curled between him and Pepper and the other in time-out across the room. Once Gran had fallen asleep, they'd done other things that still had him grinning, and now he was stretched out on his bed, skimming Facebook while Lucky purred in his lap.

This dating thing was nice.

No pressure.

No worries.

Just two people who had more in common than they thought, enjoying each other's friendship and company, with no expectations about the future.

He'd always wanted to take care of Tabitha. To be her knight in shining armor.

Pepper, though, didn't need a knight.

He'd thought that would bother him. That she didn't need him for his stability, for his strength, for his money, for his support. She didn't *need* him for anything.

She simply *wanted* him. Which was so much more powerful than he'd ever known it could be.

A breeze fluttered the old curtains that had come with the house, and with it came a voice.

"I'm telling you, Margie, she's pregnant. There's all that food she's been eating, then the glow all week, and now she's in the house, puking her guts out."

He dropped his phone.

That was Cinna.

Numbness crept into his feet and clawed its way up his ankles.

"I don't know," Cinna said. Her voice was hushed, as though she didn't want to be overheard.

Or maybe she did.

Did she know Tony's bedroom faced Pepper's backyard?

"Wherever she's keeping everything about her IVF treatments, I can't find it. So I don't know if it's Tony's or not."

That numbness was spreading fast now. Up his calves, his thighs, shrinking his nuts, icing over his chest. He leapt off the bed, stumbled, and Lucky shot out the door as fast as her little limp would carry her.

This wasn't real.

This was some kind of prank.

She'd said she couldn't get pregnant. She'd *sworn* to him she couldn't get pregnant. So why—how—but—

He didn't even bother with shoes. His lungs were heaving, his heart shredding itself in his chest.

Cinna was wrong.

She was *wrong*.

He didn't feel the wet grass under his socks. He didn't feel his hand pounding on her front door, and he didn't see either of the dogs when he charged past Gran.

All he knew was that this was *not* happening to him again.

The woman he loved—*fuck*, when did he start loving her?—was *not* having another man's baby. "Where. Is. She?"

She wouldn't do this.

Not Pepper.

She wouldn't.

261

He didn't hear Gran answer, because he was taking the steps two at a time to the bathroom upstairs. The door opened before he could bang on it, and there she was—his Pepper.

Pale. Unnaturally bright-eyed. Hand to her lower belly.

Just like Tabitha had been.

Every single morning of the first two months of her pregnancy.

The condom. It had broken. The fucking condom had *broken*.

"Tony?"

"Are you pregnant?" he demanded.

She went a shade paler and drew back into the bathroom.

"Are you?" he repeated.

"Why would you ask me that?"

Why? Why, why, *why*? His heart wouldn't stop. His brain wouldn't stop. His lungs wouldn't stop. They were all too much. Too heavy, too fast, too hard. "You were trying to get pregnant."

Her lids snapped as she blinked over her bright green eyes. She grabbed hold of the sink. "Who told you that?"

"It's true. It's true, isn't it?"

"It doesn't matter."

"It fucking *does* matter if you're sleeping with me and carrying some other asshole's baby," he roared.

He grabbed his head, because he couldn't grab his heart.

Not again. This was *not* happening again.

"You need to leave." He could barely hear her over the panic raging in his ears, but he knew that tone.

It was a Pepper Blue special.

She'd gotten what she wanted, and he was excused.

"You owe me the truth," he ground out.

"It's becoming pretty clear that I don't owe you a single damn thing. Get. Out."

"I swear to god, if you're—"

"*Get out*." She didn't touch him, but her words were a slap in the face.

Because she wasn't saying *get out* for now.

262

She was saying *get out* for good.

"The goat worked?" Gran said behind him. "*Yes*! I knew I could count on that goat!"

"Gran, *shut up*."

Tony didn't wait to hear any more.

He'd heard all he needed.

Pepper Blue wasn't the woman he thought she was.

And he was a damn fool.

2 0

*P*epper's stomach was roiling, her head ached, she was feverish and chilled all at the same time, and she was on a warpath.

She found Cinna walking into the kitchen from the backyard thirty seconds after the front door slammed shut behind Tony.

"What. Did. You. Do?" she demanded. Every word made her stomach bubble and protest, but she wasn't letting this stupid bug get her down.

She was too furious.

At Gran. At Cinna. At Tony.

How could he *think* that about her?

Cinna reached into the cabinet for a box of Cocoa Pebbles. "Pregnancy test is in my room. Not that you need it. Pretty sure we all know what the puking's about."

It took every ounce of control not to grab that box and fling it across the room. "You told Tony I was pregnant."

Cinna started. "What? No. That's your job." She jerked her thumb toward the back door. Outside. In the open. "I told Margie."

Oh, *god*. Pepper's knees threatened to give out. His bedroom—her backyard—he'd heard every word.

And he'd believed Cinna. He *knew* Pepper couldn't get pregnant, and he'd believed Cinna. "*Why?*"

"Because you *are*."

Hope flared to life right alongside the searing pain of knowing her sister was wrong. "I'm going to say this one time. And one time only. I am not now, nor will I *ever* be pregnant. Whatever you think you know, you *don't*." Dammit, not the tears. But her throat was clogging and her nose was burning and her tongue was getting thick. "I. Can't. Have. Babies. Not now. Not ever. And there's not a family pool or a stomach bug or a fucking *goat* that can change it. Ever."

The know-it-all in Cinna's stance was shifting into something far worse.

Something that looked like pity. "Pepper, I—"

"Don't talk to me. Just—don't."

Her stomach heaved again. She clutched her midsection, turned and stumbled past Gran—who, for once, looked every bit her age—and hurtled herself up the stairs.

Now they knew.

Now they knew, and now she'd have to tell the story a dozen more times.

Alone.

Because the one person in this world who knew, the one person she'd thought could possibly understand how much this hurt, wasn't the man she'd thought he could be either.

And she hadn't realized until right now just how much she'd wanted him to be.

Tony's basketball game sucked the next Monday.

It sucked so bad, the other team started missing easy layups out of sympathy. Probably because they were up by fortyish points.

When the bloodbath was over, his legs were tired, his lungs ached, he had a newly jammed finger that would be a bitch to work with when he was making pizza dough later today, and not a single woman in their little audience would look at him.

Not even Mikey and Dahlia's baby. Probably not Kimmie's babies either, even though they were still baking.

Babies, babies everywhere. Everyone got babies except Tony.

That should've been the biggest rub. If Pepper was pregnant—and he didn't have a fucking clue if she was or wasn't, but he'd heard through the grapevine that she'd told her family she'd been going through fertility treatments the better part of the last year, intent on doing motherhood alone after too many failed relationships—she'd fight him tooth and nail to make sure he saw that baby as little as possible.

If it was his.

The Pepper he knew—the Pepper he *knew*—wouldn't do that to him.

But the Tony he was would never recover from that horrific moment, staring down at a perfect little girl with dark hair and blue eyes, screaming her lungs out like she already knew she was her mama's girl, when a burly, dark-haired guy he recognized as a regular customer had come barreling into the delivery room.

The nurses had tried to stop him, security had been rushing in, but he'd cried, *Tabitha, is she mine?* and Tony's whole world had unraveled.

Everything he'd known, everything he'd loved, everything he'd dreamed of, just gone.

And when he'd had that moment of panic that Pepper was doing the same thing to him, he'd done the one thing he'd been fantastic at for over a year now.

He made sure he got out first.

But he'd forgotten how much it hurt like a bitch.

Four hours after the game, he was surprised when Max showed up at Pepperoni Tony's back door.

Dammit.

He was going to have to change his pizza joint's name.

266

"You look like a man in need of a beer," Max said.

Tony grunted.

"Grab a pizza and get your ass over to the garage."

So he could play kumbaya with someone who'd been Pepper's friend first? Max might've gotten out of The Aisle, but he still had it in his blood. Didn't matter that Pepper wasn't native.

She fit in.

And Tony didn't.

Not in Willow Glen. Not in Bliss.

Apparently nowhere with normal people with normal problems.

Should've moved to Nebraska. Or Mississippi.

"Heard a rumor Lindsey Truitt's on her way to see you," Max said. "It's me or her, and if you're half as smart as you usually act, you're gonna grab that pizza and get over to my place."

Fine.

But he wouldn't like it.

Since he'd lost his mind over Cinna's conversation last Thursday, he hadn't liked much of anything. Not pizza, not beer, certainly not bourbon.

Definitely not himself.

He still liked Lucky, but he wasn't so sure his cat liked him. She'd been sneaking outside more frequently, delivering fewer sacrifices to her water bowl, shredding more toilet paper, and he hadn't caught her on his bed even once.

He also hadn't seen Pepper at all. Not getting in her car, not coming home, not walking her dog or letting any dogs out into her backyard.

Possibly because he'd shut all his curtains, gotten to work before sunrise, and refused to go home until late into the night. Working was what he was good at.

Not people. Not relationships. Not anything that involved emotions or commitments or family. And his own family had been a bear lately too. All of his brothers and sisters—step, half, and full—had stopped by at least once since the wedding. Dropped in for pizza. To

PIPPA GRANT WRITING AS & JAMIE FARRELL

chat. To ask if he'd bring Pepper to this graduation party or that family dinner or this play or that basketball game that one of his nieces or nephews had.

They liked her.

Hell, *he* liked her. He'd more than liked her.

But he fucked up everything he touched. And he was done.

Just done.

As much for her benefit as his own.

He left Pepperoni Tony's in his assistant manager's hands and took a chicken bacon ranch pizza next door. Merry wasn't around—on a deadline at home, according to Max—so they settled into the office over beers and pizza.

"Merry dumped me once," Max said.

Tony grunted. He didn't give two anchovies about someone else's love life.

"Up and disappeared completely," Max continued. "No warning, no note, no nothing. Just gone. For a year."

So now Tony knew Max was a moron. No wonder he was willing to be friendly today. He was too stupid to know better than to try to make friends. Tony chugged half a beer and tossed the empty can toward the trash can.

Missed.

What a surprise.

If Max was picking up on the *shut up* vibe, he ignored it. "Found out her dad was a jewel thief. Then I caught her trying to sneak into my family's jewelry shop just before Christmas."

Now the story was getting good. "You're an idiot, you know that?"

Max grinned. "I'm gonna pretend like you didn't just insult both me and the love of my life."

"And I'm gonna pretend you're not here trying to tell me some deep lesson about how we need to understand women's motives."

"Actually, this is your last shot to explain to a few of us what the fuck's going on in *your* head before Pepperoni Tony's gets blacklisted on The Aisle. Which I'd like to avoid, because this is actually damn good pizza."

Six weeks ago, that would've inspired terror.

Failing at Pepperoni Tony's—that would've killed him.

But even though pizza was his baby, he didn't care. He didn't have it in him to care. What good was pizza without someone to share it with?

His heart was broken. His dick was broken. His soul was broken.

What difference did any of it make?

"Merry likes you," Max said. "She has good instincts. Better than most after everything she's seen. She says you're a decent guy. But that only gets you so far when no one knows why you broke up with Pepper. Especially while she's been so sick."

And there went that knife, twisting in his gut again.

It didn't actually matter if Pepper was pregnant.

Because Tony could never be the kind of man she needed.

Or wanted, for that matter.

He grabbed another beer and stood. "Thanks for lunch. We should do this again sometime."

"Not a guy here who hasn't been there, Tony. Don't want to talk, that's fine. But don't be an ass either. Gonna break my lady's heart if you take away her Merry Cheese pizza."

"I'll send you the recipe."

This wasn't like when Tabitha destroyed him.

This was worse.

Because this time, he *knew* he was doing it to himself.

PEPPER WAS FINALLY BACK at work, in the full swing of things, by Tuesday. She'd peed on a stick to appease Cinna, who had gone out of her way to be an utter angel while Pepper battled her stomach bug. Mom had come and picked up Gran and George—so Gran didn't get sick, she'd said, but Pepper knew her mother.

So you can have some time off to recover.

And not from being sick either. From the dating and the goat of fertility and the beauty that was an old lady who'd lived a full life with nearly everything she'd ever wanted, now trying to influence her granddaughters' lives to be the same.

Which wasn't entirely fair—Pepper knew Gran's heart had broken when Grandpa had passed away, though she'd been too young to really understand or feel anything when it happened.

But Gran had had her babies. She'd had a solid husband. She'd traveled the world, and she was still grabbing life by the horns and riding it with carefree abandon.

The only thing Pepper had ever come close to doing with *carefree abandon* was dating Tony.

She got it—his ex-wife had hurt him in probably the most painful way a woman could hurt a man.

But she also knew she and Tony wouldn't have lasted forever. Sooner or later—probably sooner—she would've wanted to take the next step. Talk about moving in together, or getting engaged, or even eloping.

And Tony didn't want marriage.

Even if he did, he didn't love her. She'd been his rebound. In a lot of ways, he'd been her rebound. Was she stronger and better for it? She didn't know.

But it would've ended eventually. Her relationships always did.

Might as well be over now.

The whole family knew the entire story. Margie had come and stayed with her this weekend too, strong and clinical and unemotional as only Margie could be.

I was worried was the extent of Margie's chastisement. *And it's not weak to need help from time to time.*

Felt good to be back at work, and she blamed her still mildly tender stomach for not feeling the usual enthusiasm for tackling the day.

Even though she knew better.

She was closing up shop after doing what she did best—solving problems, selling dresses, and making other women's dreams come true—when she caught sight of someone leaning against the wall beside the back door.

Her traitorous heart had leapt—maybe it was Tony?—but of course, it wasn't.

They'd already said all they needed to say.

Even if she hadn't wanted to let him go. She hadn't been ready. She understood why he'd flipped out. She didn't even blame him.

Not really.

Even if her heart hurt more than any other part of her had in the last week. Or possibly ever.

"Tarra?" she said to her sister.

"Men are assholes. Let's go get ice cream."

"And cupcakes?"

"All the cupcakes."

It was the best plan she'd heard in days.

THIRTY MINUTES LATER, instead of sitting at Kimmie Cakes or at Dahlia's ice-cream shop next door, Pepper and Tarra were surrounded by friends and family at Suckers, CJ's bar. They'd overtaken the entire floor, except for the bar area, and were loaded down with cupcakes and ice cream—of course—along with those cheese fries that Pepper hadn't had in entirely too long.

"I can't believe you didn't tell us," Nat said. She'd passed baby TJ off to Will, who was sitting beside Mikey and singing softly to both babies. Lindsey and Kimmie both looked ready to pop, despite neither of them being due for at least another few weeks, though in Kimmie's case it was easy to blame the twins. Dahlia was glowing, Merry was enjoying her own personal cheese plate, and Max, CJ, and Josh were pretending they weren't listening in.

"If I'd told you I was using sperm donors to try to get pregnant on my own, what would you have done?"

"I—" Nat started.

"Liar," Tarra said easily over an Earl Gray cupcake. Which was something only Tarra could enjoy, pregnant or not.

"Okay, *fine*. You haven't dated *all* of the single sons on The Aisle yet." Nat humphed. "I know how hard single parenting can be, okay?"

"I wouldn't have been alone." Pepper squeezed Tarra's hand. "You won't be either. You know that, right?"

"Oh, I'll happily do this alone," Tarra replied. "As soon as I'm well and truly annulled from my Sin City misadventure. That was *years* ago, by the way. Freaking fake Vegas attorney. I hope he dies of dysentery."

"I was thinking scorpion bite," Cinna called from behind the bar.

"Desert exposure," Dahlia said.

"I had a dream my mother was a scorpion once." Kimmie licked the frosting off her cupcake while murmurs of *yep,* and *I believe it* went through the room. Josh stopped pretending he wasn't eavesdropping to scan the lot of them suspiciously.

Not because of his semi-awkward relationship with Kimmie's mother, Pepper suspected, but because usually Kimmie only talked about her dreams when she was nervous, and he wanted to know who was making her uncomfortable.

Josh might've fallen on the overprotective side.

Which was utterly perfect for Kimmie, who was munching on her cupcake without a seeming care in the world, apparently happy to contribute to the conversation without any underlying meanings or stress this time.

Cinna set a glass of red in front of Pepper. "It's on CJ."

"I wish we could get rid of her as easily as we can get rid of Tony," Nat muttered.

"You don't need to get rid of Tony." Why did it freaking feel like her heart was being ripped out of her chest when she said that? It was like finding out she couldn't have babies all over again. "It wasn't ever real," she added, which hurt not just her heart, but also her very marrow. "I asked him to be my date to Tarra's wedding to get Gran off my back because I was…preoccupied. He did everything he was supposed to and more. We both knew it wouldn't last."

It was like someone was using her heart as a punching bag.

And that someone was her.

God, she missed him. Her friends were being amazing and supportive and everything friends were supposed to be, but they didn't *get* it.

Not like Tony did. Yet he'd still accused her of being pregnant.

"Doesn't mean you didn't get attached," Dahlia said. "I was using Mikey for some extra cash, and look how that turned out."

"And I was using Josh to make my mother mad," Kimmie chimed in with a grin.

"I was using CJ for the same," Nat lied.

"I was using Max for sex," Merry offered.

Lindsey was the only one who stayed quiet. In fact, she was the only one who hadn't uttered a word all evening.

"No opinions?" Pepper asked her.

"She's got 'em." Will looked up from the babies and eyed his wife. "But she won't tell me either. Says she still has to keep some secrets from her lawyering days."

"You two have *no* secrets," Nat said.

"Didn't say she was *successfully* keeping it a secret from me. Said she wouldn't *tell* me. There's a difference."

"So?" Nat prompted.

Pepper's breath hitched. Lindsey had become Bliss's unofficial matchmaker—supposedly she was psychic with it, which Pepper didn't believe, but of everyone in this room, she knew Tony the best. She probably knew more of Tony's secrets than Pepper did.

But Lindsey simply shrugged. "If Pepper wants to know my opinion, she'll ask me herself."

It didn't matter what Lindsey thought she saw or didn't see. Neither she nor Tony was in a place to commit to a serious relationship. He wasn't over what his ex-wife had done to him, and she didn't know if she'd ever get over not being able to have babies. "Have you seen him?" she asked.

Lindsey shook her head.

"I did," Max offered.

He didn't say how Tony was doing.

He didn't have to. Because she knew.

In her heart, she just *knew*.

"Take care of him," Pepper said.

She reached for her wine with one hand and a fresh bowl of triple chocolate something ice cream that might've been called chocolate orgasm, and that was the last she talked about Tony for the night.

Because saying any more would've been like ripping the bandage off over and over and over again.

21

S ales were holding steady, Tony had been able to give his staff more hours, and he could legitimately relax and kick back if he wanted to.

Instead, he was searching real estate. Up near Chicago. Over in Indianapolis. Maybe Milwaukee. Hell, there wasn't anything honestly stopping him from moving to Canada.

If he sold his places both here and in Willow Glen, he could get out. Make a fresh start.

Forget these last few years. Put some distance between himself and family expectations.

He'd tried to hit on a customer yesterday. Pretend everything was great. Put on that show.

He'd gotten halfway through, "How's that pizza?" and choked.

Hadn't even gotten close to a pickup line, lame or otherwise.

"Hey, Tony, got somebody up front asking for you," one of his servers called through the office door.

He didn't want *somebody*.

He wanted…

He just *wanted*.

Things he couldn't have.

Out front, he found Bella and Francie waiting for him at the counter.

More family. More questions. More bullshit. "Lunch?" he asked.

"Nope, an ass-kicking," Bella replied cheerfully. "But we'll take some pizza with it."

He snapped his fingers at one of the passing servers. "Table for two. Lunch is on the house."

"Mom hated Tabitha," Francie announced.

He'd had a knot between his shoulder blades for almost a week now, and his sister wasn't helping.

"She really did," Bella agreed. "Said she wasn't good enough for you. And if she'd tell *me* that, you know it was bad."

"I'm going back to work."

"You're not like our brothers, Tony." Francie grabbed his arm before he could walk away. "You could make it. We *want* you to make it. But we don't know how to help."

"I might."

The new voice put Tony's teeth on edge.

He hadn't heard her since she'd inadvertently dropped a bombshell while talking to one of her sisters on the phone in Pepper's backyard.

"This is my fault." Cinna looked at Francie and Bella, then back to Tony. "Can I have just a minute? Alone?"

"Don't let us stop you," Francie said so quickly Tony suspected a setup.

Bella, too, angled back. "We'll just get a seat and wait."

Though he would've rather pried his toenails out with rusty pliers, Tony gestured Cinna out to the street.

She didn't get to go into his office.

Foot traffic was low—it almost always was on his street, though The Aisle was another story as the weather was slowly warming toward spring.

"She's not pregnant," Cinna said. "And even if she was, if you were half a man, you would've been there to be that baby's father anyway."

He couldn't decide if his teeth were about to crack because she was a brat, or because she should've been right.

But he knew what that waver in his heart was.

Pain.

Pure, raw pain.

He'd accused Pepper of being pregnant—of being the one thing she'd wanted badly enough to try to do it on her own, the one thing she'd failed at. He'd thrown it in her face.

Told himself *he* was the wronged party. That she should've been honest with him about trying to get pregnant.

When he should've manned up and trusted her instead of hiding behind his past to keep himself from getting hurt.

"I'm sorry I butted in," Cinna said. "I'm sorry she's not pregnant. I'm sorry I thought she'd do that to you. But mostly I'm sorry that neither one of you will get over yourselves long enough to admit how much you care. Because Pepper might look strong. She might act like she has it all together. But those are the people you have to worry about most. And I thought, of all her boyfriends, you might have finally gotten it."

He should've.

Look what he'd done before he met Pepper. He'd become a one-date wonder. Expanded his booming business. Moved into a house he'd told everyone he was going to renovate and flip.

Pretended everything was fine when nothing was right.

Nothing except his rescue cat, who was just as broken on the outside as he felt on the inside.

He didn't look at Cinna.

Didn't step back into his restaurant.

Instead, he turned and walked away.

Somewhere.

Anywhere.

He wasn't okay. He wasn't all right. He might never be.

But he didn't want to be alone. He shouldn't have *had* to be alone.

Not anymore.

PEPPER HAD HIT the sugar and wine too hard too soon after being sick. This sucked. When she'd been a kid, she'd bounced back from the flu in a matter of days. As a grown-up, a stupid stomach bug had taken her down for almost a week.

Her doctor said it was normal.

Her doctor had also confirmed that this *was* a lingering stomach bug, completely normal, and not morning sickness.

She left work early and headed home. Tarra had stayed the night and had no plans for leaving anytime soon, which suited Pepper fine. She liked the company.

Especially Tarra's company right now.

The two of them made an odd couple—Tarra on the path to unwanted single motherhood, Pepper mourning her own chances to ever make it happen—but with Tarra's job being mobile, she was talking about moving in for a few months.

While she waited for her own private detective to find her long-lost Vegas husband so they could get the annulment they should've had years ago.

But Tarra wasn't there when she got home. She let Sadie out—poor Sadie, who seemed to actually be *missing* George, if that were possible—and set a kettle on to make herself a pot of tea.

She was flipping through the teas Tarra had brought with her when she heard Sadie erupt in barking outside, followed by a yowl of sheer terror.

Without thinking, she flew out the back door. "Sadie! Sadie, no, puppy. Lucky, get back. Back!" She snagged Sadie, narrowly missing getting clawed by Lucky, who darted on her bad leg through a teeny opening in the chain-link fence and toward Tony's house, where the back door was also flying open.

She closed her eyes and buried her nose in her dog's wiry fur. "Leave the kitty alone, Sadie," she whispered.

She hustled back inside, because she knew what she'd see if she didn't.

Tony.

Accusing her of letting her dog terrorize his cat once more.

Accusing her of keeping secrets.

Reminding her of her very worst failures in life. Of all the things she'd never have.

Or worse, Tony being a reasonable man who still didn't want her. Who might've already found a woman to move on with.

The door shut with a definitive click behind her. She inspected Sadie for cuts or scratches while the pup tried to lick her nose, which was when she realized her eyes were leaking.

She got herself back under control, poured a cup of green tea, and carried it to the living room. Afternoon talk shows were on, and Tarra's baby would need a blanket, so she grabbed her knitting needles and the knotted mess of yellow yarn and once again set about tackling this cast-on, cast-off, purl-this, purl-that stuff while people danced and laughed with Ellen DeGeneres.

Sadie curled up at her feet, and for all of fifteen minutes, life went on.

Until someone knocked at the door.

Sadie leapt up and charged it in full fast-bunny-hop mode, as though she'd suddenly become a guard dog, which either meant Gran was back, unannounced, or...

Or something worse.

She set her knitting aside and forced herself to walk on unsteady legs to the door.

And when she swung it open to find her favorite pizza-delivery guy standing on the other side of her screen door, not with pizza, but with a bouquet of flowers in hand and guarded terror in his eyes, her knees almost buckled.

"Hi," he said before she could find her words. "I'm Tony. I moved in a few months ago, and I just fucked up the best relationship I've ever had with the most amazing woman I've ever known. She told me once that I'd fall in love and marry the next woman I dated after her, so I was wondering...are you free tonight?"

Yep, her knees were going to go. So were the tears. Definitely her heart.

Of everything he could've said, of everything he could've done, he'd done *this*.

The one thing no other man could *ever* offer her.

"Tony," she whispered.

"I was wrong. I'll be wrong again. Probably all the time. But I want you. Every day. I want to teach my cat to get along with your dog. I want to let your grandmother goose me on the holidays, just because it'll make her happy. I want—Pepper, I just want *you*. You're the patch holding my heart together, and I—I love you."

"I'm not pregnant," she forced out.

"Even if you were, even if you *had* been when we met, I'd still want you both. But I don't need babies. Pepper, I just need you."

Those eyes. Those dark, desperate, terrified eyes. The flowers were wobbling in his hands, he hadn't shaved in days, and he wasn't in a coat.

No, he was standing there, baring his soul, asking her to be his.

Forever.

She flung the door open and almost took his nose off, then squished the flowers between them as she grabbed on to him and hugged him for dear life. "I love you," she whispered. "I love you so much. You're everything I never knew I was missing and everything I've ever needed."

He finally got his arms untangled and wrapped her tight. "I'm a mess," he said into her shoulder.

"Oh, god, Tony. We both are."

That earned her a reluctant chuckle. "I'm sorry, Pepper. I'm so sorry. For everything that's my fault and everything that's not."

"I'm sorry too," she whispered. "I should've told you."

He was holding her and stroking her hair and pressing his lips to her forehead, almost shaking in her arms, and for the first time in her life, she was *glad* she wasn't perfect.

"You would've," he said. "In your own time, you would've."

"You have too much faith in me."

"I love you."

Three simple words.

And she knew just how much those words cost him.

He pulled her tighter. "Pepper, I mean it. I'm going to fuck up again. Probably all the time. But I swear to you, I will *never* hurt you like *that* again. Just please—please promise you'll always be mine."

"Tony, I already am." She lifted her head, went up on tiptoe, and pressed her lips to his.

And what started as a simple kiss rapidly turned into a heated mesh of mouths and tongues. The flowers landed somewhere on the porch. They somehow stumbled into the house, tripping over Sadie, touching and kissing and stroking and peeling their clothes off amidst whispers of *I love you* and *forever* and *never go another day without you*.

And two hours later, as Pepper held on to the man she'd never let go again, a slow rumble started in his throat.

She lifted her head off his chest and looked up at him. "Care to share?"

"I was just wondering if you'd order pizza for your bachelorette party."

She burst out laughing. "You're thinking about pizza? *Now?*"

"One of my two favorite things in the world." He cupped her head and bent his to touch her lips. "Right after you."

EPILOGUE

*T*here was nothing like a cloudless summer Saturday at the softball diamonds in Bliss. Especially when it came with pizza, Pepper, and their oldest in the championship game.

Erica might not have had his or Pepper's genes, but she still hit like her mother. "C'mon, E! You got this," he called through the fence separating the field from the stands.

Pepper was in the dugout, chewing her nails.

Happened when they were down by one at the bottom of the seventh inning, with two outs and runners on first and second.

"Go, E!" four-year-old Chloe yelled at her big sister.

"BaaaEEEE!" echoed two-year-old Bria from Tony's hip.

Today's game might've been between two teams full of seven- and eight-year-olds, but the stands were still packed. Probably because every last one of the girls' aunts and uncles and grandparents had come out—on both sides of the family—along with Pepper's closest friends.

Including the one responsible not just for Pepperoni Tony's Bliss location, but also for Pepper and Tony having to buy a bigger house last Christmas.

When Lindsey Truitt had called and said her nonprofit foundation had been contacted by a woman dying of cancer who didn't want her daughters going to the state, he and Pepper hadn't even had to talk about it before they'd hopped in her car and driven out past Willow Glen to meet the family.

They hadn't been actively pursuing adoption—they'd been making the most of their time as a couple the last year and a half before that—but fate happened sometimes.

The girls' mom had passed away just after the new year, which had gutted him and Pepper more than the younger two daughters they inherited. Erica—as the oldest—remembered her mom more.

But she was coming out of her shell and loving the hell out of having so many doting aunts and uncles. She also got special pizza time with Tony a few times a week—especially during the summer—and dress time with Pepper a few other times a week.

And he and Pepper were learning the real meaning of *balance*.

"I wouldn't want to be Dan right now," Lindsey Truitt said beside him.

Tony glanced at Erica's fiery eyes and the determined set to her jaw as she stood at the plate and stared down Dan Gregory, Max's brother and acting league pitcher for the girls' game today, and he grinned. "And if she's like this at seven..."

"God help you all," Lindsey replied.

Will stepped up beside her with Stella, their one-year-old. She was happily sitting in his arms, playing with his baseball cap. "My sister was like that at seven," he offered.

"As I said, god help them all," Lindsey repeated with a smile.

Dan tossed a soft lob at Erica.

Tony held his breath. His heart might've even paused. Erica drew the bat around, and—

Cling!

Pepper jumped in the dugout. "Run! Run, E, run!"

The ball bounced up the center of the diamond, sending Dan scuttling out of the way while the other team's shortstop and second baseman scrambled too slowly to nab it before it drifted into the outfield.

The crowd was on its feet, cheering and yelling as Erica pounded her little legs on her way to first base.

"Hits like her mother," CJ said on Tony's other side. He rubbed the back of his head while he held onto TJ, whose real name was *still* a mystery. "Don't ever let her get her hands on a tailpipe."

The runner coming from second rounded third to whoops and hollers. Chloe was shrieking. Bria stared at Tony with big round eyes, obviously debating if she wanted to cry or join in the fun.

Or possibly she was filling her diaper.

Potty training would be fun with this one.

In the outfield, a blond little girl grabbed the ball and tossed it at the first baseman while the third base coach waved on the adorable little pixie who'd been on first. "Run! RUN!"

And there was Erica.

Running like her little life depended on it, legs pumping, arms too, rounding second while the ball rolled to a stop at the back of the dirt between first and second bases, the throw not nearly strong enough to make it halfway to the pitcher or first baseman.

"Go, Erica!" Tony called.

"Go, E! RUN!" Chloe was jumping now, hanging on to the chain-link fence while her sister approached third. Sadie, who'd come to the ball field with them, huddled behind Tony's legs on her leash. "Run to the house! RUN TO THE HOUSE!"

The third base coach told her to stop.

She ignored him.

Tony grinned and pumped a fist in the air. "That's my girl!"

Pepper was jumping and cheering at home plate, hugging the two girls who'd already scored while the other team scrambled for the ball again and lobbed it at the catcher.

Too late.

Because Erica was crossing home, diving into Pepper's arms, who swooped her up and swung her around and kissed her oversized base-ball cap.

Pepper met his eyes, and that wide smile, so full of pure joy and happiness, made something catch in his throat.

This.

His wife. His girls. His cat. His dog, who still thought she was a rabbit, and who still spooked his cat sometimes.

If he had his life to do over, he wouldn't change a damn thing. He'd take every heartbreak of his own, and he'd take on Pepper's and the girls' too, if he could have this.

Today.

Every bit of pain and turmoil had been worth it, because his life had brought *this.*

He and Chloe and Bria trotted onto the field, trailed by the bunny-hopping Sadie, to Pepper and Erica and the rest of the team. He traded his youngest for his oldest to swing her up in a giant bear hug. "You, little lady, are amazing," he told her.

She squeezed him back with all the strength in her little arms. "I hit a home run, Dad!"

"You sure did. You're a beast with that bat."

Family crushed around them, hugging and cheering and squealing.

He set Erica down and slipped an arm around Pepper. "Nice job, Coach."

She went up on tiptoe and pressed a kiss to his cheek, her sweet scent tickling his nose. "You too, Dad."

He grinned, she smiled back, and Chloe dove into both of their knees. "Pizza time!"

Pizza. And family. And love.

Everything he'd ever wanted. Nothing he'd expected.

And it was all perfect.

ABOUT THE AUTHOR

Jamie Farrell is the alter ego for *USA Today* Bestselling romantic comedy author Pippa Grant. She believes love, laughter, and bacon are the most powerful forces in the universe. When she's not writing, she's raising her three hilariously unpredictable children with her real-life hero.

Visit Jamie's website at:
www.JamieFarrellBooks.com

THE COMPLETE JAMIE FARRELL BOOK LIST

The Misfit Brides Series

Blissed

Matched

Smittened

Sugared

Married

Spiced

Unhitched

The Officers' Ex-Wives Club Series

Her Rebel Heart

Southern Fried Blues

Jamie Farrell's Pippa Grant Titles:

The Girl Band Series

Mister McHottie

Stud in the Stacks

Rockaway Bride

The Hero and the Hacktivist

The Thrusters Hockey Series

The Pilot and the Puck-Up

Royally Pucked

Beauty and the Beefcake

Charming as Puck

I Pucking Love You

The Bro Code Series

Flirting with the Frenemy

America's Geekheart

Liar, Liar, Hearts on Fire

The Hot Mess and the Heartthrob

Copper Valley Fireballs Series

Jock Blocked

Real Fake Love

The Grumpy Player Next Door

Standalones

Master Baker *(Bro Code Spin-Off)*

Hot Heir *(Royally Pucked Spin-Off)*

Exes and Ho Ho Hos

The Bluewater Billionaires Series

The Price of Scandal by Lucy Score

The Mogul and the Muscle by Claire Kingsley

Wild Open Hearts by Kathryn Nolan

Crazy for Loving You by Pippa Grant

Co-Written with Lili Valente

Hosed

Hammered

Hitched

Humbugged

Printed in the USA
CPSIA information can be obtained
at www.ICGtesting.com
LVHW050502210624
783560LV00007B/778

9 781955 930062